Grabbing Fog

Also by Sophia Kim Apple, MD:

***

COVID-19, a gripping novel inspired by real events
(The Unseen Doctor, Book 1 of 2)

***

Forgive to Live

***

Nonfiction:

Who Says You Have Breast Cancer?

Grabbing Fog

Sequel to COVID-19, the Unseen Doctor, Book 2 of 2

Sophia Kim Apple, MD

Cover design by Hal Apple
Cover layout and production by Stephanie Robinson
Edited by Hal Apple

For inquiries contact:
www.unseendoctor.com

"America suffers from a deficit of imagining the lives of other people."

— Sophia Kim Apple, MD

Table of Contents

The essential purpose of my first book, released in 2021, was to document the coronavirus pandemic upon its arrival in 2019. This book continues that story as the pandemic also continued. Similar to my first book surrounding COVID-19, this is a story inspired by many actual events during the pandemic, primarily in the US. The palatable format of a novel brings our focus through the eyes of people in the field of medicine, how we lived during this portion of human history. — *Sophia*

This is a work of fiction, based on many actual events and facts. Medical and scientific information is true, such as descriptions of vaccines, historical background on viruses, vaccines, diseases, and the depiction of a human body dying from COVID-19.

The information regarding immigrations into the US and treatment of people living in the US is true, such as those who came from China and elsewhere.

All data regarding hospitalizations, deaths, and impact of the pandemic within hospitals and within society are true, including impacts as those described in the states of New York, California, and Florida, and many New York City events including mask requirements, garbage pileups, and city streets lined with trucks filled with dead bodies.

Specific events at Wuhan are not based on fact, such as a researcher from the US meeting the 'bat woman' (although such a person in China does exist) and secretly transporting the virus to the US.

Names, characters, certain companies and company names such as Abby Labs are products of the author's imagination and are used fictitiously.

Prologue

June 2020

Life goes on. The living continue to live and those in death are dead as the pandemic goes on. Freezer trucks full of dead bodies occupy hospital parking lots, and a few nearby city streets are lined with additional trucks to accommodate increasing deaths. This is the new norm, hoping the summer heat does not bring an overwhelming smell permeating the city. Desensitization becomes a key to survival. Mingling with people becomes something to avoid and being alone is an expectation, and a desirable condition.

Dr. Samantha Parker's one-bedroom Bronx apartment appears anything but desirable after she accepts two additional roommates, Drs. Giti Schwartz and Roxanne Brown, first-year pathology residents. Samantha opened her apartment to them until they can find better and more appropriate places to live. Soon, hopefully.

Chapter 1

The injury

June 5, 2020

"The pandemic is less painful than suffering age-old racial discrimination and hatred!" shouts Roxanne Brown to other women in the jail cell. Her hands, face and hair are bloody. A cellmate sees the blood and screams at the officers, "You beat her! Get her out of here, get her to the hospital!" A detective pushes past a few officers and enters the cell as he partially carries and escorts Roxanne into a patrol car. He slams the door shut and watches it accelerate away from the station. In a few minutes the car arrives at the Bronx hospital Emergency Department where an officer drops her off and drives away without charging Roxanne for inciting violence at a protest, nor for resisting arrest.

Roxanne has now lost significant amounts of blood, with dimming consciousness, and is unable to tell the ER attending physician who she is. The doctors and nurses search through her pockets to register her, and find her badge: Roxanne Brown, MD, Pathology Department. Their own hospital's ID. They transfer her into a private room, farthest away from probable COVID-19 patients. Fortunately, COVID cases are decreasing but tremendous fear and precaution remain in the emergency department where COVID-inflicted patients are congregated.

***

Roxanne has not returned home after she left before dusk. Samantha is watching the breaking news around 1:00 am as cameras show the area where Roxanne and the protestors were planning to walk. Initially it was a peaceful march with banners, chants of *Black Lives Matter!* and *No justice, no peace!* or *I can't breathe!* This protest is a part of a larger organized effort across several sites in each of the five New York City boroughs that began a week ago on May 28, 2020. As the night deepens,

Roxanne's protest march becomes chaotic with looting and direct conflict with police. More than 1,000 people are arrested by the end of the night. Roxanne is one of them. She spends the night in a jail cell packed with 25 other women, and is the only person wearing a mask. Blood pours out of her head, beaten by police using batons. Her bleeding will not stop. Blood covers her face, she cannot open her eyes from the swelling of her forehead, which is now split open. Her adrenaline is pumping so hard she does not even realize she is severely injured. Roxanne bears thirteen stitches in her forehead performed by a first-year internal medicine resident after CT scan, to rule out possible concussion. Tonight there is a severe shortage of ER attending doctors to cover the shift. She is given intravenous fluid to compensate for the blood loss. After Roxanne improves into a stable state, she calls Samantha at 4:30 am and explains what happened.

Samantha runs to the emergency department. Due to the curfew, the Bronx streets are particularly quiet with no trace of sound from any living thing, not even a homeless person, an eerie feeling on the dark streets of New York. Samantha can only hear her own breathing, muffled by the moist mask she wears. She left without telling Giti, who was deep asleep when Samantha rushed out of the apartment.

Chapter 2

Three realities

June 4, 2020

Giti is a tiny woman, barely 100 pounds, five feet tall. She has been commuting two hours every day by subway from Brooklyn to her residency training in the Bronx hospital. Her community in Williamsburg, Brooklyn is home to a large Hasidic Orthodox Jewish community, population about 57,000. With the pandemic, her commute became unbearably long as subway trains run infrequently. This is dangerous to Giti for two main reasons: risk of coronavirus transmission on mass transit systems, and lack of safety as she leaves the hospital late at night after her heavy workload. As an Orthodox Jew, she is unable to work from Friday sundown to Saturday sundown. Their residency director and fellow residents knew about her situation, but this still causes difficulties for their on-call schedule coverage. Residents began complaining about their Friday and Saturday work schedules to cover for Giti and they resent her absence every weekend. Other complaints are voiced by their faculty members, also known as their professors; their 'attending physicians.' To compensate, Giti is exceptionally conscientious, hard-working, and helpful to others in times of need that are well beyond her duties. Giti desperately avoids causing further inconvenience to other residents, so she commonly works extremely late into the night, allowing her to complete each week's work by early Friday afternoon. Subway travel at night is risky and dangerous to anyone in New York City, especially a woman of her physical stature. Samantha had cautiously agreed to welcome Giti as a roommate who agreed to pay one third of the rent, and Giti typically stays from Sunday morning through Friday early afternoon, then she departs for her Williamsburg home for arrival before sundown.

Roxanne's residency salary is not sufficient to find appropriate housing in an environment where she can study.

She is the only Black female pathology resident in the department. Roxanne grew up under a single mother who had five children. She's a street-smart, first born child helping to raise her young brothers, both physically and financially up to this point in her life, and perhaps for years to come. Her poverty-stricken Bronx neighborhood is unsafe. Roxane never gave up attending schools and making excellent grades, graduating from college and medical school by achieving full scholarships among few other black students. At one point her whole family lived on the street, homeless, searching for food from garbage dumpsters for several months. She knows the ins and outs of every government system to avoid living on the streets and they spent countless nights in homeless shelters. Her father is a drunken man, in jail for reasons unknown since she was young. Roxanne last saw her father when she was a young teenager. Only to Samantha and a few others does she reveal portions of her past family history and current place in life. Her story is a heart-breaking tragedy, far removed from the reality of most doctors and residency trainees. Despite the hardships, she has never given up her dream to become the first doctor in her family. Her junior high school teacher is an influential figure to Roxanne who often told her never to give up on the power of education. Mrs. Rose, the teacher, is also Black, and perceives Roxanne as an unusually smart girl and often reminds her, "The only way out of the misery of poverty — and maybe discrimination — is to get an education." Roxanne takes this statement into her heart. She tends to her family's needs, leaving little time to study. Persistent, she stays focused on the things she needs to learn, and she learns quickly. Now, with a stable medical resident income, the family is living in a studio apartment, somewhat safe and protected. Modest help from social security welfare has recently allowed the entire family to eat regularly. They skip fewer meals and avoid sickness that always arrived when eating rotten food they found in garbage.

Roxanne has longed to be out of her family's noisy studio apartment and to focus on her residency training. She begins pleading with Samantha to accept her as a roommate. Samantha respects Roxanne for her commitment and dedication despite all her circumstances, and agrees to Roxanne's request, accepting only 25% of the rent until Roxanne finds a better place to live.

Samantha knows it is unlikely Roxanne will be able to move out anytime soon on her small salary as a resident. Aside from rent to Samantha, the rest of Roxanne's monthly salary is given to her family. The residency program allows $15 per day to eat meals from the hospital cafeteria, except for weekends. Roxanne gathers her manna from each weekday allotment and spreads out her meals by rationing the free cafeteria food to cover a few weekend meals.

Samantha grew up with no needs unmet. She always had abundance, not just what she needed but also what she wanted, and more. While not fully understanding the poverty or religious obligations of her two roommates, she respects her female colleagues who have enormous challenges, and she wants to help them somehow. Initially, she was hesitant to lose her independence, freedom, and quietness, but the stories from both women led her to be sympathetic and empathetic to their unique challenges.

Roxanne and Giti take the living room and Samantha takes the bedroom. Since Giti pays a little more toward rent, she chooses the small corner window area, and Roxanne takes the middle portion of the living room and sleeps on the couch. Roxanne has no material possessions; just a few books, clothes, and herself to move in. Giti brings the same, plus a small bed and a few tiny furniture items.

Chapter 3

Attacks based on protein levels

June 4, 2020

The Bronx hospital where the three women work remains in turmoil with COVID–19 patients, and the dying continues. Education of doctors in their medical residency training is no longer a priority. Daily struggles are minimized. Everyone lives in survival mode, disoriented, straining to make sense out of the continual chaos. The entire country and the hospitals appear goal-less and unorderly. After the first wave of COVID, with deaths exceeding 28,000, New York City began to reopen in early June 2021 with reduced occupancy ceilings for many businesses. Our lives begin to restart after the initial shock of COVID, inching into the new normalcy by taking baby steps.

This was interrupted on May 25th as George Floyd, a Black man, dies during an arrest in Minneapolis after a store clerk alleges Mr. Floyd passed a counterfeit $20 bill. One of four police officers who arrived on the scene methodically knelt and placed his knee on George Floyd's neck for 9 minutes and 29 seconds as spectators recorded the events on their cell phones. Immediately, the harrowing death of George Floyd is broadcast around the world. After this incident, outrage toward police brutality toward Black citizens quickly spread into protests across the US and internationally. To many, this amount of brutality against a Black person is a total shock. To others, including most Black citizens, the incident is routine, a common but rarely documented treatment continuing after hundreds of generations. This entire episode of a man slowly dying under the knee of a police officer is recorded by a 17-year-old teenager, and broadcast to the nation. Other spectators capture additional footage, pleas for help, and outrage from witnesses.

Roxanne's outrage remains vehement because she saw this kind of brutality growing up among her neighbors. Her younger brother who is now 21 had experienced police brutality and was arrested for being a Black person while crossing the street with his two other friends when they were minors. For no apparent reason, her younger brother was captured, handcuffed, forcefully brought down to the street with a policeman's knee on his neck, not too dissimilar to George Floyd. Although it was not 9 minutes and 29 seconds, it was long enough for her brother to choke up and say the exact words, "I can't breathe." Her brother and his two friends were arrested and jailed for over 24 hours simply because they were Black and held until Roxanne bailed them out. The police arrested them because a clerk at a recent robbery in a nearby grocery store described three young Black men whose identifications and profiles appeared to be similar to her brother and his friends. To many who are White, all Black people must look alike. Roxanne once again watches the footage of George Floyd slowly being killed by the police officer, wailing as three officers on the scene do not intervene as Mr. Floyd was obviously dying. She quickly prepares to join a protest tonight outside the mall at Riverside, Bronx, a location featuring expensive and trendy shops.

"Samantha, Giti—please come with me. Just walk with me to protest! Our Black lives matter!"

"Roxanne, sorry, but I'm on call tonight," Samantha responds.

Giti also declines. "I've got 20 specimens to gross in, and I'll be at the hospital almost all night." Roxanne is sorrowfully disappointed to recognize these are not her close friends who can understand how important this protest will be to show the world the outrageous police brutality, lack of police accountability, inequality, and racism against Black people.

Protests began one day after George Floyd's death in the Minneapolis-Saint Paul metropolitan area of Minnesota, and quickly spread nationwide. Over 2,000 cities and towns in over 60 countries rapidly show support for the Black Lives Matter movement. The largest demonstrations in the US are expected to have a total participation of 15 to 26 million people. Day after day, public media features thousands of people protesting without masks, violating personal distance of six-feet rules, shouting at police officers and to each other. It's a sure way to spread COVID-19. These uncomfortable scenes contrast with the strict lockdowns and social distancing policies the protestors have just experienced. Some demonstrations escalate into riots, arson, vandalism, looting, and eventually street skirmishes with police and with counter-protesters. Tens of thousands of stores and restaurants are boarding up their windows to prevent looters from breaking in. They had already begun closing businesses due to the pandemic, and many are now expecting destruction and loss of precious inventories on top of their economic miseries. At least 200 cities in more than 30 states impose curfews in the US. Washington DC activates 96,000 National Guard, State Guard and 3rd Infantry Regiment service members, the largest deployment of military operations other than wartime. National television news presents continuous coverage, warzone-like images, violence between civilians and police forces, and physical conflict against other law enforcement officers.

Joining Roxanne in the protest and traveling to the Bronx shopping mall is the last thing Samantha and Giti would consider.

Roxanne shouts, "You only care for your wellbeing and comfort. You don't understand any of the racisms in this country. Wait until you get this racism against your own!" She yanks the door open in front of them, then turns and slams the door shut and kicks it as she leaves.

Samantha and Giti face each other, uncomfortable to talk about what just happened. Samantha takes courage and speaks.

"Do you think she is going to be okay? I hope she took some masks with her from the hospital."

Giti irritably responds, "The hospital gives out only one mask per day. How can she bring masks?"

She is correct. All the staff and doctors are given one mask per day, not even an N95 because the N95 masks are only distributed to staff in the ER, OR and COVID units. Recently, the masks Samantha and Giti were given are much thinner than the usual surgical masks. Though it is easier to breathe through the thinner mask, they are both worried about the risk of getting coronavirus, particularly during their daily encounters with patients who must be transported in the hallways where doctors and staff walk, even when walking to the bathrooms or cafeteria. They are also worried their 100-year-old hospital with God-knows-what HVAC system is bringing in stale air while they work for more than 10 hours a day. The hospital administrators and leaders never address these concerns, and nobody dares to ask what they are afraid of knowing. On top of this, the residents' area is next to the morgue, in the basement. One night, soaked with the smell of formalin as the residents cut patient tissue specimens needed for their medical diagnosis, one of them jokes, "I hope formalin vapor can kill coronavirus in the air!" Behind their laughter, everyone is doubtful the hospital leadership cares to protect the medical doctors who are in the pathology residency training program.

Samantha asks Giti, "Do you think you would go out to protest if one of your fellow Orthodox Jews was killed like George Floyd, and risk getting COVID?"

After a long silence, Giti says, "How about you? What if it was an Asian person? Would you go out to protest?"

"I don't know, Giti. I am not sure. Our people generally suffer in silence. We are not comfortable speaking out in public and making a scene."

"Why?"

"We do not want to be seen. We try to live as a model citizen in this country. Over the years, since the railroad builders came from China, all Asians regardless of the difference in countries are lumped together as 'Chinese' and often receive anti-Asian slurs. I was born here in the US, and my father is Caucasian. So, I am somewhat removed from the protein-level attacks because most people cannot figure out what I really am. But my mom is Korean American and has experienced several incidents of discrimination and racial slurs. Asians are forever seen as foreigners since the Chinese Exclusion Act of 1882, which barred Chinese laborers from immigrating to the United States. This was followed by incarcerating people of Japanese ancestry living in America following the attack by Japan on Pearl Harbor during World War II. These American citizens experienced extreme racism, and fellow Americans questioned their loyalty. No one could determine who was Japanese, Korean, or Chinese. Even now, we are all lumped together to receive attacks. Furthermore, South Asian people including those from Thailand, Malaysia, Vietnam, the Philippines and others are all lumped together as Pan-Asians. We are a part of the Asian mass. The White is always the individual. I am not seen as an individual but always as a group. Discrimination is easier to carry out toward a group of people.

Giti looks intently at Samantha and replies, "You are not alone in this. We face a long history of anti-Semitism, and personally received relics such as the 'Judensau,' or 'Jew pig,' and you know the history of a xenophobic holocaust resulting in 6 million deaths."

Giti is very agitated and adds, "You guys are nothing in comparison to what we experience every day in America. Our synagogue got vandalized with Nazi propaganda graffiti, and we cannot even enter our own synagogue without checking our bags, our bodies are patted down like TSA procedures in the airport. You can go to your church every Sunday without any fear of getting bombed or shot by pellet guns unlike our synagogue. The acts of anti-Semitism are also spiking after nearly 15 years of decline. There have been more than 2,100 acts of vandalism, harassment and physical assault against Jews since 2016." Giti inhales, breathless.

Shyly, Samantha continues. "I am sorry, I didn't recognize your point of view. Your appearance is similar to Caucasians. But Asians are easier to identify from the Caucasian race. At least you may not get the constant question, 'where are you from?' We are never viewed as an *American* American, but always as the guest, a foreigner. We are told to go back home, but our home is America."

"You may be surprised, Samantha. We get that question all the time too. We don't really look like Caucasians. Most of the white supremacists can easily point us out. To answer your question regarding whether I would join the protest with Roxanne, the answer is no, because I am busy with my own challenges of facing anti-Semitism, so I cannot see George Floyd's death as my own kind. Intellectually I can sympathize with the historical brutality the Blacks face, which continues even now. But since I also confront the same brutality from the world, and amid much of my own torment and pain, I cannot get up and fight right now for them. During this pandemic, people are gathering shoulder-to-shoulder, marching, chanting loud without mask. It gives me chills, and I am worried about the viral transmission. How long do we have to prolong this nasty virus? Why aren't the people more responsible to end this pandemic first? Don't they know the virus doesn't care about our emotions? They are making an ideal situation and haven for the virus."

Samantha considers Giti's perspective and replies. "I think the Blacks had enough. Pandemic time or no pandemic time, this amount of brutality in the human race cannot be tolerated. To demonstrate and protest in the time of pandemic is expressing how serious they are to say, *'enough is enough.'* They are risking their lives to say that. We are making excuses not to join Roxanne tonight, but in time, we need to face this issue of human equality whether we like it or not for our own sake. The constitution of America states *we are all created equally* but obviously this is not true for Blacks and other minorities."

Chapter 4

A darker reality

June 4, 2020

As the night deepens, Roxanne's protest march becomes chaotic with looting and direct conflict with police. Many enraged frontline protestors are not wearing masks, shouting at police, demanding justice for the Black people's lives. Protestors are frustrated with COVID-19 lockdowns and lashing out with unexpected but justifiable causes, cries for freedom, and pleas for others to be outside in the street; a crowd showing defiance. The protesters are without weapons, met by police with shields, helmets, and batons. Police use the kettling method and line up to block the streets and soon the protestors are confined, then pressed into a mass against the police force, causing direct face-to-face conflict leading to physical contact and excessive force by the police. A patrol car drives into the crowd, an officer pulls down a protestor's mask and releases pepper spray, and other officers throw tear gas and shoot rubber pellets.

On the opposite side, protestors shatter police car windows and set several vehicles on fire. Several monuments in Central Park and other areas including the Bronx are vandalized by certain cop-haters who wear shirts spray painted with *ACAB*, an acronym for *'All Cops Are Bastards.'* The protestors throw empty bottles and rocks at officers who are wearing armor. It is no match against police armed with far superior weapons.

The opportunists dash into the luxurious and trendy stores, breaking the glass of storefronts and swarming in to steal expensive items, especially designer shoes and sneakers, gathering as much as possible, arms full of stolen goods and running away into the dark streets, as if this is the way to show justice to the world. Because of the COVID shutdowns, stores and restaurants were already facing dramatic decreases in sales, people losing their jobs, families lining up blocks upon blocks at food banks for the first time in their lives just to get their next meal, as if it is the great depression of the 1930s or the deadly

1918 influenza pandemic.

More than 1,000 people are arrested by the end of the night. Roxanne is one of them. She was placed in a jail cell packed with 25 other women, but was the only person wearing a mask. Blood poured out of her head, beaten by police using batons. Her bleeding would not stop. Blood covered her face, she could not open her eyes from the swelling of her forehead, which had split open. Her adrenaline was pumping so hard she could not realize the severity of her injury.

Samantha arrives at the hospital after the call from Roxanne. Seated at the bedside as Roxanne sleeps, she places her hands on her roommate's arm, but her cold hands awaken Roxanne. She cannot easily recognize Roxanne due to the severe bruises and swelling of her face; a heavy bandage over her head covering one eye.

"What happened?" Samantha asks.

"I am so cold."

Samantha notices only a thin white sheet covering Roxanne.

"I'll get some blankets." Samantha immediately gets up and talks to the nurse outside the room. The irritated nurse glares at her for asking non-urgent matters when she must deal with COVID patients and countless wounded demonstrators shot with rubber pellets. One protestor lost his eye, and another died moments ago from rubber pellets shot by police. The nurse appears tired and anxious for her shift to end. Getting a blanket is not something she will be bothered with. Samantha searches the area, opening all the drawers until discovering a closet full of thick blankets, and takes two for Roxanne. All Samantha cares for at this moment is to get a blanket for her friend who is cold and shivering.

"Hey, what are you doing?" barks another nurse to Samantha, who wears a hospital scrub to blend in with the nurses and other health care workers.

"Just getting a blanket for a patient," Samantha replies as she hurries to Roxanne's room and covers her with both blankets.

"Oh, thank you," Roxanne says.

"What's going on? What happened to your head?"

"I got into a fight with police officers."

"Why in the world would you do that?"

"Long story. I got 13 stitches. I will be okay."

"How long are they keeping you here?"

Roxanne points her finger at the IV fluid bag which is almost empty.

"Until all the fluid is in my body. I'm dehydrated and lost a lot of blood. But I will be okay and back at work this morning."

"Roxanne, I don't think you can go back to work in this state. What service are you on this month?"

"Surgical pathology. GI service."

"Are you out of your mind? One of your eyes is covered by the bandage. What were you doing? During your GI service you know you cannot skip even a single day."

"Samantha, this protest is very important to me. It's more important than my own life. The GI service is secondary."

"What can be more important than GI service when you are a pathology resident?"

"Oh, Samantha, only if you can live in my skin for one day, will you understand what I go through as a Black person in this country? Where do I even begin to explain to you?"

"Why don't you try!"

Roxanne gives a long exhale before she begins. "It started on July 17, 2014. My father witnessed an NYPD officer kill Eric Garner, putting him in a prohibited chokehold while arresting him. The only thing Eric Garner did was sell single cigarettes from packs without tax stamps. Many Blacks do not have a privilege called a 'job' to make ends meet or just to eat. The policeman wrestled him to the ground, put his arm around Garner's neck. Garner said the same words George Floyd used, "I can't breathe!" spoken 11 times before he died on the sidewalk on Staten Island. The autopsy was done and the medical examiner stated Garner's death was a homicide, a death caused by the intentional actions of another person resulting from compression of neck. Despite that, Garner's asthma, heart disease and obesity were cited as contributing factors and the grand jury decided not to indict the police officer. There were small demonstrations nationwide in response to this case but there is no justice for the Blacks, then and now. The police officer was fired five years later. The video of this murder was released to the press, and you could clearly see how the police choked Eric Garner, and yet he was not found guilty. My father was outraged, so he vandalized the police station on Staten Island with spray paint and he got caught. Now he is in prison for a 20-year sentence, accused of demonstrating with violence, and falsely accused of stealing retail goods by looting. It wasn't him who was looting, but to police, all Black men look alike, and they accused him. Garner's family received 5.9 million dollars but what good is that when so many Black people, especially Black males, are repeatedly brutalized by police every day of their lives? What did George Floyd do to deserve murder from a police officer on the street in Minnesota? Both of the cases are surfacing only because someone videotaped the incidents. There are so many Black people who suffer police brutality who are not videotaped. I have four brothers who are in their early 20s and in their teens. They are scared even of death by police who confront them without any reason. The only reason they are targeted is because of their color, nothing more. They haven't done any crime but are often arrested. Once they are arrested, it becomes a life-and-death situation. My second brother was just walking with friends after school on the wrong side of the street, the side where Whites live. Neighbors complained because they didn't like the fact that groups of Black kids walk in their neighborhood. A police car arrived in under five minutes and officers beat them up. My brother got broken ribs. I am tired of this harassment just because we are Black. I am angry beyond my control, and sad beyond my expression." She wipes her tears and continues.

"This demonstration is not just protesting for injustice, but it is my life, my purpose in living, fighting for dignity as a human to be treated with respect. We have been treated worse than animals throughout history in America, even today. This cannot continue. We already paid so much of a price in our losses. We lost our people, land, history, the truth, and dignity!"

Samantha is speechless. She has not realized how Whites have twisted their version of American history to subside and minimize Blacks' rights. For that matter, people of color in general. Documentation of American history is heavily influenced by Whites' perspectives, their truth, not the point of view of Blacks. History taught in her grade school was completely tainted by White textbook authors. Samantha does not recall reading any perspectives from Blacks or Asians in her American history classes.

Regarding Asian American history beginning in the early 19th century, three major waves of Chinese immigration to the US occurred, primarily laborers for the transcontinental railroads, and mining workers. Many were virtually slaves, and all were treated as cheap laborers, suffered racial discrimination, and always regarded as aliens. In 1882, the US Congress passed the Chinese Exclusion Act prohibiting Chinese to become naturalized citizens, or to buy land, and even from marrying White women. Thank God that these laws are now abandoned. It is strange that White people have thought this country belongs to them, without respect to the Native Americans, who are called Indians. They originally lived in this land until they too were pushed aside with brutal force to live in isolation. At the same time in America, White people were relatively new to the country, immigrating mainly from European countries. They were mere guests in this country.

African Americans experienced slavery in North America beginning in 1619, when a ship carrying 20 captives landed at Point Comfort in Virginia against their will. In 1776, the Declaration of Independence was written, whose principle states, "that all men are created equal, that they are endowed by their creator with certain unalienable rights," but this does not extend to African Americans. By 1860, the population of African Americans grew to nearly 4 million, 13 percent of the total population, and eventually they gained the right to vote under the 14th amendment in 1868 — but only the Black males could vote.

Meanwhile, eight of the first 12 presidents were slave owners and the country was divided by the organization of new, segregated institutions, and extralegal violence by White supremacist ideologies that prevented Black people from being truly free. Primarily White citizens used their ability to control the laws and wrote the history of America for hundreds of years. Blacks do not receive true freedom. Greed of American capitalists exploited Black workers for hundreds of years, and their rights to be 'equal' is prevalent even today. Unsung African American heroes are forever hidden within the 400 years of history in this country. Police brutality and racial inequality are constant companions of their lives. What's another Black life lost? What's the difference between the current death of George Floyd and lynching? Killing by hanging for an alleged offense without a legal trial? How much longer can African Americans wait until they get the same respect for their lives in this country? Even after Barack Obama — the first Black president in America — stories of Black discrimination continue.

***

Samantha can begin to understand Roxanne's point of view, just by putting herself into the situation of racial discrimination by the police. What if George Floyd was one of her relatives or herself, her father or brother? Even though her father is White, and she does not have a brother, it is easy to think that anyone in the same situation will have the same angry feelings as does Roxanne. Samantha is ashamed she did not walk alongside Roxanne to protest for justice and humanity. Under God, no race is superior, nor deserves more respect or recognition. We are made of God's image equally, whether we are White, Black, Asian, Brown or any color for that matter. Samantha cannot express all her complex emotions of shame, frustration, guilt, anger, and defeat, so she holds Roxanne's hand once more and sits close to her.

"I will do your GI service work until you get better." That is all she can say gathering her courage.

Chapter 5

Sifting true heroes

June 10, 2020

The new Scientific Director at Abby Laboratory faces a monumental challenge to be accepted by his new team. Ed Liu is acknowledged for his brave act at the Wuhan Institute of Virology (WIV), where he secretly obtained the COVID-19 virus and brought it back to the US and quickly cloned it. Unfortunately, heroic acts are soon forgotten in our feeble memories during the pandemic, and like most people, Ed's team can focus only on the item at the top of a to-do-list. Dr. Benson, a Black female manager and well respected scientist was the team's leader until 'the golden boy for Dr. Allen' was introduced as a new Scientific Director and their team leader. Everyone but Ed knew that Dr. Benson was a more appropriate person for the director position.

On January 11, 2020, the World Health Organization (WHO) tweeted that they had received the coronavirus genetic sequences from China, and the official race to generate a vaccine began. Apparently, Ed's brave acts and cloning of the virus in petri dishes had been unnecessary. By the time he returned from Wuhan, the team at Abby was already underway with first phase trials. Rumors abound that Dr. Allen rushed his decision to appoint Ed the scientific director of Abby laboratory and overlooked Dr. Benson because she is a minority, a female, a quiet scientist with no focus on self-promotion. She works under the radar of company leaders, as Ed soon learned.

Abby was co-founded in early 2010 by Steven Allen, PhD, and evolved into a biotech company pioneering new ways to deliver medicines using messenger RNA (mRNA) to fight back viruses. Dr. Allen's doctorate degree in biochemical engineering from MIT led him to build connections with numerous scientists at MIT and NIH, while he promptly learned the essential mission and basic character of mRNA concepts. He believed it could change the planet, but every scholar and colleague disagreed.

"It's not going to work," he was told, and his humble start began with rejections of his first nine grants. Critics became notoriously sarcastic, citing over 200 reasons why mRNA won't work.

Abby was originally established upon the research and findings of a female scientist—a Hungarian-born biochemist. In early 2000, she and a colleague were working in a University of Pennsylvania lab when they later met Dr. Allen, and together they created the current company. 23 mRNA drugs and vaccines were created, with 14 in clinical studies, but not a single product was approved by the FDA. The business was losing money. Dr. Allen apparently possessed business savvy, so they agreed to appoint him as CEO. He obtained some private funding and expanded the work on mRNA while he hired additional scientists. The most prominent was Sandra Benson, an MD and PhD specializing in virology. She formerly worked at NIH studying the human antibody response to viruses, specifically the Zika virus. Ed Liu, PhD, studied Ebola and Dengue viruses and was hired much later. Sometime in late 2019 Ed suddenly traveled to China for an extended trip, reportedly to visit the Wuhan Institute of Virology. Not long after his return, the entire team of over 90 scientists came under the direction and leadership of Ed as they further concentrated on a coronavirus vaccine with new technology in vaccine development by using non-traditional methods.

Sandra knew of her capability to lead the entire scientific staff in the company's vaccine portfolio, but Ed Liu became the new director, although his education and experience was far less than Sandra's. Her numerous years working on experimental mRNA for the Zika virus led to development of a Zika vaccine in 10 months, a company record for completing such a task. It was natural for Abby to adopt her template in making a new vaccine for the coronavirus and to utilize the coronavirus's genome sequences that were published in early January. In just two days, her team in the lab established a COVID-19 vaccine candidate: mRNA-1273. The team quickly identified the spike protein and engineered mRNA sequences to stabilize it to induce a strong immune response against coronavirus. The FDA had never approved or authorized any mRNA-based vaccine. The company gambled and proceeded to direct valuable resources toward a new novel virus, although no scientist could predict if a possible pandemic would last more than a few months.

This was the first time in history that a synthetic vaccine was used for administering in humans, an experimental technology to fight against the virus, rather than traditional methods such as inactivated or killed virus. The mRNA vaccines are made on a computer and in vitro, not from the viruses themselves. By mid-June, there were more than 100 companies, commercial laboratories, and academic institutions joining the race to make a vaccine against COVID-19.

Pfizer in particular is a competitor to Abby and a more established scientific entity. This 171-year-old Fortune 500 powerhouse also takes on the project to use mRNA to manufacture a vaccine. Pfizer has thousands more employees, an established name recognition, and has not taken any money upfront from the US government. Rather, the federal government promises to pay the company $1.95 billion for at least 100 million doses if their vaccine is approved. Time is of the essence. Abby Laboratory is an unknown smaller company no one even knew about until their surprise announcement about their vaccine undergoing a Phase 1 study in late April of 2020. The very first clinical trial data from Phase 1 had very promising results and is a significant but momentary relief to the team. But they face hurdles: Successful phase 2 and 3 trials, application and then acceptance of emergency use authorization by the FDA, cash flow, new workspaces, new equipment, more scientists, and enlisting thousands of volunteer subjects for the phase trials.

The traditional way to develop vaccines is a sequential method; make an animal-grade vaccine, test it successfully, and then manufacture. Then, wait for the animal data, and when successful, make a vaccine for human trials. Abby Laboratory decides to do all these steps simultaneously, a gamble of significant risks. If they chose the wrong path, how long can they absorb the time and expense at a point of no return? The most significant scientific challenge is to get RNA delivered into cells. RNA molecules need to be wrapped up in nanoparticles made of lipids, but those nanoparticles can have undesirable side effects. Late one night Ed's team successfully concocts an ideal amount of lipids enveloping mRNA for successful delivery into cells. Their first attempt soon results in successful data in both animal and human trials. They have proven that mRNA can carry instructions into the human body to make antibodies that are primed to attack a specific virus, in this case the coronavirus. Remarkably, they learn that the same method can be used to attack cancer cells, extremely promising for a treatment modality to fight against cancer cells. It is a pivotal breakthrough they must momentarily set aside.

***

Other vaccines notable to mention are from the British Swedish rival AstraZeneca, and the Johnson & Johnson (J&J) vaccine, both not using mRNA. The J&J vaccine uses double-stranded DNA which is not as fragile as mRNA. J&J adds the gene for the coronavirus spike protein to another virus called Adenovirus to enter cells, while preventing replication or illness.

AstraZeneca similarly uses a weakened version of Adenovirus (which causes common cold) from chimpanzees, modified to contain genetic materials of the coronavirus. ChAdOx1nCoV-19 is the name of their vaccine which requires two doses given 4–12 weeks after the first dose.

J&J's design utilizes a protective touch protein coat of adenovirus and more stable genetic material of DNA, and hence, the J&J vaccine can be refrigerated for up to three months at 36–46°F, whereas mRNA-based vaccines need to be frozen in minus 94°F for transport and storage until they are ready to be used. After thawing, a vial of the Pfizer vaccine must be used within five days. Abby Lab's vaccines are stable at refrigerated temperature much longer, 30 days, and at room temperature, 12 hours. The J&J vaccine can be stored at room temperature for a longer time, with another advantage that only a single dose is needed. AstraZeneca's ChAdOx1nCoV-19 vaccine can be stored at refrigerated temperature for up to six months.

Different vaccines in different stages of clinical trials may soon be available for consumers. This generates havoc and chaos in people's minds: *'Which one do I get, which one will be most effective, what are the most optimal doses, how many times should I get vaccinated and at what time intervals, can I have two different types of vaccines, what are the logistics to get vaccines into people's arms, what side effects shall I expect, how long should I observe for the signs and symptoms of side effects, where to administer shots and monitor the side effects appropriately — hospital settings or in drug stores like flu shots — and who will administer the vaccinations to appropriately address potential side effects, what is the priority list for receiving vaccines, what are the varying efficacies for each vaccine, and finally, will the vaccine cover virus variants, mutations?'*

Answers to these are unknown at this point. Throughout the country solutions appear unplanned, not discussed, and not communicated in a systematic manner.

***

On a granular level, Ed must smooth out his relationship with Dr. Benson, who is focused on her work and has no time to discuss personal feelings with Ed and politely declines his meeting invitation to dissolve any personal issues. The company is nearly in chaos; a single mistake from a lab technician is cause for dismissal, staff turnover abounds. Every man for himself is the unspoken principle in the company. Ed chooses to ride its wild horse and bear the pressure inside himself until their vaccine is produced. No time to haggle over political power with Dr. Benson, and her silence is a blessing to Ed.

Research scientists within the competing companies commonly work 14 or more hours per day, condensing their work into one year that would normally take four years. These scientists are heroes, the 'other group' that is unseen, in no spotlight compared to frontline doctors and nurses. Researchers make personal sacrifices equal to or greater than health care workers, sleep in their labs at nights, miss family events. Partners and spouses relinquish their own personal time and typically handle all family matters, homeschool children since most schools are closed, often quit their jobs to fulfill these duties, both men and women, but predominantly women. Meanwhile, researchers perform repetitive work that must be meticulous and super precise, their motivation is purely a genuine desire to end the pandemic, as quickly and safely as possible. These scientists are not familiar with being the center of attention, unlike the frontline workers who are typically paid more than scientists. Researchers quickly began receiving additional space, staff, or equipment unlike prior to pandemic. Apparently, unlimited funding is available.

Ed began with 90 researchers in his group, expanded this to

250 by mid-June but he has high turnover rates. He is consumed daily in reviewing research data with his scientists, but he also oversees expansion of workspaces, hiring additional scientists, bringing in new equipment, and quickly becomes bogged down with HR issues. These have become his major work. His unexpected new position in management provides headaches and stomach aches. He prefers working on experiments, hypothesizing theories, and proving or disproving his theories. He is a scientist.

Dr. Allen enjoys the spotlight, visits the White House to discuss progress, and brings the media to the company to generate a broader image of his company. Hence, Ed practically runs the company and makes daily decisions on all major scientific and HR matters. In time, Ed develops reasonable, sound judgments and decisive leadership under these circumstances. Amid the urgent timelines, most researchers including Dr. Benson have no major issues with him. Ed works hours comparable to other researchers, sleeps in his office each night, and often skips meals. He has no time to think about personal interests, including Dr. Samantha Parker.

When success is on the platform, declaring who is the real hero or heroine can become muddy in identifying such a person or persons. The ultimate pedestal of who receives recognition can be far from the truth. Everyone claims they are a part of the whole picture of success, and that may be true.

Chapter 6

Pillow of Tears

June 12, 2020

Emily Parker settles down somewhat with her routines after the death of her husband Robert on April 1. They were on a cruise ship offshore at Santorini, Greece, celebrating their 50th anniversary.

The power of mundane everyday chores, busyness and irritations can substitute for even the greatest of losses. Her friend Mahalia has lived with her for three weeks, but now must go back to the Philippines because cruise line workers like her have a narrow window to repatriate. So, Mahalia must quickly go back to her country, even though she has a visa to stay in the US one more week. Emily buys armfuls of gifts for Mahalia's family and her friend ends up with eight suitcases of goods, packed with expensive gifts the family has never seen or dreamed of having. Emily also buys her a first-class ticket that allows for the additional baggage at no cost.

Within three weeks, Emily and Mahalia had become best friends. "You are my Jesus in flesh," Emily says daily to Mahalia. "After losing Robert to COVID-19, and being accused of bringing the virus on board, I lost all sense of who I am, the purpose of living, and the sheer exhaustion of the prolonged trip caused my nervous breakdown. People around me don't normally hate me. I began to hate myself and my life, thinking that I must have brought death to my own husband and everyone on the ship. I wanted to vanish from the face of the earth. I couldn't bear the pain of losing my loved one and carrying the blame. Why am I living, and my husband died?"

Hearing this, Mahalia could only hug Emily, like she did after pulling her back from jumping overboard and saving Emily's life. Mahalia is uncomfortable staying in Emily's beautiful mansion house, eating Emily's food and enjoying the privileged life which she never dreamed of, feeling indebted to Emily for her unusual kindness. Mahalia was comfortable living on a small cruise ship, on the bottom deck with multiple workers living in crowded rooms without windows. Now she lives in a huge house with a 270-degree Bay view, floor-to-ceiling windows, often eating Korean beef kalbi which Emily painstakingly prepares by spending four hours in the kitchen. Mahalia never imagined any Asian person to live in this kind of luxury in real life, as if she's living a scene from *Crazy Rich Asians*. Such a spacious home for just one person in San Francisco, arguably one of the most expensive real estate views in the world. In her country, more than 15 extended family members often live in small shacks, crowded and packed side by side.

"Emily, at least four people can fit in your king-sized bed in this guest room." To that, Emily just smiles and says, "Mahalia, you can roll over many times."

On Memorial Day less than three weeks ago, two cruise workers had arrived at Emily's house, a woman and a man in white cruise line uniforms, appearing like marine officers early one morning. They came with an urn containing Robert's remains, and stiffly said, "Our profuse apologies for the loss and delay in transporting Dr. Parker's remains," and offered condolences to Emily. She placed the urn on top of the mantle of the living room fireplace. Once the officers left, she placed it on the floor next to the fireplace. She feared the contents might spill during a big earthquake in the Bay area like the one in 1989. Emily holds her husband's cremated remains in her bosom often at night, and cries until there are no more tears left in her eyes. Mahalia hugs Emily and rocks her to sleep. "You are indeed one who God sent in the time of darkness," Emily says. Mahalia makes sure Emily can easily function and take care of herself every day.

In the first week of June, Samantha visits her mother as promised. Mahalia is pleased to see Emily with a beautiful and decent daughter to look after her. All three visit the funeral home and Emily purchases a columbarium that houses cremated remains. They've brought a few recent pictures of Dr. Robert Parker, some showing Robert in his doctor's white coat. Alongside his stethoscope they brought, it seems to create a dignified final resting place for him.

Two days later, Samantha meets the lawyer who managed her father's assets, including his insurance. She learns her father purchased a large life insurance policy for his family's financial security, not including his pension and savings. With the house fully paid off, Robert knew his wife and daughter would not worry about finances for the remainder of their lives. Samantha reviews all of her father's finances and teaches her mother how to write a check. At first, Emily is frustrated with so many responsibilities but soon realizes that she must learn quickly, for Samantha will not be there forever for her. Emily's most difficult challenge is reading her bank account balance once all the money is wired to her bank account. Emily was comfortable up to a few thousands of dollars, but not in millions.

"Too many zeroes," Emily says.

After Samantha and Mahalia leave, Emily finds herself alone. She imagines Robert walking out of his library office and calling her name to request masala chai or oolong chai that he always enjoyed in the afternoon. Emily can hear his voice calling her. She turns to the voice but there is no one besides her, hearing an imaginary voice. Emily does not want to sleep in the master bedroom where he laid next to her. So, she sleeps in Samantha's room after her daughter departs to New York City. During the nights, Emily finds herself crying, wetting her pillow but no number of tears will bring her husband back. The only thing she can rely upon is God. Underneath the wing of God's hand, she finds her soul resting in peace that surpasses her understanding. She repeats the words, "We all die one day. I am indeed alone. I was born alone, and I will die alone. And I should be content being alone on this day with my God."

Chapter 7

Too many zeroes

June 15, 2020

Mrs. Kong visits Emily more frequently to play Ba-duk and check on a recent widow to make sure Emily is not doing silly things all by herself. Mrs. Kong sees Emily struggling with her bank account that has too many zeroes to count.

"You should not have that much money in the bank!" Mrs. Kong says, looking through her bifocal glasses.

"What should I do then? My husband had a life insurance money recently added to the checking account."

"You should diversify the money. Spread out over many things like stocks, bonds, bitcoins, and precious metals. The bank cannot guarantee all that money you have if they go under. And the stimulus checks of $2,000 the president is giving again are not going to come to us. That's for the poor people." Mrs. Kong is referring to the $1.9 trillion relief plan the president signed to give a maximum of $2,000 to families of certain incomes to navigate the financial difficulty during the pandemic.

Emily is puzzled. "What are you talking about? How can a bank go under?"

"Remember 1930s, the great depression?"

"No, I was not here."

"Trust me! The whole bank system can shut down. I don't even trust these FDIC-insured banks. Diversify money! You can join classes I attend. You must learn how to make more money from the money! We have four other older Chinese women, and we meet. We follow the stock market every week. Sometimes when stocks are up and down, we meet twice a week. We go to classes to learn more about the money. Classes are very good. Join our group. You have so much time now. You don't know what to do with all that time you have since Robert is gone. Don't worry, I am not taking your money. I have enough money. Sometimes we just play mahjong and eat Chinese food," Mrs. Kong says smiling.

Emily always notes that Mrs. Kong can be intrusive, pushy and demanding, and especially with her broken English, it can sound harsher. But having a very long relationship with Mrs. Kong, she trusts her. Emily decides to join the group, at least to learn more about the finances and extend her friendship with others, not just church groups. It is true that Emily finds more time than she knows what to do with since Robert passed away. Also, Mrs. Kong has much more money than Emily, which she is sure about. Mrs. Kong would not damage the friendship over the money with Emily.

Chapter 8

Mother's wish

July 18, 2020

Her mother Emily's birthday was a week ago, but Samantha had to remain in New York and take the pathology GI service for Roxanne. Now, Roxanne has mostly recovered from her injury and returns to GI service, allowing Samantha to fly back to San Francisco for her mother's belated birthday. Since Mahalia had left for her home country, Emily is now living alone in San Francisco with no one to care for her. Samantha plans to visit her mom as often as possible and help with finances, house chores, and to be her companion. Mrs. Kong lives next door, but Mrs. Kong herself may need care from someone. Her children had often visited each year prior to the pandemic, but they are afraid to risk transmission of the virus to the elderly and avoid physical contact. Samantha is also concerned about the risk of transmitting the virus to her mother after air travel.

Emily drove to the airport and picked up Samantha, and they promptly discussed the condition of the large home. Three weeks ago Emily called her daughter and explained that "the ground is always wet, killing plants and grass." Samantha called a pool expert, who determined the swimming pool was leaking, water seeping into the foundation of the house. The plan is to re-patch the surface of the pool, but first they must drain countless gallons of water. It is painfully difficult to hire pool experts because a growing number of families with kids are installing pools in their backyards due to the pandemic. Since nobody can travel during the pandemic, putting a pool in the backyard has become a popular thing to do this summer. Construction workers are scarce because they're booked months in advance as they renovate and build homes. Housing prices are relentlessly increasing, not enough homes for buyers, especially in the suburbs where the city people are moving to escape the virus. Working from home during the pandemic is suddenly required by employers, followed by the high demand for home renovations to create work-from-home office spaces. Simultaneously, the price for wood and nearly all other home building materials began to skyrocket. One benefit for workers is having no rush hour traffic.

Samantha increasingly believes her mom should move into a condo or a small apartment, but is afraid to bring up the subject. Perhaps Emily could move to New York City, but Samantha knows her mom does not want to move at all, and changing residency to another state is out of the question, at least for now. Emily has lived in California most of her life and she loves the diversity in Asian food, her church, her friends in San Francisco.

Surprisingly, Emily asks, "Do you think I should move to Jeju Island in Korea?"

Jeju Island is the largest island in South Korea formed by the eruption of an underwater volcano approximately 2 million years ago. Jeju is a popular holiday and honeymoon destination relying on tourism, known for its pristine clear water with rock formations around the island and a unique climate to grow delicious Jeju Island tangerines.

"Mom, no one from your family lives on Jeju Island. Why would you want to live there alone?"

"I don't know, I've been thinking, why should I live here in San Francisco when Robert is not even here with me. At least I can go back to Korea and live among people I can relate to, speak the same language and eat the food I really like in my old age."

"But Mom, San Francisco has many Asian people including Koreans, although the majority are Chinese Americans. You lived here more than you lived in Korea. Besides, Korean people are not the same as when you left Korea. You might be romanticizing the idea of living in Korea. You will feel like a foreigner in your mother country because you lived in America for so long."

"You might be right. I probably romanticize living on Jeju Island, back in Korea. But I am increasingly nervous going outside my home these days. Many Asian people are getting random attacks, even in Chinatown. These perpetrators are mostly Blacks, and Arabic-speaking people. Why do you think these people are attacking us?"

"Mom, do you think they are Blacks and Arabic-speaking

people? Don't you think the most common people who attack Asians are Whites? It's the media that talks about this and shows these incidents. They tend to focus on Asians who are attacked by Blacks and Arabic-speaking people. I think the majority of the hate crimes against us are conducted by the Whites. There have been more than 3,800 hate crimes against us during the pandemic, mostly slurs, shunning, and physical attacks against the elderly women, the easiest targets. They cannot fight back. The cowards are acting out because our president said it is the 'China virus.' They always had prejudice against Asians just like they have against Blacks. Now, they feel justified to manifest preconceived notions that we are foreigners who brought tragedy into America. And you know how Asians are, they rarely report any crime against them. If they reported 3,800 cases, then you can easily assume twice that number."

After some silence, Emily says "Yes, you are right." She never told her daughter she had suffered racial slandering on the cruise ship. For some reason, Emily wants to hide her painful and shameful experiences from her daughter, as if by hiding these, her daughter will avoid similar racial bias or attacks. Emily also never revealed her suicide attempts, and neither had Mahalia. Emily appreciates Mahalia for not explaining how they became intimate friends. The hurt is too deep, indeed too personal. She is ashamed to admit the event, sorry to live in this land, always viewed as an immigrant who was never welcomed in the first place. Although she is a naturalized citizen of America, married to her White husband for decades, she never felt that America accepted her as one of its own. She is an uninvited guest in this country, and should behave with utmost decency because she did not want her mother country blamed for her personal behavior. Emily had secretly hoped her daughter would take on more of Robert's looks to avoid discrimination in this country. She encouraged Samantha to dye her hair blonde or light brown, to look more like a White person growing up.

Samantha always thought her mother was odd and never understood the concept until recently. Samantha keenly observes her surroundings, glances in many directions, sometimes stopping to turn around when walking in New York

City during the pandemic.

"Mom, there is something else that I have to deal with in medicine, as a female doctor."

"What is that, sweetheart?"

Emily braces herself to hear her daughter's painful experience.

"There was this new young White scrub nurse who was next to me when I was in medical school doing surgery rotation. She said, 'It's all guys here!' and the attending surgeon chuckled and said, 'as it should be.' And then that doctor added a statement to me, 'Don't tell your med school dean I said that.'"

Samantha immediately adds, "I was there; a woman, a minority race and my presence did not deter his comments. It was painful. Sexism and glaring racism continues in medicine, yet more than 50% of medical students are currently female. The fundamental hierarchism and male White dominance cannot change. It is a product of a pervasive cancel culture. They argue in blindness, 'Why are you so sensitive? Why do you encourage inclusion so much, while we can't say anything in public about LGBTQ, women, minorities, gay and lesbians?'"

"How can doctors and medical students treat diversity of patients without bias, when the prevailing culture idolizes the cancel culture which is a form of vigilante justice? In medicine, we have collectively fed the concept of cancel culture and now we are finding that it stands directly in our path toward inclusion, justice, a foundation of honesty, humbleness, and a spirit of wisdom over mere knowledge." Samantha's passion rises, approaching anger.

"So, did you report that to your dean?" Emily asks.

"No, I was a coward, feeding the idol myself. I am not too proud of it, Mom."

"Well, you were just a medical student."

"It's not just that. It's not safe to speak up and be a whistleblower. The institution and the system are supposed to protect me if I speak up, but I will get retaliation. Indirect hostility, frequent put-downs, ostracizing, pushback in my residency education. Residency training often places non-White people and women in undesirable situations, fewer professional opportunities, and inhibits career development. Ultimately, my own self-identity and significance will be questioned. In a way, the system promotes silence by instilling fear of speaking up, reinforces reliance on male power by minimizing encounters with 'troublemaker female' colleagues. Not a single person who seems to be alongside me has risen to support me. A few have turned against me because they must protect their own positions and jobs. I know how this 'cancel culture' works in medicine, and I will not fight to un-cancel the silence, at least not now."

Emily is silent for a moment and says, "The topic is beyond my comprehension. Let's just eat!"

As usual, Emily has cooked Samantha's favorite dishes, and enjoys watching her daughter eat.

"You are malnourished. Look at you, how skinny you are."

When visiting her mother, Samantha feels continuously full. "Mom, no one will marry me or want me because I will be so plump like a rolling ball," and they laugh about it.

"You know Samantha, you need to seriously think about marriage and having at least one child." Samantha knows what's next. "You are not getting younger." Emily says this all the time, but now she adds another comment. "What happened to Ed? You know, I like Ed. He is smart, handsome, nice to me and to his parents. He is a firstborn son. A nice boy. Very responsible and filial son. It's very hard to find such a man now."

"Mom, Ed and I broke up. I told you that before. The last time we saw each other was at the end of April. It's been almost four months."

"Why did you break up with him?"

"I told you mom; I met this other doctor I fell in love with."

"But you said he died."

"Yes, he died but I am still in love with him."

"I know that feeling. I am still in love with your father. But you are different. You need to look for a man who can take care of you. You are still young and have a whole life ahead of you. I'd like to have grandchildren. You can bring your grandchildren to me. I can take care of them while you work." Emily smiles, imagines holding a grandchild in her arms.

"Mom, I need to have a husband before I have this child that you are dreaming about."

"Yes, of course, Ed can be your husband."

"No, I can't marry him."

"Why not? Ed has been your boyfriend for over a decade. I've seen him throughout your adult life. We even went to Yosemite National Park with him. He is a nice man!"

"Mom, I am not going to marry him. His family is suffocating."

"You are marrying him, not his family. It's hard to find a nice man like Ed these days. Old boyfriend is the best because you can trust him."

"I don't want to marry someone who does not share my religion. He is a Buddhist. The whole family is Buddhist. They go to the Buddhist temple."

"Oh yes, I forgot about that. Yes, I can understand. I won't push you too much on Ed then."

"Thank you, Mom!"

With that, they settle the matter of Ed. Tomorrow, however, her mother will continue with a conversation, 'when are you going to be married and have a kid,' as though a woman is not a complete human being without a husband. Samantha cannot figure out if these nagging questions and cultural values of women originate from Korea, or from Emily, a mother who thinks women need men to fulfill their identities.

While deep in thought, her mother interrupts.

"If you are not going to be married soon and bring me a grandchild, I will think more about moving to Jeju Island along with my sisters from Seoul. I don't want to live in this house. I suddenly hear Robert's voice calling me and I turn to see him, but he is not there. When I go to bed at night, I feel him next to me, but he is not there. When I turn certain corners of this house, I expect to see him, but he is not there. The house is too big for me, and I am alone here. I was thinking about visiting Korea and to see Jeju Island with my sisters. First, to just take a look and visit them. I have not seen them in over a decade. I don't want to live here anymore."

Samantha understands the decision is non-negotiable, but chooses to not think seriously about her mom moving to Korea. Not at this time. Perhaps hoping her mom stays in San Francisco is too strong to imagine otherwise.

Chapter 9

Women at warp speed

July 28, 2021

Abby Laboratory had the first potential vaccine for clinical trials, but Pfizer completed the first clinical trial using a similar mRNA with a different snippet of genetic code which is deployed into cells to stimulate a coronavirus immune response. Both vaccines require two shots, three to four weeks apart. Each dose of Pfizer contains 30 micrograms of mRNA whereas the product from Ed's company contains 100 micrograms. Since it has a higher dose per shot, it is expected to generate a more robust immune response by producing higher antibodies. But a government program named Operation Warp Speed asked Abby Labs to test lowering their dosage of the vaccine without eroding the vaccine's protection. And because of this, FDA approval is expected to be delayed until after the Pfizer vaccine approval. The government had pledged to buy at least 100 million doses from Abby Labs for $2.48 billion, which works out to roughly $25/dose, a great profit. Suddenly a non-visible small company becomes the center of a global hope. Their company stock reaches to the sky.

Dr. Allen asks Ed to host a well-publicized press conference for the company. The next day, Ed provides a laboratory tour as the media rushes to capture images of the researchers in their labs. Camera crews surge forward as Ed leads their approach into the laboratory spaces. The press does not know what to expect within the laboratory, so they immediately film research technicians pipetting the RPMI, pink fluid into test tubes, or anyone they can find who is peering through a microscope, or working under sterile hoods. The scientists do not know how to react to these people who surround them, so they continue working in absolute quietness.

Some reporters ask, "What is that? What are you doing?" but receive no reply because technicians and scientists do not know how to answer these generic questions. Outside the labs in a large meeting room, Ed finally provides more detailed information and brings some calm to the media. Dr. Allen is not acquainted with many of the details in laboratory work, so Ed is the appointed person to interact with the media. His image is featured across national evening news, online platforms, and numerous outlets around the world. The stories often include footage of lab workers pipetting. His team members ask Ed, "What's the deal with pipetting? That has nothing to do with vaccine development!"

Most Americans will assume vaccine development is primarily pipetting a pink solution into test tubes by expressionless, serious research technicians. After the media event, Dr. Allen and Ed host a celebration for their successful and promising preliminary results from Phases 1, 2 and 3. Their early small Phase 3 data shows over 94% effectiveness in their vaccine subjects; an incredible result.

"Why don't you say something Ed, my shy and brilliant scientist?" says Dr. Allen with a grin. Looking toward the small group of people in the courtyard, and hundreds of scientists and other employees via Zoom, Ed responds.

"Thanks, Steven, for your kind words. I'd like to recognize my colleague and dear friend Dr. Sandra Benson, who tirelessly worked for over a decade to develop a Zika virus vaccine using mRNA technology. Only through her behind-the-scenes work and dedication over the last 10 years can we celebrate this COVID-19 vaccine that has become our reality today. We are seeing an extraordinary vaccine developed by all of us, led by Sandra, and we want to honor and recognize our team for their hard work, long hours away from your families, hearts and souls poured out to make a new history on our planet. Our accomplishment came from having a single goal, a single focus, being of one mind."

Sandra Benson speaks next, through Zoom. "Thanks Ed and Steven for recognizing our work, the incredible teamwork. At times I was saying, 'what in the world am I doing here?' but we never gave up as we ran the invisible race to compete with dozens of other companies. Here we are, about to finish number one or two at the final finish line. Let's make our vaccine available to Americans by early November, and end the pandemic here in America and then quickly across the globe."

Sandra knows most staff members placed great trust and faith in her previous work, and supported the theory that her Zika virus technique could also work in fighting the coronavirus. Dr. Benson thinks that her work as a woman scientist, a Black person, is often overlooked, regardless of her credible and impeccable scientific training and proven scientific work. However, after leaving a recent meeting she overheard a few people grumbling that she was given special treatment because she is Black, and a woman.

***

The Pfizer vaccine is also led by a woman scientist, Dr. Oz, along with her husband, Dr. Sahin. As a couple, these scientists have been creating a vaccine against coronavirus using a similar mRNA technique. Dr. Özlem Türeci is a native of Turkey and became interested in immunotherapy to treat cancer by mRNA, and cofounded BioNTech. These formidable entrepreneurs are now leaders at BioNTech, derived from Biopharmaceutical New Technologies. Its US headquarters is in Cambridge, MA. Sahin is the CEO, Türeci the chief medical officer. They had been working for two decades and now have developed the mRNA vaccine against the coronavirus within 11 months. Together with Pfizer, their vaccine's blended name is Pfizer-BioNTech Covid-19 vaccine.

***

The dichotomized, inside jokes flow through the Abby Laboratories. "They should never overlook the power of women in science," and others reply, "These women are driving us insane."

Because Dr. Benson works quietly without self-promotion, her work would have dissipated in importance had Ed not mentioned her work in public, even though employees in companies typically know who does what. Dr. Allen appears to overlook Dr. Benson's work and continues to rely on Ed's leadership of the team. Favoritism from a leader is the sure way to divide a team.

Several months ago Dr. Benson had commented to Ed in a passing comment, "We African American, Black women are at the bottom of the list to get any recognition or power. Look at the history of voting, in order. First, White men, then Black men, White women, and finally Black women. But science could not become what we have now, unless Black women were working behind the picture. The history repeats itself again and again in America and the whole world; White race with unalterable pride, selfish and unholy people exploiting Blacks to supply their excessive luxury by depriving us. I am tolerating you Ed, a Chinese man because you also experienced deprivation of your rights in this country, not too dissimilar to my race. You are placed into the position you have because you are a man, but God certainly knows 'who is who,' the person truly deserving credit for the scientific discovery." Ed was stunned by her feelings, and her words mostly true; speechless after such a powerful emotion composed of undeniable facts. Ed was intentional in acknowledging Sandra's point of view in public, giving her credit where credit is due to set the record clear.

Ed addresses the small crowd again. "Okay, now we got this vaccine working. Who is going to be first in line to get an injection?" Laughter and raising of hands fills their Zoom screens. "I nominate and volunteer Dr. Allen to be the first to get it! How about that?" Ed says, winking at Dr. Allen.

Chapter 10

Shame on us

October 8, 2020

The wedding day for Giti's little sister has suddenly arrived. Giti has often made it known to her sister that the wedding date and the husband are all arranged by their parents. Giti's sister has no word to say on the decision and must follow the strict ultra-Orthodox Satmar Hasidic Jewish culture. Giti's parents came to the east side of Williamsburg, Brooklyn, in the late 1940s from Hungary following World War II. Most of their family members were killed in the Holocaust. Now they are part of a large population of about 57,000 Jewish residents in a community admixed of other religious and non-religious groups. The Hasidic community dominates the area's population percentage, and is known for having one of the highest birthrates in the country. An average of eight children per family is the current statistical rate. Each year, the community celebrates 800 to 900 weddings of young couples, usually between ages 18 and 21. Women and men alike in the Hasidic community do not receive a secular education. Women tend to be homemakers and men study Torah. Lack of college degrees and secular professional skills leads to sparse economic opportunities which are far behind the rest of the population; over 60% are at the poverty rate and live in subsidized government apartments. More recently, tourism is rising in the Williamsburg area as visitors frequently take photographs of those living in the Hasidic community; Giti and her family have been followed by secular people who take photos and videos of Orthodox Jewish people as if they are exotic animals in a zoo.

"What's up with your side curls?" is the most frequent question tourists ask the Hasidic men. The practice is named *'payos'* according to the Jewish rule that a man must not cut or trim his hair from each side of the face, so it grows indefinitely. The origin of payos is from a Biblical (Torah) scripture stating that a man shall *'not round the corner of your pe'ah,'* which is generally interpreted from the zygomatic to temporal areas of the head. The details of restriction of cutting or trimming is not specified in the Torah, and hence, there are many interpretations and variations on how best to follow the rule among different groups of Jewish people. Hasidic Jews adhere to the strictest guidelines, which is to never cut hair from that region. Women are expected to not expose their natural hair after their wedding, and it must be covered with a headscarf, called the *'tichel'* or a wig. This is a signal to the public that they are married and that they comply with traditional notions of propriety.

Giti has seven siblings, five girls and two boys. She is 27 years old, a second-born girl and highly educated, very unusual for a typical woman in Hasidic culture and still single, never been married. She seems to be an outcast among her family and is treated like a black sheep in the family. Her extended family does not consider her as a part of their family, but still expects her to attend their major celebrations like weddings and funerals. Her extended family of more than 250 people religiously gather for all celebrations. When she chooses to attend the family events, everyone talks about her as if she is the only subject for their communication. Dozens give Giti their unwelcome advice; how she should live, behave, have a husband and you should have several children by now, how to dress more politely, how not to talk with such confidence, you should cut your long hair to be less sensual, and on, and on. Her parents made exhaustive efforts to convince Giti to fit within the extended family's expectations but eventually gave up on her. Even the intermediary marriage consultant hesitates to introduce Giti to any of the Hasidic Jewish boys. Giti has too many sins, including her acceptance of a secular education by completing college, medical school, and now her medical residency. Most significantly, her old age and deviated mindset is a strong deviation compared to the other Jewish women which hinders her to get married.

Deep down though, her mother is secretly proud of Giti. Her daughter has courage to succeed and become an outsider from the suffocating culture from the women's perspectives, but her mom dares not to share her thoughts with the rest of her family members. Only once, she whispered in Giti's ear when her daughter was moving out from Brooklyn and into Samantha's

Bronx apartment.

"Go and be free from this bondage of subservience and become a doctor. You make me proud of your strength. You are my daughter!"

Giti's little sister is only 17 years old, the last child and last to be married. Giti is particularly close to her little sister because Giti practically raised her from infancy. Her parents were busy with a small Kosher restaurant in the neighborhood and left all the siblings under the care of Giti and the oldest daughter, who married shortly after the last daughter was born, and hence, Giti was left to babysit all of her other siblings. Giti's little sister was an 'oops' child from the parent's point of view, seemingly neglected by everyone, so Giti took special care of her as if the baby was her own child. For these reasons, Giti and her little sister became best friends despite a huge age gap.

Giti's dilemma is whether she should go to her sister's wedding because of a rapid increase in COVID-19 cases and deaths in their Hasidic community. One of her uncles recently died of COVID after worship and prayer in the synagogue. His rabbi also contracted COVID and died. The rabbi had not considered this virus as real, and defied restrictions for gathering. Despite a significant number of deaths, several synagogues and rabbis joined to file a lawsuit against the state of New York, claiming the state's limit of gathering for worship to 25% of a congregation's membership deprives them of their religious worship and holiday observances. From their point of view, the city and state officials allow massive Black Lives Matter protests, but cracks down on religious gatherings and singles out the Jewish community with 'unanticipated and draconian limitations' authorized by the New York governor toward their synagogue attendance, a deprivation of their constitutional rights.

In March and April of 2020, during the first wave of COVID, the virus hit Giti's Hasidic community in New York with devastating force and hundreds of people died. At one point, the death rate in the Hasidic community was three to four times higher than the state average. The New York City mayor, the state governor, and even the White House advised and urged the community to "shutter key institutions and adhere to social-distancing protocols." More than 500 cases of COVID were found in one urgent care center serving Giti's ultra-Orthodox community. Residents of the community wake up each day to find out who died, including prominent rabbis. The Orthodox communities do not wear masks in public, ignore social distancing and continue to gather in large numbers. They have not closed schools, businesses, and continue their weddings, funerals, and worship gatherings in large numbers. While the city, state, and federal government push for testing, the Jewish community discourages COVID testing with a message in Yiddish and the entire community exhibits rampant COVID denialism. Misinformation abounds in the community as rumors claim that public health officials who visit are 'Nazi storm troopers.' The community is particularly susceptible to misinformation about COVID because they avoid news from the main media outlets, and only a few isolated families own a television. This creates a fertile ground for misinformation on the concept of herd immunity. Only 8% of their population test positive for the coronavirus, simply because the majority of their community refuse to be tested. The ultra-Orthodox community claims they will reach herd immunity naturally. Giti personally knows hundreds who believe that the pandemic is fake or overstated and liken the government's approach to the virus as a joke. Yesterday, the ultra-Orthodox community came out to protest. It turned violent, with at least a hundred Hasidim setting fires, burning masks in the streets, and denouncing the governor and the city's mayor after many in the Jewish community were fined $15,000 for attending a wedding event in their synagogue.

In 2019, measles outbreaks occurred within this community that did not trust nor practice vaccination of children, even though the measles vaccine is known to be safe, extensively researched, and abundantly used for decades. With COVID, the sentiment is harsher than their reaction toward the measles vaccine. It will be a formidable challenge to introduce a COVID vaccine to a wary and untrusting community such as the Hasidic Jewish community. Interestingly, Israel campaigned in favor of a national vaccine program and succeeded with 85% of Israeli adults completing vaccinations, making Israel the best country for studying vaccine efficacy.

Giti has lived in two distinctive cultures and environments

where both parties clash with no mode of communication for understanding each other. Her current communal dissociation is insurmountable for a person like Giti, who grew up knowing the beauty of belonging in a small community, while also possessing scientific knowledge, a secular scholar with a degree in medicine.

In frustration, Giti explains to Samantha and Roxanne, "I expect that hundreds of people will gather for weddings without wearing masks or social distancing, yet most won't take the virus infections seriously. Mask wearing is scorned, a sign of not trusting Almighty God even when everyone knows someone who recently died or became sick."

"Can you *not* go to the wedding?" Samantha asks.

"I have to go. Otherwise I will truly be outcast by my family. This time, for real."

"How can you go knowing your uncle died just a week ago and your entire family is probably infected with COVID?"

"I know, I will wear a mask," Giti shyly replies.

Roxanne bursts with anger, "Then when you come back to this apartment you will infect all of us!" Giti looks at Samantha, not knowing how to respond to Roxanne.

"I am not having that!" Roxanne shouts. "I don't want to get sick from you. As it is, we go to the hospital every day and expose ourselves to COVID. You're headed to an epicenter. Based on current data, more than a quarter of all people who attend the wedding in your community will be infected. We don't have vaccine availability yet and God knows when that will be!"

"But you're going out to another Black Lives Matter protest. Who do you think you are, bringing COVID into this apartment after your virus exposures at protests? Samantha and I are patient with you, but God only knows how many people you're shouting and marching with have COVID. You get mad and sometimes you remove your mask and yell at the top of your lungs! I saw you on TV. Shame on you telling me what to do. Americans are protesting that Black Lives Matter in every large city and in larger numbers than my entire Brooklyn neighborhood. When we protest for our religious rights, you become critical and intolerable because you are anti-Semitic. Your people are the villains. Black people spray paint our synagogues and have killed Jewish people throughout history. That's because you are jealous that we worship our God who says we the Israelites are the chosen people and chosen nation to be blessed by God." Giti is breathless, Roxanne is enraged.

"You stop there! You have no right to say that! You have no idea what it is to be a Black person in this country. You have not been disgraced as a whole, never murdered simply because of your color and never suffered a relentless force of brutality against you from the police."

"Oh, I know what you are talking about. You simply forgot that I suffer anti-Semitic curses and disgustful comments every day of my life. Equality is not part of my equation; you ignore that I am a descendant of Holocaust survivors. Roxanne, large genocides are not in your history!"

"Giti, you don't seem to have a good education in Black American history. Sure, there was genocide, and more. After your holocaust, this country was still fighting and protesting to eradicate Black families from owning their own land, keeping us from voting, taking our money and forcing us to bow down and sit somewhere else. Countless people were hung and burned alive. Jews are not the only race who experienced genocide. And if you are the chosen people or nation from the Almighty God, what have you and the Jewish nation done for the rest of the world? There are certain responsibilities if you are truly a chosen person to reflect who God is through your nation; but what have you done that is beneficial to us? You just demand special treatment from all of us while you do nothing beneficial to others." After a pause Roxanne shouts, "Throughout history, each one of you is selfish!"

"Enough! Both of you!" Samantha finally demands. Giti and Roxanne look at Samantha as she gets up from the sofa and walks toward the apartment door.

"Shame on you, both of you. We should embrace our little united nations living in this tiny apartment with harmony. If we cannot tolerate and understand each other, how do you expect our country to be united? Please just stop attacking, and please listen to each other. I know for sure Giti must attend her sister's wedding, and Roxanne must go out to protest for her people's rights. It's for all of us—our rights. Let's just deal with the facts of each other's needs. Whether we get COVID and die, is God's control. Let's be cautious for ourselves and for each other. I wish both of you would not go anywhere except to the hospital to work, but that's not going to be our common reality. I will leave it up to you to decide what actions to take. We are responsible women and doctors." Samantha opens the door and turns, "I am going for a walk. Some fresh air. With my mask on! I will be back in 45 minutes."

Chapter 11

Hasidic wedding

October 11, 2020

Giti attends her little sister's wedding. As expected, the entire extended family are in attendance and her entire synagogue joins the celebration hosted by her parents featuring an elaborate four-tiered pink wedding cake, dancing, and live music from a band. This wedding may be the last for a child from the Schwartz family. They gave up on Giti's wedding, for sure. She learns that her parents' restaurant is doing very well; Jewish people are still going out to eat. Business as usual even during the pandemic. The indoor wedding celebration is planned for seven hours, with no proper ventilation. Three people wear masks, children run around coughing at the food buffet, and Giti sees one elderly guest picking up food dropped on the floor to eat it. Many guests hand pick their food, change their minds and then pick up other food items. Conversations are in close proximity amid coughing and sneezing, hugging, singing, touching, handshaking, sharing dishes with each other and occasionally circulating drinking cups to sample different fruit juices, sharing cigarettes and cigars; these are extremely bothersome and horrifying scenes for Giti. She has seen in her hospital what the coronavirus can do. No one in the hospital would ever imagine walking around and wearing no mask for seven hours. Giti observes certain guests are clearly sick with fever, probably with COVID-19. It is truly a heavenly environment for the virus to transmit and reproduce. Giti is double masked and always wears her glasses, never takes a sip of water or eats any food. She would like to wear a hair bonnet and hazmat suit from the hospital to protect her ears, hair, and body but she could not go that far. She escapes touching anyone and carries alcohol swabs to clean after using the bathroom, sickened by the invisible world of virus transmitting and infecting in front of her among ignorant people.

Meanwhile, her family members, mostly women, are giving

her well-meaning but unwelcome advice, how to live appropriately. Several even follow her as she walks away from them to admonish her, "Such a shame that all your younger sisters are married, and you are still a single woman." Women are genuinely sympathetic toward Giti for not having a full life with a husband and children of her own.

"Get rid of that mask, Giti, don't be ridiculous. Let us see your face."

One of her cousins forcibly takes off Giti's mask and intentionally coughs directly at her.

"There, finally you are one of us!" as he runs away, laughing. Giti is in disbelief of his cruelty, and immediately puts her masks back on, which are now torn. She places her hand over the masks to keep them in place.

Her reality in the hospital and the devastation from COVID is drastically different from her reality at the Hasidic wedding. How can the same world have such different realities under the sun? Once again, she realizes how far she has been removed from her roots and the family. The battle between the things seen and unseen exists. Both are as real as life and death, but only she seems to acknowledge or recognize it. Knowledge of the virus-world prevents someone from going back to the innocent and naive world. It is unbearable for Giti to see how the innocent or ignorant people live. It is not a matter of not trusting God, nor is it a political issue. Arguments about wearing masks do matter to a virus. Virus will do its thing — duplicate by transmitting it from person to person. While persons stubbornly debate politics, religious differences or human rights, the virus is proliferating and doing its business of replications. The naive choose not to accept the microscopic world of truths and facts. It is an unseen or non-existent world to many. Indeed, 'truth shall set you free.'

Giti runs out of the wedding celebration after two hours. She couldn't take it anymore and said goodbye to no one. She rapidly walks to the subway station and worries how Samantha and Roxanne will treat her when she enters the apartment. She will certainly not share how a family member removed her masks and intentionally coughed at her face.

Chapter 12

Anosmia

October 24, 2020

Giti notices her loss of smell. Anosmia, the diagnosis she learned during her second year of medical school. It began a week ago. First, she experienced a low-grade fever, mild cough, and sinus headache and hid her irritable symptoms from her roommates out of fear from blame and accusations. Upon arrival at the hospital for work she is stopped at the entrance by a worker who is checking the temperature of every employee. A rapid loud beep alerts everyone to her temperature of 100.2° Fahrenheit. Employees quickly distance themselves from Giti by six feet or more. She feels their blame and judgment. Her temperature is rechecked.

"Dr. Schwartz, you cannot get in. Go back home!"

Giti returns to the apartment and meets Samantha and Roxanne as they leave for work. Perplexed, they ask, "What are you doing back here?"

Giti merely says, "I forgot to bring something. I will get there later." Giti lies. She is an early morning person who reports to the hospital at 6:30 am sharp every day. Both Samantha and Roxanne are night owls, barely able to arrive at the hospital by 7:30 am. As doctors, they both intently peer at Giti and notice her reddish, possibly feverish appearance. "She must have run back home. She looked hot," Roxanne later says as they approach the hospital.

"Yeah, she looks different, maybe sick," Samantha quietly adds.

A conference for medical residents begins at 8:00 am almost every morning via Zoom. Today, Giti is absent. Highly unusual for someone like Giti who works like a clock, reliable to the degree of a machine, her work ethic flawless.

Samantha texts Roxanne, "What's happening with Giti?"

"Maybe she is sick with COVID-19."

"Don't even joke about that!"

"I am not joking. She attended that wedding and said two of her extended family were hospitalized after the wedding."

"Oh, no, we wore no masks at our apartment."

"Yeah, right, I told her not to go to the wedding. Now what are we going to do?"

"Don't know but I will call Giti."

Samantha calls but Giti does not answer the phone. No one knows where Giti is, and her co-residents are upset as they are forced to accommodate additional piles of work from Giti's service in her hematopathology rotation. They're complaining about Giti's disappearance until an attending physician arrives and reports that Giti has confirmed her illness. Samantha is nervous. How does she tell Roxanne about Giti? Samantha has a bad vibe about this as she considers that a COVID-19 patient is living in her apartment.

Late afternoon, Samantha texts Roxanne about Giti. Moments later, Roxanne runs from her own rotation in the blood bank and rushes into Samantha's surgical pathology rotation work area.

"Samantha, what are you talking about? Is she sick?"

"Yeah, I think so. One of the hemepath attendings got a call from Giti saying she is sick and not coming to work today. And one of our residents saw Giti this morning being blocked at the entrance because she has a fever."

"Oh, no, she has COVID!"

"Well, let's not get there yet. Maybe she is just sick with a cold."

"Wishful thinking, Dr. Samantha Parker. I am not dying with COVID-19."

"You are jumping into a conclusion. No one is dying now."

"I am not taking that chance, and you know our people, Blacks die with COVID-19 more than other people."

"OK Roxanne, but what will you do? Are you going to stay at your family's place? You know you might already be exposed. You should not go anywhere near your family."

"What about our workplace, Samantha? We both should not be here and infect the other residents."

"Yeah, you are right. Let's check into the free housing the hospital has for doctors. We need to get tested and be quarantined for two weeks."

"OK Samantha, but first, what about Giti? Is she going to be alone, fighting the disease? Shouldn't we look after her?"

Samantha is confused while considering what to do. As Roxanne says, they should first go and see if Giti is doing better or getting worse, and then decide what they should do. Many complexities enter the equation: Who will cover their service work during their own time in quarantine? Who will take care of Giti if she becomes extremely sick or unconscious? What if Roxanne and Samantha become sick with COVID? How can Samantha tell her mom in San Francisco about the situation? Her mom Emily is expecting to see Samantha during Thanksgiving, which is coming soon, and Emily is not doing well alone in San Francisco, especially after being attacked while leaving a grocery store with Ms. Kong. The incident was reported as an Anti-Asian hate crime committed by a White guy. Samantha has seen her mom only once, a video call after her mom was hospitalized with multiple facial bruises. Even though it is not safe being in a restricted space on planes, Samantha promised her mom she would come for Thanksgiving and comfort her.

Samantha switches her thoughts to Giti. She becomes frustrated. *Why did Giti attend her sister's wedding, knowing the risk she was taking?*

Chapter 13

One of our own

October 24, 2020

Roxanne leaves work early at 4:00 pm, relieved that her Blood Bank rotation has a second resident on service. The hospital has not yet fully adapted to any normal surgery schedules ever since the first wave of COVID-19 cases in April and May. Citizens in New York City are driving less, resulting in fewer car crash incidents and a reduction in traffic, although rates of accidents and traffic are picking up slowly. Need for blood is directly associated with the number of surgeries and traumas, even while the city's hospitals and the Red Cross are experiencing blood shortages. Alarmingly low numbers of people are traveling to donor centers during the pandemic.

Roxanne is nervous and increasingly worried about Giti who is alone and sick, and she's eager to find out Giti's state of health. Taking a full gear of PPE and stealing an N95 mask from the OR, Roxanne also grabs hair bonnets, facial shields and other masks, and a handful of gloves as she prepares to face Giti at home. An OR nurse raises her hands and scolds Roxanne, "N95 masks are only for OR staff!"

"I'm prepping to scrub in for a rush case," she lies. One of the advantages of wearing hospital scrubs is no one will notice who's who unless an ID badge is checked. Everyone wears a mask and often eye protection goggles during a pandemic, so distinguishing between specific staff, identifying doctors, nurses, or other professional roles one from another is difficult throughout the hospital.

Rushing out of the hospital at a brisk pace, Roxanne arrives at the front of the apartment in a few minutes. Panting and fully geared up in full PPE, she opens the door, and pauses. Giti is motionless, lying on her makeshift bed, a mere mattress on the floor in a corner of the living room. Roxanne wonders, *Is she alive, sleeping quietly, or dead?*

"Giti, Giti!" Roxanne calls louder and louder.

No movement. "Giti!" Roxanne shakes Giti's arm. No reaction. Her anxiety becomes fear. She touches Giti's neck and detects a weak carotid pulse. Giti is not wearing a mask, so Roxanne does not want to get close to detect if Giti is breathing. She shakes Giti's entire body without a response. It appears she passed out, probably from the dehydration, which would easily occur in Giti's tiny body that weighs less than 100 pounds. Giti likely did not eat nor drink the whole day. Roxanne touches Giti's forehead; hot from fever. She calls the paramedics. Roxanne lies down next to Giti, crying for her friend.

"Why did you go to the wedding, you silly girl. Now look at what happened to you. You are risking your own precious life!" A period of ten minutes seems like eternity until the ambulance arrives.

Roxanne calls Samantha and tells her to be at the emergency department waiting for Giti and her to arrive.

Samantha runs to the emergency department, grasps an attending physician's arm and boldly states, "Giti, our pathology resident—she is coming here, most likely a COVID case, passed out due to dehydration and fever. Where is she?"

The attending physician turns and sternly replies. "We already prepared a bed for Giti, and we sent one of our own dispatchers to pick up Giti by ambulance."

The hospital medical staff had become a unified body to collectively help countless COVID patients, especially one of their own who will arrive shortly. They have perfected the art of isolating the COVID units, even within the emergency department, and became extraordinarily efficient in handling cases following the first and the second waves of COVID. Temporarily, they found relief during October. Now, a third wave is forecast for the holidays in November and December; the largest wave yet. Doctors and staff ask, will the American people listen and obey CDC guidelines to not gather or travel? Can they not see what the coronavirus has done for the past six to seven months? Can we follow the actions of citizens in Asian countries, who cooperate and follow medical recommendations instead of selfishly asking, "When can I go to a wedding? How about having a family party, or just family and maybe a few close friends at home? I'll only invite young people—maybe 20 people? How about 15?"

Samantha is at the ER entrance when paramedics bring in Giti, on a gurney. In tears, Roxanne tells Samantha, "She wouldn't get up. No response even after vigorous shaking!" The ER doctors and nurses acknowledge Giti and Roxanne are wearing their hospital's scrubs, with their hospital name badges.

"This is Dr. Giti Schwartz." Roxanne says to one of the doctors.

"Yes, we already know from Dr. Parker," he abruptly replies. "So the patient attended her sister's wedding party in Williamsburg, Brooklyn?"

"Yes, against our wishes," Roxanne emphasizes.

"There is a spike in COVID within that community. We will treat her as a COVID patient. We will get the test immediately."

Samantha and Roxanne nearly run to keep pace with the doctors and the moving gurney.

"How long do you think she was in this unconscious state?" another doctor asks Roxanne.

"Not sure. I arrived home to check on her at 4:10 pm and found her like this. She reported to work this morning but could not pass through our entrance checkpoint. She had a fever."

"Okay, let's push some fluid in her," says the doctor to the receiving nurse.

"My count of three. One, two, three!" The doctor counts as they lift up Giti's tiny body and onto the ER bed. Quickly they hook up several lines, check her temperature and push the long swab into her deep nasopharyngeal space. Giti does not respond to the forceful stimulus. Samantha and Roxanne step back to give room for their colleagues. Roxanne is fully protected with PPE, and Samantha is the only one without an N95 mask.

"I better get back to work," she says, realizing every patient in her midst may be a COVID patient, and Roxanne replies,

"Okay, I will stay here and watch what happens to Giti."

"Okay. Text me with updates."

Samantha heads to the pathology department, worried about Giti and concerned to be the only person not wearing complete PPE.

A few hours pass. No text from Roxanne. It is late and dark outside. As fall season deepens, the city's temperature is noticeably colder.

Chapter 14

Attack in Chinatown

October 24, 2020

While Samantha reaches her phone to call Roxanne for an update on Giti, it vibrates and rings. Mrs. Kong is calling from San Francisco.

"Hello, Samantha?" Mrs. Kong asks, with her usual heavy Chinese accent.

"Yes, Mrs. Kong. How are you? Is my mom okay?" Samantha is immediately worried about her mom. Mrs. Kong is not a person to call and chit-chat or share polite greetings.

"No. That's why I call you. Did you know Emily was in the hospital four days ago? Well, I was with her the whole time. She sick, you know. Somebody kicked her in the street. No reason. She was with me going to grocery store in Chinatown. I was still in the store paying and Emily went out to parking lot to bring the car close for me with many bags. She knocked down in the street and no one helped her. I got all the bags in my hands and saw her in the street, face down. No moving. The guy already running far away. I screamed and screamed. Then, the Chinese people came out from the grocery and restaurants, and helped me. Emily face was all blood. She is okay, talking to me but her face terrible, bleeding a lot. Someone called ambulance and I left all the grocery bags in the street. I don't know what happened to those bags. I left them there and go to hospital. My first time in ambulance. Emily was crying holding her face. Terrible, terrible."

Mrs. Kong cries as she speaks, as if experiencing the event again. Samantha has known only a mild and benign version of the event. Mrs. Kong's version is shocking and painful to hear.

"Is she better now?" Samantha asks cautiously.

"No, she was doing better and ready to go home yesterday with me. Now she not doing good. She fell out of her bed going to bathroom in the hospital. They did some test again and she no good. Something wrong with her head. She not... passed."

"What? Is she dead?" Samantha is in shock.

"No, not dead but pass."

"You mean passed out?"

"Yes, passed out!" Mrs. Kong says.

"Is she conscious? Is she talking?"

"No, she passed out, no talk, no eat. They moved her to another bed, more serious."

"You mean the intensive care unit?"

"Intensive care, yes. They said they need to do some surgery to remove blood in her brain. You need to come right away. I don't know what to do here."

Samantha is stunned, disbelieving, silent for a moment, a flush of thoughts like a tsunami; what to do with her surgical pathology rotation this month, how fast can she buy a plane ticket, how long of a trip, what will happen with Roxanne and Giti, what if her mom dies, it sounds like a concussion and subdural hematoma that they need to evacuate, and what else is happening with Mom?

"Samantha, you still there? You know you have to come here. This might be the last time you see your mother," Mrs. Kong says in a shaking upset voice, Samantha's silence is a clue she is wavering on her decision to come.

"Oh, yes, I will, Mrs. Kong. I will leave tomorrow. I will leave tonight if I can. There is no question about that. I am just shocked; nothing I can think of, not anything for a moment."

"Okay, that what I expect to hear," says Mrs. Kong with relief in her voice.

"Thank you for staying there with my mom. I will be there as soon as possible."

"No worries. I will be here until you come. I had to sign for your mother's surgery." Mrs. Kong ends the call.

During her call with Mrs. Kong, texts from Roxanne appear.

"Still in ER, COVID test positive. Fever, 101. Oxygen level 86."

"Moving to ICU. Intubate soon. Still unconscious."

"Frustrated with Giti."

Samantha cannot move or think. What is happening, so suddenly? When it rains, it pours. It seems all the calamities are paired together at once, suffocating me from thinking rationally.

What should I do first? Take time to book a plane ticket to San Francisco, or go down to the emergency department to see Roxanne and Giti? I lost my father to this pandemic, then lost my first love, Dr. Falkner! I assumed my calamities were over and done with. No, this pandemic is relentless. It brings more and more challenges into my life, beyond my capacity to absorb and digest.

Samantha's thoughts are in a state of paralysis; her mind is unable to determine or act upon the next logical step. The pandemic and tragedies exhaust her, and now the racial hate speech, beatings, and violence against non-White races grieve her to a point she cannot bear to ponder. *My mother, attacked in the middle of Chinatown? What has this world come to? Why my mother! A victim of hate crime — in San Francisco? It's the safest place for Mom to live. A third of the people are Asian!*

Police have not caught the person who punched Emily's face and pushed her onto the street. Samantha has not seen surveillance camera footage but was told a man in a dark hoodie walked toward her mom from behind and pushed her so hard that she fell down, her head striking hard against the concrete sidewalk curb. Then, the man punched her face several times as her helpless mom lay on the pavement, then he fled running. Her car key was still in her hand and her handbag was still wrapped around her body. She was not robbed, and nothing was taken from her. Samantha imagines her mother could easily have a subdural hemorrhage as the result of the violent impact of her head against the curb, and the punches to her face.

What kind of jerk would do such a thing to an old lady who is just going about her own business? Her mom had no time to respond or defend herself. What did Emily ever do to deserve such harsh and cruel violence?

Chapter 15

Human touch

October 24, 2020

Crimes targeting Asian Americans and Pacific Islanders in the US have risen dramatically since the beginning of the coronavirus pandemic. 3,800 instances have been reported. Asian Americans are known as hesitant to report negative things; the actual number of incidents is estimated to be much higher than 3,800, especially when one includes verbal abuses and the vandalization of Asian-owned businesses. It all seemed to begin when the US president labeled the coronavirus as the 'foreign virus,' which was not a simple rhetorical flourish, and he deliberately stated 'the China virus' more than 20 times in March 2020, and downplayed the consequences of COVID-19. When asked, the president said, "It's not racial at all. It's from China. It comes from Wuhan. It's a Wuhan China virus. I want to be accurate, and I am not being a racist."

Maybe he had no racist intentions, but the words are powerful. When the president of the US says, 'China virus,' some of us laugh because of the unfiltered and uninhibited language he uses, as though we laugh at words used in cursing and swearing for lack of better things to do. Higher emotional intelligence tells us not to mention or joke about politics, nationalities of other people, racial or religious issues, especially in public settings. But when the president speaks, he somehow justifies negative or corrosive words and brings justifiable hate toward China, a target that 'brought the virus into the world.' It personifies, and personification is metaphorical. The word 'Chinese' is problematic as it associates the infection with a particular ethnicity and country. COVID has brought countless deaths, so the association of 'Chinese' brings resentment, fear and disgust toward people associated with this word. His intention matters less than the effect it subsequently brings. His own Department of Homeland Security (DHS) issued a warning that white supremacists may act against Asian Americans.

Muslims and Black Americans are also joining in acts of violence against Asians. The Americans who are ignorant think that all Asian Americans are Chinese, and all Asian nations are the same, whether they are Japanese, Korean, Vietnamese, Thai, or any others. Pacific Islanders as a group are now coming together to join the taste of Anti-Asian violence.

There has always been an underlying notion among all Asian people of feeling that we do not really belong as Americans; we are considered as the 'foreigner' and 'people of color,' regardless of whether we are born here and live in America for generation after generation. Some Italian folks suggest, "Change your last name and forget about it because we went through Anti-Italian discrimination in New York in the early days and we are fine now." Not true for Asian immigrants; the second and third generation Japanese soldiers who enrolled in American military service during World War II were questioned of their loyalty as American citizens. Where do those people then belong? Certainly not Japan, and America rejected them as true Americans. Fatigue and impatience grows among Americans who hear stories of racism. Those who face bias and racism know such impatience is from ignorance; a deflection, a lack of interest and time to hear from others who are not like them. Samantha is stifled and devastated from Americans who cannot think beyond the protein levels of humanity. This mindset is in all nations and countries where multi-racial people live together. The world will never seem to accept this melting pot as unity, under God, made in His image, equal in significance, beautifully and wonderfully made with diversity for His purpose.

All of these thoughts come to Samantha as she purchases a ticket for a flight leaving tomorrow morning at 6:00 am from JFK to San Francisco. She packs her things and sends a quick email to her attending pathologist. "I won't be back tomorrow to sign out the cases, but all the cases are written up and prepared as best I can." She briefly explains what happened to her mom.

She goes downstairs near the emergency department to meet Roxanne and tells her what's happening with her mom and that she will be in San Francisco for at least a week. Roxanne volunteers to take over the surgical pathology rotation Samantha is on, partly to pay back Samantha for taking over her GI service when she was injured in June while out protesting.

"Thanks," Samantha says. Unable to control her emotion any longer, she sobs and wails.

Roxanne holds her, hugs her tightly. "It's going to be all right. Don't worry, it's all right. God is with you Samantha, and you know I will pray for you and Giti."

Samantha feels out of place, touched and hugged by a human's warmth. Samantha has not been held by anyone for six months, and it seems unnatural to be so close to another person. She feels abiding comfort in human touch. She has been unaware how warm and comforting it is to hold someone. This place is indeed the united nations covered by the blessing called love. Roxanne, a Black woman hugging Samantha, a half-Asian, is an image the world needs to see, knowing we will make it together no matter how long or how hard it will be to overcome the protein level differences in humanity.

Chapter 16

What about the stuff?

October 25, 2020

The red-eye flight is pretty much empty, less than 15 people on the plane, hard to believe it covers the airline's expenses to continue operating. Strangely, the passengers are seated in one area, separated only by an empty seat in alternating rows. Passengers opt to spread out and go far to the back of the plane, but flight attendants discourage them from doing so. Samantha settles in with a cozy blanket and wears an N95 mask tightly sealed around the nose and mouth, goggles, ear plugs, ready to starve and not drink during the entire trip and eager to sleep in a window seat for a five-hour trip. The COVID culture even affects airplane etiquette; no one wants to chat and that's perfectly fine and expected from each other. People are all into themselves, not even a polite and short pleasantry, afraid of physical contact. This works out for Samantha, an introvert. Some of the effects COVID-19 brings are for introverts; she secretly enjoys the freedom of not meeting people for social obligations, going out, visiting people in homes, no fake smiles since nobody can see what you are doing behind the mask anyway. No forced small talk, no makeup especially lipstick, money saved by not shopping for clothes and no concerns about fashion statements. Less laundry since scrubs became a mainstay in fashion, less eating out to spend money on food. No criticisms of being a homebody or party pooper, no money spent on vacations or travel, fewer business or conference meetings, and more Zoom meetings where she can turn off the camera if needed and still listen in, able to work at home and get things done without distractions. Less traffic and non-existent tourists in New York City, less hassle getting coffee from her favorite Starbucks in the morning—less noise in general. No worries about bad breath, everyone wears a mask. Perhaps most of all, understanding the feebleness of life draws people to connect with their inner selves more naturally to know what's really important in life.

Samantha thinks of all kinds of possibilities—the what-ifs in her life. What if she loses her mother? What if she cannot go back to finish her residency; she has one more year to finish. What if she has to stay in San Francisco for more than a week? What if she must stay with her mom for month after month as Mom's caregiver and eventually take over the financial obligations? What if she needs to sell the San Francisco house? It is too big for just her mom and Samantha. To where will they move? Will her mom agree to move out of the house where she has lived her entire married life? What about the *stuff?* All kinds of furniture and stuff, five bedrooms full of knick knacks her mom gathered for nearly 50 years while she lived there with Dad.

Samantha gets the chills thinking about dealing with all the irritable knickknacks her mom has collected. Samantha is a minimalist, almost to the degree of a Zen Buddhist enjoying a room with nothing except her bed and desk. Emily collects little bells and toy boots from all over; 100 countries or more. What if her mom does not function well mentally and physically after her surgery? What if Samantha becomes the sole caregiver throughout the rest of her mom's life, and what if Emily needs a 24-hour nursing care facility costing a thousand dollars per day for the rest of her life, and is there enough money?

Samantha enjoys her work as a pathologist, never about the need of money when she decided to become a physician. She yearns to work and be a successful career woman in the society, using her gifts and talents to be useful and not bored with her life. For her, it is a privilege to pay her income tax. Paying taxes is merely a byproduct of being a useful person in society. She has many what-ifs to worry about, but first, she'll see her mom and understand the situation before succumbing to her nonsense ideas that may not become reality.

Chapter 17

The surgery

October 25, 2020

Samantha enters a calm sleep on the plane by taking several deep breaths, and prayers. "God, help me. You know where I am exactly. Show me your mercy and your kindness. I am in your hand as always. I never did have any control. These are my momentary misunderstandings, as if I have any control in my life. And these worries are mere manifestations of not being able to trust you entirely. Provide me with your peace, the peace that surpasses my understanding, Almighty Jesus' name. Amen."

It is still nighttime as Samantha lands in San Francisco, gaining three hours. She takes Uber directly to the hospital. Her mom is still in the operating room getting her craniotomy. Mrs. Kong is in the hospital waiting room, dozing off as Samantha rushes in alongside the rolling wheels of her luggage.

"Oh, Samantha, so nice to see you!" Mrs. Kong hugs Samantha. Her hug feels foreign, then a thought, *What if Mrs. Kong has COVID?* naturally flashes upon Samantha as she returns the hug.

"Your mom is supposed to be out soon." Mrs. Kong looks at the clock. "How was your flight?"

"Good. I came as soon as I could."

"I know, thank you. Your mom will be happy to see you. I had to sign the consent form for the surgery." Mrs. Kong pats Samantha's shoulder and looks at her as if she is her own daughter, satisfied to have such a dutiful offspring. A neurosurgeon arrives out of a side door from the surgery.

"This is Samantha, Emily's daughter," Mrs. Kong proudly announces. "She is a doctor too. Came from New York City."

The neurosurgeon acknowledges Samantha as "Hello Dr. Parker, your mother's surgery went successfully." He sits across from Samantha and Mrs. Kong as he explains in detail how he did the surgery. He adds, "Emily's symptoms were a little unusual in that she had mostly GI symptoms, nausea and vomiting at first, and slowly confusion, and falling easily with problems in walking. At first, we thought your mother had a stroke or possibly meningitis. We did not realize there was a very slow subdural hematoma developing."

They eventually performed further imaging and saw blood collecting.

He explains to Samantha, "The complication due to surgery may include further bleeding on the brain, infection of the skull flap, deep vein thrombosis, seizures, stroke, and death. We must watch for all these symptoms and signs. Your mother will be in the hospital for at least a few more days. Then, she will be moved to a rehabilitation facility and trained for further improvements such as walking, talking, and regaining weakness of her limbs. How fast a person recovers will be variable from person to person; some people may recover to normalcy within a few weeks and some people never make a full recovery."

He then apologizes for the event that happened to Emily even though he is not associated with the hate crime perpetrator. Samantha and Mrs. Kong profusely thank the neurosurgeon for his kindness and compassion toward them both. He asks Samantha to sign all the paperwork Mrs. Kong had previously signed, since Samantha is next of kin to Emily. Normally, they would not begin the craniotomy before such paperwork is signed by next of kin, but Samantha was already on a plane when they decided to take Emily into emergency surgery.

An hour later, Emily is brought out of surgery which releases waves of emotions that pour out from mother and daughter. Emily's head is covered with white bandages, even hiding one of her eyes. Her face still badly bruised, deep blue and purple in color, and swollen, Samantha can hardly recognize her own mother. *What kind of an evil person would do such a violent act of shoving an innocent elderly woman to the ground?*

Samantha cries out, "Mom, are you okay? Can you hear me? I am here. I am here by your side. Please don't die on me, please." Mrs. Kong pats Samantha's back quietly, trying to wipe her own tears. "Okay, okay, she okay, Samantha, don't cry, don't cry." Mrs. Kong is tearful, speaking calming words to Samantha.

Gradually Samantha calms herself, regains her composure, and asks Mrs. Kong to go home. Almost two full days have passed while Mrs. Kong has been with Emily, having little or no sleep, nor meals. Mrs. Kong herself is a fragile lady in her late 70s. Emily is moved to an ICU bed and Samantha accompanies her, the echo of luggage wheels trailing behind. Samantha smells like diesel fuel from a jet. Sleep comes quickly as she curls up on a sofa, close to her mom. The dawn reveals the spectacular Golden Gate Bridge through the hospital window. Emily has not awakened.

Chapter 18

Korean blood

October 26, 2020

Samantha is sitting next to Emily's hospital bed, resting her head against her mother's arm. She began worrying why Mother had not moved for over an hour, so the surgeon came in to assess Emily's status. He reassuringly comments, "Dr. Parker, your mother will wake up when she is ready, in her own time. It's okay. Your mother did great."

Suddenly Samantha feels the touch of a warm hand on her head, a familiar comforting hand which regularly stroked Samantha's head as a child when her mother repeated, "You are precious, my child, the one and only, my daughter."

Although her mother is not offering these words today, the touch from her hand reminds Samantha of the lifelong unconditional love from her mother. How lonely and unfriendly the world would be without a mother.

"Mom!" Samantha raises her head and calls out.

"My daughter, you are here," a muffled sound due to her oxygen mask.

"Yes, I am here Mom, how are you feeling?"

"I am okay. I feel beaten up." She tries to smile and adds, "I am really beaten, you know?"

"I can't believe a monster like that is still out there. What kind of person is he to beat an innocent old lady!"

"He is not a monster. Don't talk like that. He is still a child of God."

"Mom, how can you say that after all this? He is worse than a monster!"

"Samantha, hush, the important thing is you are here. My baby! But why are you here? What about your work? You are supposed to come at Thanksgiving time. I am okay. You should go back," her reply filled with many worries about Samantha's interrupted residency training.

"Mom, you are more important than my work now. I want to

be with you."

"No, you should go back. Did Mrs. Kong call you? I told her not to call you because then you will worry and come. I will be okay very quickly. I will get up and walk and jog soon." Emily sounds ready to get up at that moment and presumably begin walking down the hall and exit the hospital.

"Mom, the doctors said you need to recover and regain your normal activities. First you will need to get stronger here at the hospital, then be discharged to a rehab place for a few weeks. You just had major surgery."

"Is that what the doctor says? I was ready to be discharged the other day. I thought I was getting much better."

"Mom, you had a blood clot in your brain. Subdural hematoma. The doctors needed to remove that bleeding."

Emily cries. "Will I be able to walk again? I don't want to be a burden to you. I want you to go back and finish your doctor training without worrying about me. I want to be independent."

"Yes, Mom, they said you will recover. You will walk, cook, jog and be independent. You just have to go through this little setback for a few weeks. You will work hard at it in the rehab place. If anyone can make it, you will, with that Korean blood of yours—nothing is impossible if you work hard at it and failure is not an option. Remember Mom? You used to tell me that all the time."

Emily smiles, "Yes, Korean blood, work hard and you can do anything. The sky is the limit."

"I can't believe you have to go through such a difficult time, Mom. You suffered hate speech, blame, and cursing from passengers on the cruise ship, and now this violence, of all places in San Francisco. Where is God in this?"

"God is with me and you. He must have a reason for us to go through these tough times. We may never know the reason in this lifetime, but we shall ask Him when we go to the heaven."

"Do you think so, Mom? Would He tell us about the reasons in heaven?"

"Yes, maybe we don't even need to ask. We will know anyway. I read the Bible the other day in my morning quiet time. It's from Habakkuk 3:17–19. He asks God why there is so much injustice and violence everywhere in his time. He cried out to God complaining about the situation and God answered him that He is disciplining the people of Judah for they have forgotten their God of salvation, and they worship idols. In the end, Habakkuk says these verses. I want to read it to you. I wrote it here in my notebook."

She struggles to find her notebook but can't find it from the drawer near her bed. She asks Samantha to read it from her phone's Bible app.

"Even though the fig trees have no blossoms, and there are no grapes on the vines, even though the olive crop fails, and the fields lie empty and barren; even though the flocks die in the fields, and the cattle barns are empty, yet I will rejoice in the Lord! I will be joyful in the God of salvation! The Sovereign Lord is my strength! He makes me as surefooted as a deer, able to tread upon the heights."

"Yes, these verses comfort me. Even in the midst of violence, hate and injustice, my God is my strength. I may not know why these calamities happened to me: I was blamed for your father's death from COVID-19, accused of bringing COVID onto the cruise ship, and I mourned on our anniversary when I became a widow. I came home and got beaten because I am Asian, nothing is working out for me. But I will still praise God for the life here on earth, and I have many blessings. You are my beautiful daughter, and I am completely content to leave this life whenever God calls me."

"Mom, I don't want to lose you. What about me, if you leave? I am all by myself. I have no family. I want you to be with me here on earth a little longer." Samantha gently reaches for her mom's hand and puts it on top of her own head, just like before. Emily strokes, and strokes, Samantha's long silky hair.

Chapter 19

Addendum to life

October 31, 2020

The largest nighttime parade and celebration of the year occurs in New York City's Greenwich Village on Halloween night. More than 50,000 typically participate wearing costumes of zombies, witches, monsters, robots, ghouls, Jedis, and Wonder Woman. Giant puppets loom overhead, spectators often face-to-face and numbering well over a hundred thousand people. This year, the event was cancelled due to COVID-19. Roxanne usually participates with her mother and siblings as spectators; a family tradition is eating hot dogs, sugar candies, and watching the Carnival.

This year, she is in the ICU sitting next to Giti, watching her friend die. Giti has been deteriorating slowly since her admission. Her oxygen level continues to decrease even while on the ventilation machine, and she has lost 15 pounds. Giti is tiny to begin with, but now appears to be merely bone and skin. The doctors begin losing any hope to save her, so they decide Giti will no longer continue in an induced coma that might provide her a very small chance of saying goodbye to her family.

Roxanne visits Giti in the ICU every day after work, against hospital policy. No visitors are allowed in the hospital, especially in the COVID units and ICU. Roxanne does not care and goes to see Giti anyway. The ICU nurses and doctors soon gave up on persuading Roxanne to not visit Giti's ICU room and they overlooked her visits. Nurses realize both women are pathology residents here in their own hospital and are impressed with Roxanne's sympathy and empathy toward her friend.

Roxanne holds Giti's small hand. "How are you today, can you hear me? It's me, Roxanne. Can you wake up? Can you talk to me?"

Sometimes Roxanne helps nurses turn Giti's body so that she does not get a decubitus ulcer which is caused by a constant pressure sore in bed from her body's weight to the skin surface. During the turning and moving of Giti, sometimes her tiny friend grunts. Roxanne will visit for at least an hour before going home to eat and sleep.

Today, instead of going to lower Manhattan to see the Halloween parade, Roxanne holds up her iPad for a Zoom video call so that Giti might say a few words to her family. Nurse Ramos in the emergency department helps set up the conference call. Nurse Ramos's unexpected job these days includes providing IT support to connect patients for a final conversation with their families. With the remaining air in Giti's COVID-infested lungs, she says, "I love you all. Thanks to our God, it has been my honor to know you, my family."

Giti's mother is uncontrollably wailing. "Giti, my baby, don't go, don't leave us!" Giti's father tightly holds Giti's mother. Her sisters and brothers are sobbing, unable to speak. It is their last conversation with Giti. They cannot be at Giti's bedside in person. This horrible virus prevents families to be present, or stand or sit next to a loved one, even a patient on their deathbed.

Giti says her last words. "Roxanne, thank you. My God is your God and He loves you." Her tears run down onto her pillow, and slowly she takes her last breath. No one does CPR, or pushes more drugs into her vein. Roxanne's mask is totally wet by tears, and she cannot even wipe these tears.

The ICU doctor pronounces: "Dr. Giti Schwartz, the patient. Time of death is 10:52 pm, October 31, 2020."

Roxanne pulls the white sheet over Giti's head, while holding the iPad for the family to see. It is a closure of Giti's life that she felt obligated to share with her family as if they were here to witness themselves. Giti's family members wail, screaming with pain. There are no dry eyes around Giti's bedside. At some point Nurse Ramos tells the family she will end the conference, and then turns off the iPad. Roxanne helps the nurses to disengage all the lines. The hospital transport worker brings the zipper bag which is placed in close proximity next to Giti's body. Roxanne holds Giti's arm and pulls her toward herself while Giti's body enters the bag. She and the worker stretch the bag over Giti's body and then pull the bag's zipper as it closes over the tiny face of Giti, the final time for Roxanne to see.

Roxanne says to Giti, "I didn't get to say goodbye to you.

Goodbye, Giti. Thank you for being my colleague and friend. Through you, I learned of your God, family obligations, and duties, the value of family, and how to be a better doctor. Thank you for being who you are and thank you for being here to be my friend."

Nurse Ramos speaks as she touches Roxanne's arm. "This has been the toughest job for me these days, saying goodbye to family members, connecting them before death with COVID patients. In nursing school I had no idea that I had to do this kind of job. I thought I would be taking care of the physical needs of patients. This task takes me into another level of stress and sadness. I cannot bear it emotionally. I can relate to all the family and dying patients, and so I do this. But I am drenched with enormous sadness, and I cannot sleep at night."

Roxanne wants to hug Ramos but can't do that either. They must keep some distance between each other. Frustration grows within Roxanne as her tears and perspiration fog up her plastic facial cover, inhibiting her to see nurse Ramos, who also cannot see Roxanne through her own foggy face covering. Roxanne is consumed with a desire to get rid of the moisture inside her facial covering and get rid of the long impenetrable gown and head coverings of PPE. She has no air circulation, causing her to perspire constantly. This unbearable situation overwhelms her desire to tell nurse Ramos that she appreciates her, and admires her for accepting the newly found responsibility placed upon her, an unwritten life-altering addendum to her job description. Roxanne should inform Samantha about Giti, but anxiety pushes her back. Midnight arrives; she must call Samantha, who is also under pressure from watching her mother's slow recovery from surgery, anxious that her mother may fall in the rehab hospital while relearning how to walk. Samantha is heartbroken to see her mom struggling to stand up straight, holding onto the grab bars, over five minutes to take one baby step.

"Samantha, are you awake?" It's Roxanne.

"Yeah, it's just 9:00 pm here. I am with Mom watching TV in her rehab hospital."

"I am sorry, but I need to tell you about Giti."

"What's happening? Is Giti all right?"

"No, she just passed away about an hour ago."

Samantha cannot take another blow to her system, another

loss of life. She is unable to respond to Roxanne's voice.

"Are you there, Samantha? Did you hear what I just said?"

"Yes, I heard you."

"Giti was so young. Giti's father has now tested positive, he's very sick. Two of her extended family members who attended the wedding are hospitalized and on ventilators."

"Oh, no! Were you there with Giti when she passed away?"

"Yes, I was able to do the Zoom meeting with her family until she took her last breath. It was heartbreaking, Samantha!" Roxanne begins sobbing.

"You are so brave to do that for Giti. Thanks for being such a wonderful friend. Roxanne, where are you now?"

"I am with Giti in the morgue. She is all zipped up and covered. I am still arranging with her family to transport the body for burial. You know that Jewish people are required to bury the body within 24 hours and our hospital does not have 24-hour decedent services, so I am the point of contact for Giti's family."

"You should go back to the apartment and get some rest. What service was Giti supposed to be on for the month of November?"

"Cytology."

"What about you? What service are you on?"

Roxanne is not enthusiastic to answer, sighs and says, "Hemepath, again."

"Well, I am supposed to be on Chemistry rotation," says Samantha, "but I guess some other resident is expected to take care of it. I am taking a Kin Care sick day, and using all of my vacation days. I just spoke to Aaron, chief resident, and he told me not to worry about anything and to focus on caring for my mom. He was very nice about it."

"Listen to us. What we worry about is the service coverage rather than Giti's death."

"I know Roxanne, I was just noticing that too. Our duties of medical service never escape us even before we can mourn for the loss. I feel ashamed to admit that but please contact the chief resident Aaron. Tell him about Giti tomorrow morning so he can backfill Giti's cytology service coverage. You know some of the cytopathologists get angry when they have no pathology resident to assist them."

"But they have cytology fellows!"

"I know, but they perform fine needle aspiration procedures all day, in and out of signing out their cases, and they are not reliable for the service work. They have their own work and pressure."

"Yeah, yeah, I will call the chief resident. You sound like a chief resident yourself right now, Samantha."

"Sorry. So tell me, how are you doing, Roxanne?"

"How am I doing? I am in a mess! A friend died. There are 30 or 40 bodies stacked up here. I don't know if they are all COVID bodies. I can't seem to get my mind off Giti who was in the ICU still breathing and talking. Suddenly she is here among the dead. I can't ever talk to her again. It feels surreal. What if that was me who died? I am so close to COVID, it is all around me. Giti's family wanted me to come to her funeral, but I refused. Actually, I lied to them that I have to work. It's not entirely a lie; I do have to work but I don't want to go to her funeral with all those people who gave her the virus which led to her death. Is it okay not to attend Giti's funeral?"

"Definitely yes, Roxanne. You have done more than anyone else for Giti. You stayed with her until she took her last breath, and you connected Giti to her family to say goodbye. Giti will know what you have done for her, and she will understand why you cannot attend her funeral."

"Samantha, do you have a feeling that you are experiencing an out of body experience? It feels like I am there, in the cloud looking down as if I am seeing myself as someone else."

Samantha pauses, not knowing how to respond. "Roxanne, thanks for being there with Giti, dead or alive. It takes courage to be doing what you are doing. You have done more than anyone, more than her family could do. If Giti is in heaven looking down on you, she will appreciate you and be impressed with your genuine friendship and humanity even though you were sometimes tough on her. I am ashamed to ask you to contact our chief resident, worrying about the service coverage rather than grieving for Giti. But I will grieve in my own time and ways that you may not know. But right now, I have to be with my mom. Please go home and get some rest so that you can fight for humanity again tomorrow. By the way, remove her mattress and place it outside or in the hallway tonight if you still have not done that."

"I was just thinking of that too. Thanks Samantha. By the way, I did sleep many nights with her while the mattress was still inside. But I think it's fine."

Seconds pass until Samantha replies. "Okay, whatever you say. But I would move that outside for now and throw it out later."

"You don't want to lose me to COVID?"

"Obviously not. Roxanne, please take care of yourself."

"Okay, good night Samantha. Pray for me all night."

"I will."

Samantha recalls her first year of residency. Aaron was her senior resident. When she called in sick with flu symptoms, she was on surgical pathology service. Aaron commanded, "You are coming in for work unless you are dead!" That stern voice has stuck with Samantha forever in her brain. No wonder why so many doctors report to work even if they have a fever—which might be COVID these days. They are trained to work through any challenge, even sickness. Doctors take their work seriously, sometimes more important than their own physical needs, work is priority number one. Trying to save humanity, a doctor becomes inhumane. Samantha is surprised that she worries about service coverage ahead of the loss of a friend. Dead is dead and the living have to live. How cold and cruel this seems. Samantha is impressed with Roxanne, a Black person taking care of Giti, an Orthodox Jew, to comfort and support her colleague until the last minute of Giti's life. While living, they often fought over race and their differences, creating constant tension. Yet in the end of life, they unite in the name of humanity and kindness. After Giti's wedding, Roxanne chose to sleep in Samantha's room, on the floor away from Giti, and criticized Giti's selfish act to attend a large group gathering, disregarding social distancing and mask wearing. Suddenly, Roxanne was the one who attended Giti's last breath on the earth, held her hands, comforted her, and expressed the ultimate love toward a friend.

After her phone call with Roxanne, Samantha watches—but does not see—the TV in front of her. Her mother's worried face looks at Samantha. She asks her daughter to hop onto her bed. They cuddle together and Emily strokes her head. "It's okay. It's okay, my baby. God is with us. He is watching over us. He says, 'do not be afraid, I am the Lord, your God.'"

"Mom, I need to tell you about one of my roommates, a co-resident who died with COVID."

Samantha opens up her tightly controlled emotion to release her sorrow. She cries uncontrollably. Her mom prays out loud for Giti's spirit and for her family and continues stroking Samantha's hair.

Samantha came to California to help her mom, but Emily is enriching Samantha's wellbeing. Realizations within Samantha begin to emerge in her mind.

How long must we wait until this COVID is over? How many more lives must be lost until we pass this pandemic time? The world seems topsy-turvy, in utter confusion, byproducts of COVID, a systemic psychological imbalance, fear of the unknown with no end in sight. Where is God in the midst of the pandemic, in sheer chaos? Why can she not yet praise God as the prophet Habakkuk, who said, 'Even though…I will rejoice in the Lord…'

Chapter 20

Thanksgiving dinner

November 26, 2020

Emily is recovering. She can perform her normal activities, perhaps somewhat slower in pace than before her attack, but Emily is very satisfied with her progress. It has taken two weeks in the rehabilitation facility to regain and retrain herself to do things independently. Getting injured takes only a split second, but months and perhaps a year are required to regain full strength and capacity. The CDC has released a strong recommendation not to travel during the holidays, and a month has passed since Samantha arrived in San Francisco. This is a significant absence from her residency duties. Samantha is excused by using four weeks of vacation, her sick days, and a leave of absence under the law called 'Kin Care.' Nearly all of the pathology staff have avoided coming to the hospital unless their service work absolutely requires them onsite, so Samantha can work remotely if required.

She begins preparations for a Thanksgiving dinner for her mom and Mrs. Kong. It is not a traditional turkey dinner her family enjoyed when her father was living. Today, it is a Korean dinner; 'galbi-chim,' a beef stew cooked throughout the night in marinated soy sauce. A nearby Korean grocery store had all of her necessary ingredients to slowly cook the precious dish her mom had taught Samantha. Emily cannot sit and watch her daughter cook, but she can provide instructions, so she commands her daughter to do this or do that. A constant irritation for Samantha, but she secretly enjoys her mom's persistent voice. She prefers being with her bossy mom over being an orphan. Thank God her mom is thriving and living, busily providing Samantha the knowledge of complex recipes to prepare Korean dishes that her mother had learned and perfected. Samantha grew up eating these meals, but never had time or cared to learn how to cook. If Emily passes away, the precious knowledge to prepare food Samantha enjoyed as a child will dissipate, surely a regret that Samantha will carry.

Mrs. Kong's family had decided not to gather during the Thanksgiving holiday as had been their tradition. They fear transmission of the coronavirus and avoid airline travel or gathering in the home of an elderly person. Mrs. Kong is alone in her immense house and was glad Samantha invited her to join them for a Thanksgiving Korean dinner.

This Thanksgiving is unusual for them all; Emily Parker and her daughter Samantha having the dinner without Robert Parker; Mrs. Kong at someone else's house for dinner, without family or grandchildren. They must adjust to a new environment forced upon them by COVID-19.

The table is set beautifully with Korean food; several types of store-bought kimchees, japchae (clear noodle dish), broiled croaker fish, white sticky hot rice, and of course galbi-chim, the centerpiece. It is a wonderful smell of remarkable food as the ladies sit around the table, eagerly anticipating the delicious food. They hold hands and thank God for their health, food, and the opportunity for their fellowship together, and quickly wipe their hands with alcohol gel. Every moment of life such as this is a gift from God often taken for granted. Every good thing in life comes from God who grants us a moment of life such as this. Emily, Samantha, and Mrs. Kong take their first bites as tears of joy and sadness flow for the missing loved ones in their lives. This pandemic brought us a different degree of appreciation in life. How significant are family and friends, and how short is this thing called life?

Samantha is now determined to be closer to her mom during her fellowship program after her residency. She applies to only two institutions, both in the San Francisco area for this additional cytopathology fellowship training; Stanford and UC San Francisco. No fellowship training is more important to her than being close to her mom, her only family left on this earth. If she does not get into either fellowship, she will get a job as a general pathologist near San Francisco.

Emily continues to religiously complete her rehabilitation exercise routines and walks with Mrs. Kong at a nearby park for at least one hour a day. This tenacity impresses Samantha, her mother's sheer determination and willingness to get better quickly to not burden her daughter. For Emily, getting better and functional is crucial. Emily pushes herself to be 'normal' with all her might, and devotes complete determination while in rehab. Failure is not her option. She must not depend on Samantha's care or inhibit her daughter's life, forcing herself to walk outside once again and trust other people in public areas.

Samantha observes her mother's deep courage and faith. When asked, Emily replied, "I choose not to be afraid of Anti-Asian violence and not to be a victim of it mentally. I could be a victim of Asian hate physically, but I will not let that paralyze me mentally. I have nothing to lose now. I am going to march for who I am and show the world I am an American too!"

Emily is not angry at her circumstances; she simply wants to go out there alongside other Asians to show the world that she too has a voice. "It's my obligation to enlighten others that we are also Americans," she says.

When Emily is strong enough to walk well, she and Mrs. Kong become activists to stop anti-Asian racism, busy organizing peace walks alongside the Chinese Culture Connection and Chinese Progressive Association in San Francisco. The COVID brought xenophobia and racism, but it also brought courage to fight against the individual rights of humanity, whether it is the Black Lives Matter or AAPI (Asian American and Pacific Islander) rights. Emily is no longer a quiet subservient Asian woman who shies away from public eyes, but a strong warrior fighting for her own rights, willing to go out and stand for what she believes.

Samantha is amazed; proud that her mother is not victimizing her thoughts and life from the hands of a few cowards who refuse to cover their faces while coughing upon and shoving away older female Asians.

Chapter 21

Celebration day

December 18, 2020

Scientific teams work unceasingly to finish the race and be first in the US for the development of a COVID-19 vaccine. On December 11, 2020, Pfizer's vaccine was approved by the Food and Drug Administration (FDA), and an Emergency Use Authorization issued. One week later, FDA also authorized the emergency use of mRNA-1273, the vaccine from Ed's company targeting COVID-19 in individuals 18 years of age or older. Both vaccines were now authorized for distribution and delivery to the US Government would begin immediately.

A press conference is quickly arranged amid hectic schedules of Dr. Steven Allen and Dr. Ed Liu.

Steven Allen began addressing the media. "We appreciate all our team members, financial support from NIH, and many other entities who worked under this phenomenal Biomedical Advanced Research and Development Authority (BARDA) and Operation Warp Speed. With all of your support and hard work, we were able to create and manufacture our vaccine in 11 months from sequence to authorization, while advancing clinical development with the Phase 1, Phase 2 and pivotal Phase 3 studies of 30,000 participants." Steven pauses, shifting his posture.

"We also thank all the research participants undergoing clinical trials and the staff at our clinical trial sites who have been on the front lines of the fight against the virus. The Department of Defense (DoD), in partnership with the Department of Health and Human Services (HHS) and the US Centers for Disease Control and Prevention (CDC), will manage allocation and distribution of the vaccine in the United States, with the allocation and distribution according to populations prioritized and identified by the CDC's Advisory Committee on Immunization Practices (ACIP). We can deliver approximately 20 million doses to the US government by the end of December

2020. Our company expects to manufacture and deliver between 100 million and 125 million doses available globally in the first quarter of 2021, with 85-100 million available in the US."

Steven looks directly at the cameras and says, "Thanks to the FDA, for approving Emergency Usage Authorization based on our data analysis from the pivotal Phase 3 clinical study on November 30, which confirmed a vaccine efficacy rate of 94.1%. I stand here today, indeed a historical day and proudly represent our American company to fight back this terrible virus."

Ed stands proud next to Steven. In silence, he knew vaccine development was predicted to require a minimum two years. He and his company succeeded in under a year. Sadly, they are not the first, coming second by only a week.

The very first Pfizer vaccine shot is broadcast on live television on the morning of Monday December 14th. "The patient is an African American critical care nurse in Long Island Jewish Hospital, and she will be followed by other health care workers in New York."

Meanwhile, the first vaccine shot developed by Ed's company is expected to be delivered on December 22nd to a doctor in Texas, who had gone to work and fought the virus for 277 consecutive days. Roughly six million doses were being shipped to more than 3,700 locations around the country by the end of the week, adding to the nearly three million doses of the Pfizer vaccine that were dispatched mostly to health care workers starting the prior week. By the end of December 22nd, almost 615,000 doses were to be administered.

***

According to the CDC, a five-tier system is created to determine who gets the vaccines first, written with dependent clauses and run-on sentences:

Tier 1 is grouped as *deployed & mission essential personnel,* followed by *essential military support and sustainment personnel, intelligence services, National Guard, and other domestic national security personnel,* and then *Homeland and national security,* which includes *Other active-duty military and essential support personnel.*

Tier 2 is a group composed of *health care workers and community support groups; public health personnel, inpatient health care providers, outpatient and home health providers, health care providers in long term care facilities, and pharmacists and pharmacy technicians,* followed by *community support and emergency management,* and *mortuary services personnel.*

Tier 3 is composed of *Other critical infrastructure,* including *emergency services and public safety sector personnel such as EMS, law enforcement, fire services,* and *Manufacturers of pandemic vaccine and antivirals.* Then, the *communications/information technology, electricity, nuclear, oil and gas, water sector personnel,* and *financial clearing and settlement personnel* followed by *banking and finance, chemical, food and agriculture, pharmaceutical, postal and shipping, transportation sector personnel.*

Tier 4 is composed of the *general population,* with *household contacts of infants less than 6 months old and children 3-18 years old with high risk conditions,* followed by *adults 65 years old.*

Tier 5 is last, composed of *healthy adults 19-64 years old.*

***

The initial study volunteers were not composed of younger teenagers, toddlers, or infants. A requirement exists that younger groups must be tested separately, and additional trials will be at a later time. So far, these five tiers are the general CDC guidelines, but each state has some control over variabilities in the tier system of who gets the vaccine first. The federal government under President Trump gave authority to each state on how to govern the COVID-19 pandemic response. Worries exist that there are more people who need to get the vaccine than the capabilities of vaccine production.

At least for Ed, there is no shortage of job security. Scientists by nature had already been discussing their next phase of work toward vaccines in oral pill form rather than injection. Additionally, the same technology for vaccines against a virus can also be used to treat numerous forms of cancers. Coronavirus may be here with us for a long time and annual vaccinations like flu shots is the current opportunity scientists are tackling. Also under consideration is a combined vaccine for flu and coronavirus, and a vaccine for HIV is being studied in Ed's Abby Lab.

Although Ed is not the sole person who invented his company's vaccine, he is fully satisfied by his role in making history happen within 'the winning' American company, providing hope for Americans and for the world. They delivered the hope, and now they pass the baton to the next team: Successfully distribute their vaccine for injection in the arms of citizens.

It is a murky process to identify the heroes to credit for success, but at least Ed is on the winning team that provided a vaccine. A poignant fact arose for Ed's employees. Known as the creators of a vaccine, yet his team is prevented from vaccination until the 3rd tier system begins. They are considered 'Manufacturers of pandemic vaccine and antivirals,' and their hope for vaccination is pushed into late February or early March of 2021.

Ed wonders if Samantha has received the vaccine shot. She's on the front lines in her hospital. With hesitation he calls her; they have not talked for over eight months. She answers his call, to his surprise.

"Hi Samantha, I just want to call to say hi," Ed says shyly.

"Good to hear your voice. I hope you are well. Congratulations! You made the vaccine, Ed."

"Yeah, thanks. I was just wondering if you received the Pfizer vaccine shot yet."

"No, but my appointment is on Christmas day."

"That will be a nice Christmas gift. I hoped you might receive the vaccine from my company. I think it is better. Of course, I am heavily biased." Ed chuckles.

"I am sure it is. But we don't have a choice in that matter."

"Yeah, I figure." A long awkward pause follows.

"Do you think we can see each other sometime?"

"I am very sorry, Ed. I don't think it will be a good idea. I am glad you are doing well and congratulations again. Please take care of yourself. And thank you for saving the world. You deserve the recognition for doing the hard work these past months. I am sure your parents are proud of you, and I am very proud of you. Thanks for calling and checking on me. I am well and working hard from this end, dealing with many things in the hospital. We are having another surge of COVID patients and expect bigger numbers to come in after the holidays, although the pathology department is slow because no one is doing elective or even cancer surgeries. I hope you will find happiness and contentment. Thanks for everything, Ed. Merry Christmas!"

Samantha ends the call. Ed holds his phone for a while, knowing that this might be the last time he would be able to hear her voice. He cannot even be a friend to Samantha. Ed has not learned her reasons for breaking up. His mind has no clarity, no specific or clear reasons why their decade-long relationship ended. Why did she break off their relationship? It was sudden. Ed had not known a woman could be that strong to sever the relationship 'cold turkey,' as Samantha had done with him. He had not recognized the power of a woman in his life, not like this experience. *When a woman says no, it really means no,* he concludes.

Maybe after several years he can call her again. Maybe she will become a different person and change her mind.

Why bother? He wants to live his life with a woman who will love him, at least reciprocate his love. Thinking about Samantha is wasting his time. He rarely thought about her the past eight months while he embedded himself into work, so he will continue to work and forget about her. Maybe he will fall in love after meeting someone more special than Samantha. She is not worthy of any further attention. Ed turns off his phone and walks away to take a breath.

Yeah, move on! He concludes.

Chapter 22

The White umbrella

December 31, 2020

Samantha recently completed job interviews via Zoom with UCSF and Stanford for a one-year pathology fellowship that would begin in July 2022. Both gave her offers within two weeks, just as she arrived back in New York City to fulfill her December rotation. The flight was packed. Travelers generally ignore the CDC's recommendations and do whatever they want—including Samantha. Passengers wear masks, but many remove them while drinking, eating, and talking which is the majority of time in the air. Others place masks under their nose or under their chin, and receive no effect from their masks. No wonder why some statistical studies have shown no effect from wearing a mask during the pandemic; people simply do not know how to wear their masks, or ignore the instructions. One can imagine the risks of infections to a patient if a surgeon chooses to wear a surgical mask in such a casual, ineffective manner during surgery. People simply do not understand the world of microorganisms. If they do not see things like viruses, bacteria, and fungus, then they act as if these do not exist.

A passenger behind Samantha talks non-stop for five and a half hours during the flight, mostly silly things she does not want to know. His lamenting life stories are audible, even though she wears ear plugs. She then pulls her hoody over her head to prevent his saliva from flying into her hair. She feels sorry for the passengers on either side of him as they patiently endure his stories. She never realized men can talk for hours. Her men, including her father and Dr. Falkner, were pretty much non-verbal people. She eagerly rushes off the plane after landing at JFK in New York.

Samantha is thrilled to receive offers from both institutions in the Bay Area for her fellowship, and excitedly shares the information to her mom, who encourages her daughter to accept either place. "Don't worry about me. I am fine here. You do whatever you want to do. I might just move to Jeju Island in Korea to retire there. That's only if you don't get married and have a grandchild soon. I can look after your child." Her typical response. Always the subtle pressure to marry and then have grandchildren for her mom. Duly diligent to be a filial daughter and provide offspring. Continue and protect future generations. Samantha has graduated from listening and feeling guilty by her mother's demands cloaked as subtle requests. She will not fulfill her mother's wish by sacrificing her own life, nor marry before she is certain who she wants to spend her life with.

Marriage can be scary, a commitment with vows to stay together forever, until death brings them apart. One cannot jump into marriage unless blinded by love. Her biological clock is ticking, but she refuses to simply line up and devote herself to a prospective man to fulfill her mother's wish. Not that she has such a luxurious choice at the moment of deciding which man to marry.

"Mom, going back to Korea might not be a simple thing. They have changed. You may not feel comfortable there anymore and they may not accept and embrace you as one of them. We are not here, nor there. You would stick out in Korea as a 'weird foreigner,' just as in America. I would too. You seem stuck in your thoughts about Korea from the time you left and romanticize what it was like. Even on Jeju Island, you will be surprised how different they have become. Besides, I am here in America. I don't want to live in Korea. And I don't want to take 13-hour trips to see you."

"You might be right. The people of Korea must have changed. I am thinking about 50 years back when I left Korea. I may feel even more lonely in my own country. I lived in America more than two thirds of my life. Yes, sometimes I feel I am still an uninvited guest in America. Every day I recall the incident of being beaten because I am an Asian person, and I wonder if I should go back to where I came from. At least on the surface, I will look the same as the rest of the people and no one will beat me because I look different." Emily habitually conceals her pain and suffering, otherwise it might hurt her daughter's feelings if she admits and expresses what she feels, but today, she talks to her daughter as if Samantha is a mere friend. Although Emily has forgiven the perpetrator, the feelings of rejection by her country and living like an uninvited guest are not forgotten. This feeling must be exacerbated since her husband Robert died.

Samantha knows that her mom was protected by her dad under his 'White umbrella' throughout their marriage. Samantha is sorrowful and devastated for her mom speaking to her in this way.

"Mom, I want to be next to you and protect you. Very soon I will go to San Francisco when I am done with my residency here in the Bronx. I want to live with you and see you every day, so that no one can harm you."

"My sweet baby, I just want you to be happy. Don't worry about me. I want you to meet a nice man who you can marry and live your own life." Samantha interjects before the next bout of lectures on grandchildren and says, "That I can do a little later. But for now, I want to be with you."

Chapter 23

When enough is enough

December 31, 2020

Samantha accepts the UCSF fellowship. She can live with her mom and commute to the hospital, a short bus ride from home each day. She excitedly shares her decision with Roxanne, who appears reserved and noticeably quiet after Giti's death. More accurately — she's depressed.

While Roxanne is thrilled for Samantha, she immediately calculates that she must find a new apartment in less than six months. But more immediate concern is that her roommate has arrived from an epicenter in San Francisco during the highest infection and death rates in California. Samantha may carry another variant of coronavirus from San Francisco, even though she had 14 days of no COVID-19 symptoms. California has reported their highest infection rates with a dramatic 15% increase in overall death rates, nearly 26,000 over the average number of total deaths the previous three years, and these additional deaths in California are attributed to COVID-19. Latinos and non-Whites report the highest infection and death rates. Roxanne quietly observes Samantha respectfully wearing a mask in her own apartment.

Roxanne had drifted into loneliness after Samantha left for San Francisco. Countless hours passed with no conversation, aside from her necessary work-related conversations with the few remaining staff required to be at the hospital. They worked only to work and not to socialize. Roxanne's only other responsibility was to water Samantha's plants once a week. Fortunately, Roxanne had become friends with Nurse Ramos, a Philippine-born nurse who assisted in Giti's last conversation with her family via the conference call in late October. Nurse Ramos diligently performed her work over a 14-year career in the emergency department.

She speaks English with some accent, nothing that prevents efficient communication with Roxanne. Many co-workers quickly bond through emotional conversations amid their stressful environment, and seek to know their colleagues more intimately. Each is dealing with crushing and painful experiences during the last moments of their patients' lives. These experiences change people unless one is a psychopath. Nurse Ramos and Roxanne have regular lunch meetings at least two or three times a week. Usually they go outside for lunch even when it is 20 F° degrees, in wind or snow to decrease the likelihood of transmitting the virus while they eat without masks. Nurse Ramos always wears an N95 mask, which Roxanne envies. Even as a doctor she is not allowed an N95 mask, and only allotted a single surgical mask upon checking in each morning.

One day Nurse Ramos begins sharing a story with Roxanne. "My friend who is a nurse and also from the Philippines died two days ago. We reuse the same N95 mask over and over again, and 3,600 healthcare workers have died this year. Most were born outside the US. Many of our hospital colleagues were born in the Philippines and we account for a disproportionate number of the 3,600 deaths. Only a few doctors have died. Nurses and support staff are dying in far higher numbers than physicians. Many of my relatives and friends are health care workers in community hospitals that are far different from well-funded academic medical centers like our Bronx hospital. Thousands of others work in nursing homes, outside clinics, hospices and prisons where death rates are higher, more like 70%. Two-thirds of deceased health care workers are people of color. In the beginning, everyone said, 'we are all in this together.' Well, that's a lie. There are deep inequities tied to race, ethnicity and economic status in America's health care workforce. We die at far higher numbers than physicians and we're in lower-paid positions. Roxanne, I think you know that we health care workers are more than three times as likely to contract COVID as the general public, and the hospital knows this fact and yet they still do not provide sufficient PPE. We are called the true heroes and heroines but what good is that when we are still out here with no proper gear? The hospital plants a tree outside the entrance for each health care worker who dies. You saw that post from the hospital news?"

"Yes, I did," Roxanne quietly replies.

"Well, what good is that when you lose your life? The CDC first encouraged hospitals to reserve N95 masks for intubation procedures only, and we were using surgical masks which they said were adequate for everyday patient care—we put thousands of health care workers at risk. I don't think our hospital leadership consistently reports deaths of health care workers to OSHA. They are probably worried about lawsuits when the dust settles after the pandemic because the dead will be seen as victims of PPE shortages. You heard about the OB/Gyn resident's death in Texas, in September? She was only 28 years old, already had severe asthma and a long history of respiratory ailments. She was using the same N95 mask over and over, so many times the fibers were beginning to disintegrate even during her high-risk work rotations in the emergency room. Just like my mask! The hospital says a single N95 costs $79. Is that a price tag for a life these days? Well, thank God a vaccine arrived. I am grateful to be one of the first few people in our hospital to get the shot in mid-December. And thank God the hospital had a fair, tiered system to determine who would be the first to receive a shot. I was in the first tier. All the emergency department employees are tier one and got their shot. Did you get yours yet?"

Before replying, Roxanne pauses, and grins behind her mask. "Yes, I did. We are the second tier. I got my first shot on Christmas day."

"That's great, Roxanne. We as heath care workers finally received some advantage during COVID. I tell you; I didn't sign up to risk my life every day like this battle against COVID. Especially when a White patient pushed me away, saying he doesn't want Asian nurses! He said I am the one who brought this virus into America. Can you believe that? Here I am trying to help him. The guy could hardly breathe because of COVID, and I get that kind of treatment? I almost walked out of my job that day. It is hard enough coming to work in our COVID-infested environment every day in the emergency department, and now I must listen to racial insults? Why am I risking my own life and my family? I have two small children at home, and a husband. I can hardly touch them or eat with them until I do a detoxification process when I get home. I began sleeping in a separate room in March of this year. Why are some Americans so ignorant? I live in this country just like that patient does. I haven't even gone back to the Philippines for more than 20 years. All my family members are here in America. I am an American. And why don't the American people just stop acting so juvenile and listen to the CDC guidelines? Why must we continuously treat these stupid people who travel during the pandemic? They are selfish, and become sick because of their foolish and selfish behaviors. And what's all this fighting about the mask-wearing requirements? If scientific people recommend wearing masks, then we all should just wear masks. No fighting necessary. It's good for them and to others, period. And when they get sick, they're the first to rush into the hospital. Roxanne, what will happen if all the health care workers walk out of the hospital and say we had enough. When do we say enough is enough?"

***

The sentiments of Nurse Ramos are shared by most health care workers but for some reason, they dare not speak with such clarity and anger. When the politicians and the people do not trust science during the pandemic, it seems that the health care workers are given no respect and no voice to speak about their reality. Roxanne and her colleagues are disappointed to see no leadership in medicine. Nobody will say it like it is. Even respect for Dr. Fauci has dropped. The situation became worse when the president got sick with COVID. He received every available treatment regardless of cost, recovered quickly, strong as ever, showing his two thumbs up to the media.

"No big deal," he said. "Look at me, I had COVID. I'm fine after only a few days." He is ignorantly unaware that no other person can get the same medical treatment as he did. A person dies from COVID-19 every minute. His behavior shows the stronger, wealthier, and powerful person in America can fight back the virus rather easily, while the weak, poor, and powerless person dies with the virus. This is not a public health crisis, more accurately it is a crisis for the poor. We are not in this together. We lack an authentic leader who tells the truth—boldly recommending specific behaviors to the public that will make an impact against the virus— for everyone to live. Instead, weak leadership emboldens protestors who seek first to fight for their own personal constitutional rights, with little respect for others.

No one seems to have common sense. While protestors engage in conflict, health care workers sacrifice their own lives and silently plead for people to possess sensible judgment and empathy toward those of us who live among the sick, easing the pain and suffering in our endless pandemic.

Ironically, 20% of hospital staff opt not to receive the vaccines; one out of five people. Their own Bronx hospital has ordered staff to receive vaccines. Why is the small minority of self-proclaiming individuals allowed to override the interest of public health for all citizens? Did we not all receive polio and MMR vaccines before entering public schools, and accept these as a requirement for employment to earn income? As of now, there exists no scientific data that demonstrates anything other than extremely rare adverse effects from vaccines, contrary to false social media posts.

By the end of 2020 during the holidays, hospitals across the country were again filling with COVID patients. This third wave becomes much bigger than the first and the second waves combined. New York City is once again in a dire situation as COVID drags its tail much longer than anyone ever expected as death rates rise and no end in sight. Numbers become numbing, depersonalized math of the pandemic. Our brains can no longer process the numbers of dead as 'tragic.' It became a number and not a true reality. The media now avoids stories or comments about the number of deaths, unlike the first wave. December 2020 has a tsunami effect of more than 3,000 COVID-19 deaths per day, and becomes the first month in which the COVID-19 mortality rate exceeds that of heart disease and cancer combined. The state of California is at the top of the list for having the highest infection and death rates, averaging 433 daily deaths over the past week, surpassing New York. On the eve of New Year's Day, Times Square is empty. Normally, hundreds of thousands of people celebrate the countdown in New York City along with the famous ball drop and fireworks, confetti, hats, champagne toasts, and rock 'n' roll. The famous ball does drop—but with few people present. The start of a new year normally brings new hopes and a determination to achieve personal resolutions. This new year brings a heavy and persistent burden from a stubborn COVID, with no end in sight. No kisses, hugs or parties except among certain foolish people who feel invincible, and enjoy themselves with the risk of transmitting the virus. When will the definition of the United States, the nation of unitedness, come together to end the undesirable pandemic?

Chapter 24

Chief resident, Aaron

January 1, 2021

A new year arrives with new sets of hopes and unspoken expectations while incidents of COVID-19 and death rates persist. By the end of 2020, the total number of global deaths due to the COVID-19 pandemic is at least 3 to 3.3 million. In the US, 375,000 are dead. The global number most likely represents an underestimation because many countries lack functional civil registration and vital statistics systems. In the US, it is reported that the age-adjusted death rate increased by 16% in 2020, and COVID-related deaths are the third leading cause of death. Overall COVID-19 death rates are highest among non-Hispanic Black persons, and non-Hispanic American Indian or Alaska Native persons. The increase in COVID-19 infection rates and death rates become unemotional numbers as we watch the news of our choice, barely glancing at the everyday death rate with less interest than stock market numbers. We want to watch anything other than COVID-19 pandemic news, yet the media remains obsessed with never-ending personal stories of tragic loss, whether it be human life, company stock, a job, school attendance, traveling, and loss of revenue in all imaginable sorts of businesses. Surprisingly, a few industries and companies are doing better than ever: Housing markets, Amazon, construction trades. Scattered news about COVID often highlights the massive numbers of defiant younger people who think they are immune to the coronavirus while partying at night in the bars or their friends' homes. National *Nightly News* features people who are defiant even while being arrested for their activities. A more positive note from our news is the coverage of vaccine rollout plans, a new hope for humanity.

In the winter months, viruses typically thrive in their transmission because people remain inside, or travel during holidays to see families and friends, sharing food, coughs, and sneezes with other human vectors in more confined spaces.

Coronavirus is no exception; it has quickly spread.

***

Our dark moment persists in the winter of 2020. With vaccine rollouts in a very infant stage, only certain military and health care workers receive a first dose of the vaccine. Health care workers who are privileged to even get a vaccine shot sometimes question not only its efficacy, but also the safety.

Samantha is a witness to this uncertainty. In some isolated settings, doctors and nurses quietly express their thoughts. "The price to be a health care provider these days is high, not only do we treat COVID patients while risking infection, must we also become guinea pigs for experimental vaccines? We know little about these products from pharma companies, and yet we need to trust them with our bodies?"

Samantha also shares some of these sentiments but there is no other hope but to receive the vaccine in good faith. Her logic tells her that if most of the physicians, nurses and health care workers die with undesirable side effects in America, there will be no one left to treat COVID patients; an apocalypse.

Samantha is on call for New Year's Eve with her chief resident, Aaron. He freely speaks his views as a proud member of his political party.

"Did you get your vaccine shot, Samantha?"

Aaron already knows Samantha made a special trip to the hospital on Christmas day to get vaccinated.

"Yes, I did, and it was the greatest Christmas gift."

"Did you have any side effects?"

"No, Aaron, I didn't really feel anything except the arm pain for one day at the injection site." Samantha's smile behind her mask is seen through her eyes.

"How can you do that to yourself, Samantha? Are you not afraid? This vaccine you received is unknown territory in vaccine history. You know it is 'man-made,' created at warp speed. The development and production were rushed because the president pushed to get these vaccines approved by twisting arms and cutting corners. Scientific and clinical studies and research were not even completed prior to emergency use by the FDA. Aren't you nervous?"

"Nope. And don't forget it is your Republican president who

developed this vaccine at warp speed. Aren't you confident in his administration?" Samantha's sarcasm is intentional.

Aaron ignores her but adds, "The hospital did their survey, and it showed only 77% of our employees want to get the vaccine, and 23% said they are going to wait to see what happens to all those courageous and foolish guinea pig subjects and then think about getting it, or refusing it."

"Well, I am glad to add values to the data by being a nice, cooperative guinea pig."

"Come on, Samantha. Even the nurses and doctors at a German hospital were skeptical of the vaccine, and you know it's a vaccine from a company in their own country—Pfizer. Some of the arguments against the vaccine are the unknown long-term side effects; or what if the vaccine only prevents the initial outbreak of the coronavirus. Others are confident their PPE will prevent transmissions. Many people are not in a high-risk group, or afraid of pregnancy-related issues, like, is it safe to breastfeed the infant? Is it safe to neonate in the womb when the mother decides to get the vaccine? What if the vaccine has risks to ovaries when these women want to be pregnant later in life?" Aaron pushes on with his lecture to Samantha.

"I am uncertain these vaccines were tested adequately on pregnant women. Frankly, I am not sure who to believe and who to trust these days, even those in our medical field. One day, doctors say you don't need to wear a mask and a little later, yes, you should be wearing a mask. Samantha, it's not just a single physician with this view. The CDC reinforces these flip-flop ideas. Medicine should speak the truth about the illness. Sadly, medical advice is linked to a political party, and often personal agendas, instead of evidence-based messaging guidance. What's the use of getting vaccinated when we're required to wear masks, maintain social distancing and all that stuff? There is no immediate relief or benefit."

Samantha promptly responds. "A healthy dose of skepticism is good. I choose to see the 'glass of water as half full' in this. All of our current medical practice was derived from trial and error experiences; actual scientific experiments by watching what happens to the patients with certain illnesses. Yes Aaron, medical doctors in the past collapsed the lung of tuberculosis patients to attempt a cure. And later we came to know which bacilli causes tuberculosis, so we have appropriate treatment for it. If we don't try out something new, we cannot move forward," Samantha reasons, even though she is somewhat impressed with the reasons Aaron provided for his skepticism.

"The difference is, Samantha," frustration apparent in Aaron's voice, "this time, healthy doctors must take the unproven remedy as well, not just those who are sick. And I am not ready for that. Why should I risk my own body for a scientific experiment?"

"Giti died from COVID. She's from our own department, Aaron. This is a respiratory virus we are talking about which can infect you and me, not just the patients who come to the hospital. The vaccine will immensely protect us from getting sick or dying if we do get infected. We have success stories with numerous vaccines: poliovirus, measles, mumps, rabies, hepatitis B, hepatitis A, you name it. Didn't you get all these when you were young, or prior to entry into medicine? Aaron, why hesitate on this COVID vaccine?"

"Who knows, Samantha? This vaccine may cause death as a side effect, like blood clots, strokes, and heart attacks. What about autism, Samantha? What if the genetic code or composition of the vaccines made by these companies have a tracking ability to obtain your genetic codes, to know your whereabouts at any given time, to infiltrate your brain and understand what you are thinking?"

"Aaron, this is not a sci-fi movie. You are being silly," she scoffs.

"I don't know, Samantha. One thing I will not do is be first in line to get that shot. I will wait as long as possible. I need to know the side effects. I am glad the hospital has the opt-out program. Do the vaccines work against all of the expected variants? I am not going to be the guinea pig for a profit-obsessed pharma industry. Who knows, I might have already gotten COVID and be one of those asymptomatic infected persons. If I did have the infection, I don't need a vaccine because I will have antibodies against it anyway, perhaps for my lifetime."

"Whatever!" Samantha retorts with irritation, hands raised.

"But you know what, Samantha? You know Dr. Wise? The liver transplant surgeon who we all know makes millions of dollars. You know the guy who has his vacation house in Florida

Keys or West Palm Beach? I heard he brings all his rich and famous friends to his home, even international friends from all over the world, Arabs, Canadians, Mexicans, Brazilians, and Venezuelans, and people from various states in the US. They're skipping the lines and the tier system and crashing the Sunshine State to get a shot. It's the 'vaccine vacation.' They fly to Florida in their personal jets, get their vaccines because they don't need to show their residency. They simply bring an ID to show their age. So, in a way, the rich and famous people get to be first in line for vaccinations. Their justification? They pay the governor or other politicians with contributions to campaigns, then they book an exorbitant vacation destination that comes with a vaccine shot which of course is listed as a concierge service. Meanwhile, those from poor and middle income families struggle to find the locations and registration sites, and patiently wait for their turn. Some other scumbags exploit the situations and promote bogus vaccines that are probably just saline solutions and charge a thousand dollars per shot. They scam only the desperate people. The world exposes what it always has been: the 'haves' get their privilege, and the 'have-nots' get their tragedy."

"So, Aaron, what are you waiting for? Why don't you get a free shot when you are given the chance and privilege to do so because you are a doctor? A vaccine clinic is in the building."

"I am going to wait and see for at least a month or two, way past the date of your second dose. By the end of January, I will get to see if you are still healthy. It will not be too late to get my shots. Who knows, you might become a zombie or deranged by the end of January."

"Aaron, you are ridiculous! It's not even funny."

"By the way, Samantha, you want to go out with me?"

Not a question she expected. Samantha unknowingly stares at Aaron, with no answer.

Aaron is one of those proud Caucasians, too smart for his own good, an aristocratic mindset, sincerely believing he is a person *too good to be true* to the point of irritating others. Constantly praising himself for his unbeatable good looks, Aaron often comments that Hollywood is stupid not to notice his handsomeness. Furthermore, he's a Harvard medical school graduate and perhaps smarter than most pathologists who are attending physicians. Before COVID, he appeared every day wearing a bow tie from his collection, a pressed white shirt, navy blue pants, and slip-on penny loafers with no socks. Now, he abides by the COVID dress code and wears hospital scrubs fearing he may bring clothes contaminated with the virus back to his house.

Samantha has continued staring in silence, her answer still absent.

"I wasn't joking, Samantha! So, what do you say," he says meekly, "do you want to hang out with me?"

Samantha can only respond with, "I…I am sorry."

"Why not?" Aaron is puzzled to hear her response; the first time a woman has rejected him.

"Well, I thought you were a White supremacist, Aaron."

"That's an insult! How can you say that?"

"I am sorry, but you are so proud, and arrogant."

"Well, that may be true, and I have reasons to believe why I am proud of myself but not about my race. I never said the White people are better than any other races."

"Well, you imply that."

"No, I never did. I am proud of who I am. I'm a doctor, handsome, Harvard graduate, Republican, filthy rich; well actually, my parents are rich. They live in one of those West Palm Beach mansions in Florida. I'm smart and fun to be with. So, what's wrong with me having, as you said, arrogance? I am hard to come by, you know."

"That's precisely it, Aaron, I don't like people who have no ounce of humbleness. It's disgusting!"

"Don't be too judgmental so quickly. You hardly know me. I may be a humble person once you get to know me after a while."

Samantha heard his voice shake. He's upset. Has she misjudged him as prejudiced? His haughty and prideful behaviors may not derive from his race. Perhaps he simply believes to be in possession of many attractive attributes.

"You know, Samantha, you don't have to go out with me. I get it, but don't create an unjustifiable character defamation. Not all Whites are white supremacists. We may look proud but inside, we are as vulnerable as other races."

"I am very sorry." Samantha feels small and wants to hide from his sight. Gratefully, Aaron quickly responds.

"Well, I am taking the train to Washington DC to support our current president. I will stay at a nice hotel—Trump Hotel in fact—for a week to participate in a meeting and attend a major event. Do you want to come with me?"

Samantha is confused by what was asked. Is he asking her to join him for a week-long vacation in his DC hotel room? Is he joking? She recalls her own distasteful remarks to other pathology residents about the current president. Aaron is certainly aware of her political opinions. She pretends not to hear Aaron and quickly maneuvers around him as she rushes toward the women's bathroom so Aaron will not follow her.

"I'm just kidding!" Aaron yells out.

Other than his joke, she cannot understand her adversity toward Aaron just because he shows interest toward her; his sudden invitation to know each other more intimately. Besides, Aaron is chief resident and always supportive of Samantha. He covered her service duties throughout residency training the past year. She does not have a boyfriend now, but she is far from interested in having a romantic relationship. She is determined to regain composure and promptly return to her desk, next to where Aaron sits. She is embarrassed that she created a negative judgment upon Aaron that might be based on preconceived biases she developed. Momentarily she forgot that every person has traits of Christ, and made in God's image.

Chapter 25

Insurrection

January 6, 2021

Aaron arrives in Washington DC two days before the planned demonstration to support Trump. He checks into the Trump Hotel, $1,000 per night to stay with his father. He is present mainly to support his father, who flew from Florida to participate in the event. The agenda is well thought out with significant funding. His father donated 40 million dollars to an organization called QAnon. Online posts by the organization declared the January events will take place not only at the US Capitol, but throughout the country at sites which feature major federal buildings. The night before the planned insurrection, Trump and his faithful followers plan to meet at the Trump hotel where Aaron and his father are featured as invited guests, most likely because they donated large amounts of money. Now at the height of a pandemic, the hotel is thoroughly congested with Trump supporters arriving from all over the US. They are preparing Confederate battle flags to be carried in coming days, American flags, and assembling poles holding banners of Nazi emblems. Christian imagery and rhetoric are prevalent, and collections of signs and slogans profess, *Jesus Saves*, plus *Jesus 2020*, and *Christ is King*, and *God's warriors*. A small collection of protestors are self-labeled 'prophetic Christians' who hold these signs and believe that Trump is prophesied to remain in power and anointed by God to save Christian Americans. The recent photo of Trump holding his Bible next to a church in DC has become their proclamation, a sign to believe it as fact.

Other protestors and hotel guests are preparing tools they brought in hope of prying open doors. Smuggling weapons into the city is prevalent among protestors. They simply do not believe Democratic candidate Biden defeated the incumbent Republican President Trump in the November 2020 presidential election.

On Wednesday January 6th, the 117th Congress is scheduled

to meet and count the results of the votes from the Electoral College to certify the winner, typically a ceremonial affair. Trump is pressuring his vice president Pence to reject the electoral votes and stop Biden from being inaugurated, which experts argue is beyond the vice president's constitutional power.

The protest is to build momentum and pressure to disrupt the counting of Electoral College ballots. Activities are planned several weeks prior to the event including plans to storm the Capitol, although explicit calls for violence is not mentioned. The Proud Boys and other far-right groups are prepared to turn against law enforcement. They discuss war, physically taking charge at the event, and some openly consider the option of killing politicians including the Vice President and House Speaker.

Trump supporters initially informed the National Park Service that up to 30,000 people might attend their 'Save America' rally, but at least one news source estimates as many as 80,000 arrived. Virtually none are wearing masks. More than 80 buses streamed into the city carrying passengers from across the country, including Aaron and his father. Unbeknownst to Aaron, two pipe bombs were already placed near a residential neighborhood on South Capitol Street, within a few blocks of the Capitol. At 9:00 am, a call to action is pronounced: "It is up to us to save this Republic, keep up the fight." At 10:58 am, Aaron's father accompanies a Proud Boys contingent as they methodically march toward the Capitol Building. Aaron follows close behind and pleads to his father.

"Dad, I am not comfortable with this, why don't we go back to the hotel and watch this on TV?"

His dad turns around, eyes enraged. "Are you out of your mind, Aaron? We came all the way here for this. I have bear spray, and we'll break through the Capitol police lines if we have to. We are going to march into the Capitol and save our president. They stole his presidency."

"Dad, I don't want to be here. I am going back to the hotel."

"You coward! You are not my son if you do that! I will disown you if you are not fighting for America. You know the election was stolen from our president. He is the only president we have."

"Dad, think about this for a moment. Something about this is not right. People here are preparing to commit violence."

"Shut up, son. Don't pussy-about here."

"I'm here to protect you Dad, not here to support your crazy ideas. All I want to do is make sure you are going to be all right. You are 70 years old, hardly able to run. Are you saying that we will break through the police barricades, get inside the Capitol and stop the counting of the votes that were already counted in November? For the record, I will say this: I am going with you, only to make sure you are safe."

"Whatever! I am willing to die for this cause!"

"This is a crazy reason to die. I am not ready to die yet. I have a whole life ahead of me to live. I want to complete my residency and finish a fellowship and get a job. I don't really care who is the president. That has nothing to do with me."

"Nonsense, everything has to do with 'who is the president.' You will lose your rights, and once you lose your rights, it's not America anymore."

"What rights does Trump bring to you? Why would you sacrifice your life for him, Dad?"

"The right to own guns, the right to vote, and vote without corruption, the right to express the concepts of a republic, the right to protect our own country. That's why."

"Won't Biden do the same, and give you the same rights? He is an American too!"

"Don't even mention his name here. You might be killed."

"What are you going to do once you get inside the Capitol, Dad?"

"I will go into Nancy Pelosi's office and drag her out of the building. She is ruining our country."

"Are you going to kill her? Is that your right? You will be a criminal and spend the rest of your life in jail, and I will always be 'the son of a murderer.' Is that what you want?"

"Sometimes it is better to use violence for the good of the majority and the country. Freedom is not free."

"Who is the majority? The majority voted for Biden. Dad, wake up and be sensible!"

"Aaron, keep your mouth shut! If you don't want to go with me, then stop and go back to wherever you want to go. If you are coming with me, turn on your phone to listen to Trump. He is expected to speak about it now."

Aaron fumbles with his phone, opens YouTube. Starting at 11:58 am from behind a bulletproof shield, Trump gives a speech and commands, "Never concede the election!" as he faults the 'fake media,' and encourages the crowd to enter the Capitol because they have the power to prevent Biden from taking office. "We can't let that happen!" he commands.

The crowd bursts out with shouts and applause. Aaron's father and Trump's supporters begin to chant. *Take the Capitol!* and later, *Taking the Capitol right now!* and *Invade the Capitol!* Another, *Storm the Capitol!* as the crowd marches toward the Capitol. Trump concludes his speech after using the word *fight* 20 times, then returns to the White House.

Just before 2:00 pm, hundreds of rioters reach the doors and windows of the Capitol and at 2:11 pm, many of these people enter the building wearing military helmets and military-style vests. The District of Columbia Police Department was planning to respond to these 'First Amendment activities' and had not planned for what is officially identified as criminal riotous behavior. The Capitol is locked down; lawmakers and staff escape into the bowels of the Capitol while rioters vandalize the building for several hours, resulting in more than 140 people with injuries, and five deaths including a Capitol policeman. Weapons used among the protestors include metal pipes, chemical irritants, unlicensed pistols, rifles, a high capacity feeding device, unregistered ammunition, tasers and illegal fireworks. Some are later charged with weapons offenses, including carrying an AR-15-style rifle, a shotgun, a crossbow, several machetes, smoke grenades and 11 Molotov cocktails.

Aaron's father is at the west front of the Capitol. He is pushed forward by rioters who drag police officers and assault them with hockey sticks, crutches, flags, poles, sticks, stun guns, fists, and spray chemical irritants on their faces. Someone confiscates the bear spray from the pocket of Aaron's father and begins using it against policemen. The mistargeted spray hits directly into the eyes of Aaron's father. He collapses, holds his eyes as he cries in pain. The rioters begin walking on top of his father's body in their stampede to enter the Capitol. Aaron strains in panic to pull out his father. Adrenaline swiftly moves through his blood to muscles as he pulls one last time to release his father from the trampling and pandemonium. His father continues rubbing his eyes in pain, yelling profanities as Aaron clutches his father tightly around the chest and helps him to stand. Aaron pulls him back against the tide of rioters until they reach an open area, where he can escort him back to their hotel. Step by step the blinded father is guided by his son until they reach the empty hotel where he can wash his eyes with clean water. They never entered the Capitol or witnessed the destruction inside, and were fortunate to avoid arrest. Aaron immediately packs his father's suitcase to take him to the airport and back to Florida.

His father grabs Aaron's hand that holds a suitcase and pleads, "Your rights will be taken away if you don't fight now. We will be overrun by the minorities. They'll take away your rights, lands, and this country. There is no time to waste. You must fight and protect your rights, now! Otherwise, non-White lunatics will bully us to welcome all the Mexicans, Puerto Ricans, Chinese, and Blacks from Africa to infiltrate our country and gain the majority. Anyone who is White will be the minority, and your future will be doomed. Don't be naive and an idiot watching these things happen in your lifetime. Do something about it and support Trump. He will act on this. He is the only president who is courageous for us."

"Dad, is that what this is about? Your fear? Fear from being overcrowded by non-Whites ruining your rights? Trump did not even march with you. He is a coward!"

Aaron's sarcasm is unrestrained, disappointed that his father truly believes Trump is the man to protect his White supremacist ideals and concepts and this election was about racial preservation. Fear of losing privilege and changing the status quo generates strong emotions and acts of violence in the name of protection. Aaron is disgusted with the Republican party and those who participated in the insurrection; but also in his father, who will never accept someone like Samantha, who he wants to marry. Sadly, Samantha is half Asian and will never be accepted by his father.

Aaron presses his Dad again. "It is best if you go now, fly home and be safe with Mom. She will be shocked to know what you were doing here in DC. I've already called the pilot. It's over."

Aaron indeed had already called and approved the additional

fees arranging for his dad's private jet and the crew to arrive immediately and fly him home. He makes sure his father walks onto the plane and watches it take off, then boards a train back to the Bronx. He feels lucky to be away from the chaos which Trump supporters caused, never expecting violence or people in military gear would storm into the Capitol and kill police officers. It was an unprecedented sight. Aaron watches video footage of what happened that day while he was among the crowds. Rioters climb their way up to the Capitol building, break windows with sledgehammers, spray-paint offices, intentionally pursue police officers and attack anyone who opposes them with bear spray, metal rods, grab officers and begin stomping boots on their heads. Aaron now recognizes he was amid a revolution. He expects hundreds of people will be arrested. Ultimately, Congress met after the riot and certified the election. Biden is reaffirmed to be the next president in 2021.

Rebellious revolutionaries become heroes when their activity of violence results in success, but when it fails; then, these people become insurrectionists, mere oppositionists, treasonous, defiant, and rebellious. Aaron is neither of these. He merely wanted to protect his aging father. Thank God he was there to pull him out of a crowd that Trump intentionally avoided. Not that Aaron expected Trump to march alongside his followers. This reaffirms he cannot trust any politician. What did he expect, anyway? He mocks himself for his naive trust in a politician. Others are not worthy enough for him to sacrifice his life. All politicians lie. He is eager to go back to the Bronx and live his somewhat boring, normal life.

Chapter 26

Questions need answers

January 30, 2021

Ed Liu is seeking answers. New questions continue to emerge following the introduction of new vaccines, while he and other scientists are in uncharted territory as they explain the new science. Medical doctors, scientists, and government agencies are working together to develop vaccine guidelines and health care recommendations during the pandemic health crisis.

The questions and some of their initial responses or recommendations are as follows:

How long can a vaccination dose last to protect against the coronavirus? The preliminary research data shows it will last about a year, but no one knows for sure.

Is a booster shot necessary, and if so, when? Yes. Either a year after vaccination; or, within a short time. Research is needed to compare the two arms of volunteers to determine the stronger efficacy.

Is the higher antibody titer equating protection against the virus after vaccination?

Will a booster shot increase their antibodies and prolong protection against getting infected with the virus?

Can the original vaccine cover all the variants? It is unclear whether emerging variants of the coronavirus will change our vaccination needs. For example, Influenza viruses are so mutable that they require a new vaccine every year. Looking at how the coronavirus has mutated to many variants thus far; it appears the coronavirus vaccine will also need to be altered once a year. A limited result shows that the Pfizer vaccine has an efficacy of 95% against the original version of the coronavirus. But an Alpha variant from Britain shows 89.5% efficacy and the Beta variant from Africa shows 75% efficacy. However, the vaccine is seen to be almost 100% effective at preventing severe, critical or fatal disease of all variants. Virus mutation and evolution is guaranteed, like taxes to a government. More formidable variants of coronavirus may emerge in the months to come. These may spread quickly and resist or evade the original vaccine.

Is drawing blood the best method to quantify the measurement of antibodies to detect the immunity against the coronavirus? If this is so, then people who were previously infected and then received the vaccine may result in longer and more durable protection.

Inactivated viruses such as the vaccine created by China (Sinopharm) shows less amount of antibody production when compared to mRNA technology and shows less efficacy (78%).

Why is that so?

Will all people need two shots? Flu and coronavirus vaccines every winter?

What about the short- and long-term side effects due to the mRNA vaccine?

What about the children and infants? The control study for Phase 3 did not include any age group below 18. Eventually the vaccine needs to be tested for these two groups and exactly when and how are still up in the air. Also needed is safety and efficacy data for use in pregnant women.

Ed is busy creating new sets of research studies to answer these questions and contacting clinical trial sites with volunteers. His company already began developing a flu vaccine using mRNA technology to combine with a coronavirus vaccine, and this may lead to a single combined shot. This novel virus preoccupies his life and brings him unending scientific questions. His 12 to 16-hour workdays continue. He has taken no vacation time for a year and a half, nor seen his family. Ed rejects routine dental care and annual physical examinations for fear of contracting the coronavirus.

No time to think about personal matters makes it easier to forget his love life, and he pleasantly discovers his immunity to any lingering pain from his separation with Samantha.

Chapter 27

A perfect storm

January 31, 2021

Within his company, other challenges arise for Ed. A shocking number of his employees — approximately one in five people — are opting not to receive their own vaccine, or vaccines from any other company. Ed is astonished that employees in a company like his, with leading-edge technology, can have polar opinions about the vaccines. The company plans to suspend employees without pay for 14 days if an employee fails to comply with their COVID-19 vaccine requirement. Most workers signed the consent for vaccination, but approximately 18-23% refused primarily for one of three reasons: medical exemption, religious exemption, and/or personal safety. Some have requested deferrals for pregnancy. A half-dozen of his employees are threatening to sue the company and allege that the company policy mandating all staff be vaccinated against the coronavirus is unlawful, and violates their first amendment of freedom of choice and speech. Ed assumed that if the FDA approved the vaccine for an emergency approval, and later for permanent approval, the employees might change their mind and receive the vaccine, but that is not the case. The federal government may eventually decide whether it is legal for a company to require its workers to be vaccinated.

Ed chooses to speak with a dozen or more employees who declined vaccination. This one-on-one approach might prevent shaming or ridicule toward these staff during his regular town hall meetings. A few mothers in his company are adamant their children will not receive any vaccines, including measles, mumps, and rubella (MMR), and also polio, which are mandatory for entry into public schools. Parents publicly demonstrate against 'foreign substances that are causing bad side effects.' These adverse effects are not proven, but parents claim these include autism, mental retardation and attention deficit hyperactivity disorder (ADHD) in children.

This is not a new concept.

History tells us that vaccine refusal began more than 100 years ago, and even during the time of smallpox. For those who reject vaccines of any kind, the new coronavirus vaccine is just another vaccine for people to refuse. This is known as being an *anti-vaxxer*. Unless the government requires vaccinations to all, or generates vaccine passports for citizens to enjoy 'normal public activities' such as indoor movie theaters, sporting events and concerts, his company cannot unilaterally decide to fire employees for not taking vaccines claiming that the company would be violating their freedoms and constitutional rights.

Ed and Dr. Allen consult with in-house attorneys about the dilemma. It becomes apparent that when they arrive at any decision, it will evoke anger among some employees. After a full day of discussion, the company ultimately decides to suspend employees without pay for 14 days, specifically staff working onsite who fail to comply with the company's policy of its COVID-19 vaccine requirement. These employees are mostly scientists. Employees who work from home are mostly administrative staff, so the company chooses to delay a decision on this category of staff, and whether to terminate the contracts of employees who choose not to receive vaccines. Many companies and hospitals must eventually choose what to do with this issue.

*****

The pandemic seemed to start as a uniform perpetrator of infecting and killing people regardless of their race, political party or economic status, but it has already clearly divided us. We are definitely not in this together.

People can reject vaccines for many nuanced reasons, sometimes arising from a minority of religious leaders. Certain evangelicals have even linked coronavirus vaccines to be *the beast*, a symbol of the Antichrist found in Revelation, their skepticism built on the back of their growing distrust of science, medicine and the global elite. They not only oppose the vaccines, but they are also against masks and social distancing policies. Many strongly believe that they are God's chosen people and will be protected from any illness or disease, or if they die, that is also God's will. Receiving a vaccine is a demonstration of weak faith or a disbelief in the power of God. Large numbers of religious leaders continue defying authorities by hosting mass church gatherings, encouraging people to attend religious services and proclaiming the government is violating their religious freedom. Using the pulpit, certain church leaders encourage their congregations to defy business closures, mask wearing, and vaccination. Hundreds of thousands of people trust church leaders more than scientific and medical experts. Some who identify as Evangelical are spreading news that vaccines were developed by using fresh fetal tissue or fetal stem cells. In particular, they cite Johnson & Johnson, claiming their vaccine used lab-created stem cells derived from a decade-old, aborted fetus.

There are also groups of Muslim fundamentalists in Afghanistan, Nigeria, and Pakistan who have opposed getting vaccines—in particular polio—because they believe that the polio vaccination effort was a conspiracy to sterilize Muslims in the area. Many of these same groups decline to get the COVID vaccines, and certain Muslim religious leaders declared vaccines contain pork-derived products, and the consumption of pork is forbidden.

The media also influences suspicions by featuring or accentuating side effects after a person was vaccinated, especially when they provide little or no context, and avoid mention of scientific data. One such headline: "A nurse passed out after reportedly getting an mRNA vaccine." Humans are primed to pay attention to threats or negative information and the subsequent beliefs are hard to change because they are based in fear, often regardless of logic or evidence-based medicine.

Another argument used to avoid a COVID vaccine is that the COVID vaccines went through an unprecedented rapid process, with many shortcuts, and without proper vetting or concern of safety for the humans. A variation of that concern is criticism of the FDA's speedy decision for emergency usage of the vaccines. A common conclusion is the FDA was reportedly coerced into a rapid decision by the federal government or by big pharma companies, therefore no time for observations of short- and long-term side effects.

A perfect storm can lead to conspiracy theories. A storm can be triggered by asking a question, or more accurately, create a scare tactic by asking questions that may elicit fear. Such questions include:

What about the other substances or ingredients such as fatty components, aside from the mRNA genetic codes in the vaccine?

What if there is an access genetic code, or other substances that can trace people who received the injection?

What if that code can detect the private information of a person?

What if the vaccine substances that were initially created to stop the spread of coronavirus are later shown to have an everlasting negative impact on a person?

***

The reasons for *not getting vaccines* are different from *anti-vaxxers*. The reasons for not receiving COVID-19 vaccines in particular can be organized as follows:

First, a refusal to see COVID-19 as a serious threat. The former president's comments are significantly influential. Immediately upon his COVID-19 infection, the president received comprehensive treatment, and his recovery seemed prompt. He claimed that his illness and the coronavirus were not a big deal, and that Democrats were exaggerating the risks of the virus and the COVID death rates. This resulted in vast numbers in his political party to view the vaccine effort primarily as politics, rather than science.

Second, a growing assumption that those previously infected with COVID-19 will have a certain amount of natural immunity for protection, but even early research indicates that a vaccine provides stronger immunity than infection.

Third, concerns about serious or unknown side effects from COVID-19 vaccines abound. Many false concerns are floating in social media, such as infertility and other unproven and undocumented threats of long-term health risks. The scientifically known side effects are injection site pain, muscle and joint aches, low fever and fatigue, or in extremely rare cases, blood clots.

Fourth, portions of the population do not trust anything related to COVID-19. For some people, there is no trust in vaccines, institutions, companies, the government, or even the health care system in general. Much of the public has lost their trust in the CDC, WHO, and even their medical doctors.

Fifth, social media became more viral, their growth exponential and it easily spread misinformation and hearsay theories and conspiracy.

Sixth, younger people trust their own immune system to fight back the coronavirus. Their own body will protect them through healthy diets, regular exercise, and healthy lifestyles.

Seventh, those who fear long-term side effects have no way to sue the government or the pharmaceutical companies even if a person suffers severe adverse reactions. This fear arises partly because both the government and the pharmaceutical companies are protected against litigation, even a Supreme Court ruling.

People likely know someone who died from COVID-19, and someone who is not willing to get vaccinated. However, the relationship between the two are not necessarily correlated.

Perhaps the most unfortunate reason for a person not getting vaccinated is because they have no access or ability to be vaccinated. If a person is unable to access a vaccine, they become among those who do not get vaccinated. This issue remains ignored by many leaders.

***

It is important for all of us to seek understanding of why people refuse to get vaccinations. Their reasons are different, some have no clear reasons, and some are simply undecided. Vaccination rates appear to increase with easier access to vaccine sites, in-home service, and innovative ideas like a new DoorDash vaccine program. Our chances to achieve herd immunity will increase only by participation, especially through education in our communities from providers, local medical doctors, and health care professionals. Our country has qualified people who can respond to questions and help influence our culture toward a commitment of protecting each other, certainly to protect our vulnerable members of society. Ending the pandemic is socialistic: to benefit the whole community rather than arguing for individual interest.

America suffers from a deficit of imagining the lives of other people.

Chapter 28

What to say before dying

March 8, 2021

As vaccination efforts continue without pause, hospitals around the US begin to have fewer COVID-19 patients. This allows for a gradual increase in routine cancer treatments and elective procedures. Samantha has begun working more hours in the pathology department to accommodate the increase in surgeries. She and Roxanne start their surgical pathology rotation each morning at 6:00 am. They sit adjacent to each other in small cubicles among the other surgical pathology residents, intensely looking through their microscopes and writing preliminary reports for the biopsies.

On the morning of March 8, Roxanne and Samantha began working on the diagnoses for dozens of patients who had outpatient hospital procedures last Friday. Three other pathology residents are in nearby cubicles, and two other residents have been cutting the biopsy specimens since early in the morning. Normally, surgical pathology rotation requires a total of eight residents, but Troy has not shown up to work yet, and Aaron the chief resident will also be joining them this week to help with the backlog of cases. Most of the residents arrive by 7:00 am, but Troy is considered early if he shows up by 9:00 am. His tardiness frustrates the attending physicians.

At 7:10 am, Aaron rushes into the room, turns to lock the door and shouts, "Everybody, get down. There is a gunman shooting in our hospital." His eyes show fear, his posture deadly serious. He runs past the four cubicles on his right and mentally counts Samantha and Roxanne, counts four other residents in cubicles on his left and swiftly locks the door at the back of the room. It leads to a hallway near the specimen receiving area. Next, he locks the door that leads to the surgery operation rooms. In less than 8 seconds, all three doors that a shooter could enter into their room have been shut and locked by Aaron. With both hands he flips down all the light switches, leaving the room in complete darkness except for a sliver of light from underneath the door leading to the hallway and soft lights from computer monitors.

Aaron speaks softly. "The gunman in the ER is carrying a semi-automatic AR-15 and fired several shots a few minutes ago. Shut down the computers or cover them with your coats. Stay away from the doors and get down under your desks." Like a frantic cat he slides underneath the desk alongside Samantha. Her small cubicle apparently designed for children is not big enough to hide them both. Aaron's body presses against Samantha. She feels his heartbeat as he strains to avoid lying completely on top of her.

"Do you have your cell phone?" Aaron whispers.

"Yes, I have it in my pocket," she whispers back.

"Turn it on to see the news." She struggles to get her phone from her pocket, her only option is to push harder against him to grasp her phone in the rear pocket of her scrubs.

"Open up Twitter," Aaron commands.

"I don't use Tweeter."

"What? Let me have your phone!"

"You are not going to open Tweeter on my phone."

"Arghh, just open a news app. Hey residents out there, open your apps! But turn off your sounds and ringers!"

Samantha tries to open her iPhone but has forgotten her password. As she fumbles with the iPhone, Aaron takes it from her hand.

Samantha fetches it back. "Use your own phone! You don't even know my password."

Wang Li calls out next. "There is nothing on IG or YouTube about our hospital." Wang Li is a second-year resident. He attended medical school at Harvard and is proud to advertise his credentials.

"Quiet, don't shout! Aaron declares. "Gunman might hear us and break in." He then gestures the message with a finger over his lips.

Two other residents suddenly walk out from the cutting room and into the residents' room, with light spilling out and filling the room.

"Turn out the light! Get down!" Aaron realizes that he forgot to check on the specimen cutting room that is directly attached to their surgical pathology room.

"What's going on?" asks Pihu, their first-year female resident from India. Carlos, a Puerto Rican third-year resident, is standing directly behind Pihu in the doorway.

"Get the light out!" Aaron says a little louder.

Carlos turns off the light in the cutting room. Immediately he and Pihu can see nothing, standing motionless while adjusting their eyesight.

"Get under the cubicle, now," Aaron orders.

Pihu nervously responds, quivering. "I can't see. Where is the desk?" Carlos pulls Pihu with him to kneel down. Crawling forward in the dark, they collide with Wang Li and Amir, who already occupy the tiny space underneath a cubicle desk.

"Move to your left! Amir and I are under here. Go to your own cubes," Wang Li orders, and points to the next desk by using the dim light on his phone's screen.

Pihu pushes Carlos forward as they squeeze under her cubicle desk.

Everyone probably assumes the shooter would enter through the main door, something Aaron had immediately calculated, recognizing everyone should move to the front of the room and into opposite corners. The cutting room that doubles as a receiving area for specimens has limited access and is only used by hospital staff. The surgical OR entrance is only accessible by certain nurses and doctors coming directly from the OR. If the shooter enters through the front door, Aaron had reasoned that the shooter will likely point his gun directly forward, not immediately pointing to the right or left. Aaron pulls Samantha's arm to lead her further forward to the front, far right corner cube.

"Do I have to move too?" Roxanne's shaky voice breaks the silence.

"Yes, move up to the second cube, just behind Samantha."

"What are we doing?" asks Carlos, puzzled.

"We have a gunman in the hospital," whispers Wang Li. "You and Pihu should also move up near my cube, here at the front left corner."

"No kidding!" replies Carlos. "And my TikTok shows nothing about this," his phone in hand as he crawls tightly next to Pihu, underneath the second cube from the front right corner.

Pihu begins to cry, her shaking voice whimpers, "I don't want to die."

"Nobody's going to die. Just stop crying," Amir says.

"Shut up. Be quiet," as Aaron takes charge again. His body is partially over Samantha; his right arm wrapping her tight to calm her shaking. A few minutes pass, a few people softly whimper.

A shadow appears. Shoes walk past the door, revealed by the small sliver of light from under the entry door. Ten minutes pass in fearful silence. No one moves and even breathing seems to stop.

"Ooh, ooh, oh my God, my God," Pihu whimpers, her entire body shaking against Carlos.

"Shhhh," Carlos whispers. He feels warm urine, near his ankle. *It must be from Pihu. Oh crap,*" he thinks.

"I got news from Facebook," Roxanne whispers. "Someone taking a live video. It's our campus. Tanks and armored vehicles are lined up and FBI agents with serious-looking guns. Police cars everywhere. Surrounding our building."

Little lights from phones appear below their desks, soft spotlights on frightened faces. Aaron tenses up, dismayed. They might be easily detected from the outside hallway by a gunman eager to march into their phone-lit room.

Samantha speaks up. "Is there a better place to hide? Like closets or the specimen storage area?" She can't stand the smell of Aaron's body as he sweats.

"No, stay here. Specimen storage is filled with the specimen jars and bottles," commands Aaron. "We would have to remove all of those, and there's only room for one person to hide there."

Samantha persists. "I need room to breathe, Aaron." She promptly feels Aaron slowly release his arm that has been wrapped around her, and he readjusts his position. Samantha finally finds the online video Roxanne is talking about. It looks like a war zone with military troops coming toward the hospital. The streets are empty, blocked off by police cars. Several black armored vehicles are rolling slowly, with armed SWAT teams on top and others walking alongside. She fears that if all of those armed FBI agents, SWAT teams and special forces start shooting toward the building, she might be one of the casualties. There is no way to escape those heavy machine guns, grenades or other weapons. Collateral damage, other lives lost among innocent bystanders. Doctors, nurses and allied health care workers who escaped death by COVID could die by guns. Misery always compounds, and there appears no ending to this disastrous year.

Samantha cries out to God; she prays out loud. "God in Heaven, look down on us. Help us now Jesus. Give us strength and wisdom to face this harsh circumstance and let this pass so that we can walk out safely, preserving our lives without injuries. God help us now…"

"Amen, Allah, help us now!" Amir proclaims from the opposite side of the room. He crawls out from under a cubicle and positions himself in prayer, looking east and bending over to bow down. He repeats the prayer multiple times, getting up and bending down.

Aaron's voice calls out, "Amir, get back under the table. Everyone, turn off your phone!" Amir keeps to his prayers, but turns off his phone.

Roxanne's soft voice begins a hymn, "Amazing grace, how sweet the sound…"

"Be quiet!" Aaron pleads, but to no avail. Each person does what they must do, to calm their heart before their death. Pihu still shakes, and cries uncontrollably. Carlos continues to hold her, to comfort her as they lie on the stench of the carpet, now wet with urine.

Carlos begins to whimper. "I had a fight with Mom this morning before I came to work. I can't die like this. I need to apologize to her."

Wang Li joins in with his regrets in life. "I didn't visit my father who is dying with cancer last year because of this stupid COVID. He is dying in the hospital, and no one is there with him. I must go there to say goodbye to him. I didn't realize I could die before him."

"Who said you are dying? Don't even say that" says Aaron. "We are not going to die.

Roxanne speaks up. "Yeah, that's right. Why would the gunman come to a pathology room to kill people? We didn't do anything to him. He will know nothing about us."

"We should just leave this place and face the gunman and take him down!" Carlos utters.

Pihu cries out even louder after hearing what Carlos said

until Aaron exclaims, "Be quiet! Everyone, just shut up!" His irritation unfolds as people begin talking louder and louder.

Carlos rebuts Aaron. "We are a bunch of chickens sitting here, we should just get the heck out of here and fight." Carlos is fuming, intent on doing something about the situation with his own hands.

Roxanne agrees. "Carlos is right, we should prepare some plans to fight this gunman."

"Yeah, Aaron," announces Amir. "Let's get this guy down! If he walks into this room, me and Carlos will stand at either side of the door and attack him before he starts to shoot. He won't expect me and Carlos coming down on him from behind. Then, Aaron, you get the gun from him. We will tackle him and beat him up from behind." Amir is now standing at the left side of the door in the dark room, using a futile gesture to Carlos who is hesitant to leave Pihu alone, still visibly shaking and unable to function. She might yell out hysterically if he leaves her side and that would jeopardize the whole group's safety.

"Wait a minute," Aaron says cautiously. "We need to carefully plan this. We will have only one chance to tackle the gunman."

Samantha's phone lights up. "I got an email from our hospital administrator, Dr. Levin here at the hospital. It came 30 minutes ago. He says, 'our hospital is surrounded by the FBI and SWAT teams with heavy armor. Do not attempt to leave the hospital. Remain in your office or wherever you are, lock the door and try to dodge the bullets. Do not move around inside the building.'"

Aaron scoffs. "Can you believe this? He sent a regular email 30 minutes ago and he wants us to dodge bullets! People may already be killed, while he remains in his penthouse office, top floor with windows, sitting in his soft leather chair sending us an email. Email is the last thing people would read in this situation. He should use social media. Here we are in the basement, no windows to see what's going on—not that looking out from windows is a good idea in this situation—but still, we are in this slum, working hard for the hospital."

Roxanne quickly counters him. "I don't mind this place. I like my job. At least we have jobs. People are starving during the pandemic because they lost their jobs." After Roxanne's comment, no one talks for a while.

Eventually Amir starts again. "Let's go out there and take the guy down!"

"Do you have any weapons?" Carlos asks.

"No," Amir says with conviction. "But if we go behind the guy and jump him, then we can take the guy down."

Aaron shakes his head in disbelief, saying "How do you know if there is just one gunman? What if there are multiple gunmen?"

"Well, how many guys do we have here? It's Aaron, Carlos, me and Wang Li, four guys. We can manage," Amir answers.

Wang Li scoffs. "I am not going out there. Count me out. I am not going to risk my life to be a hero like that. That's just stupid, fighting against gunmen when we don't have any weapons except our bodies. Who needs that?"

"That's why you are a troublemaker," Amir shouts back. "You guys, Chinese spread the virus all over the world and do nothing to take responsibility. After all, it was your fault! China! You guys have no balls."

This enrages Wang Li. "How dare you say it's my fault! You don't know what you are talking about. You Muslims killed so many good people, how come you are not taking any responsibility for that?"

Amir moves in toward the voice of Wang Li, prepared to physically tackle him. Aaron immediately grapples with them in the darkness and disassociates the mangle of Wang Li and Amir. "Stop it you guys, the gunman might be outside. This lunatic might hear us and come shooting to kill. Just stop it!"

Amir and Wang Li breathe hard, straining to control their tempers. Aaron commands them again, "Get back to your cubicle Amir, and stay there. Wang Li, sit down, way down." Amir crawls back to his cubicle, and Aaron feels his way back to his cube next to Samantha, kneels down and warns, "Just behave, you guys. Be reasonable. We have ladies here to protect. Let's just think about getting the gunman down if he tries to come in. Keep your phones off."

A deadly silence arrives after this storm. 15 minutes pass in darkness until one by one the phones light up with social media underneath their desks, breathing quietly, keeping silent as possible. Another 15 minutes or so pass in quietness. Samantha becomes drowsy, closes her eyes, having slept very little the past two nights. Although Aaron crowds her space, she feels comfort from him that he would truly protect women among them, including her. She is puzzled by the peace that she feels even during this chaotic circumstance. This is unusual for her, and it must be from God hearing her prayers. She knows that God can give restful peace, surpassing her own understanding.

She is almost asleep when Aaron whispers, "I want to tell you in case we all die today, I am in love with you; from the moment I saw you four years ago. I never had courage to tell you that, but I don't want to die without letting you know." Samantha wonders if the whisper in her ear was a dream. *What is he saying,* she wonders. *How can I respond?*

Her thought is interrupted by his whispering voice. "I came here mostly to protect you, Samantha. I took some risks coming here. I actually came from the ER and saw some commotion. I didn't see the gunman, but I heard the shots fired and people in the ER were running outside. I ran inside the hospital and arrived here as quickly as I could. I didn't know exactly where the gunman was." This is followed by a long pause and Samantha has lost what to say.

"I realized what's most important to me when I was facing my own possible death. I have held this feeling since January when I was with my father in DC, the day of insurrection. I am in love with you. I've known this for about four years. If this is the last thing I say before I die, it will be cool." Aaron speaks softly, and she realizes no one else can hear him except her. She is in shock because she never realized Aaron had these thoughts about her. He never appeared interested in her over the past four years. The only time he asked her out was on January 1st and she thought he was just joking. She has no feelings toward him, definitely no romantic feeling. She has no answer for him and keeps quiet.

He awkwardly says, "It's okay. You don't have to feel the same. It's just me, I know. But I need to say that in case this is the last chance." He softly chuckles.

Samantha realizes how unpredictable people can be. She has thought of Aaron as a man who looks unfavorably upon others who are not White, a person from a privileged life, having it all — the looks, intelligence, tall, filthy rich, status and even a low baritone voice—probably a good singer too! He is popular among all female residents, even the hospital nurses often ask her to introduce him to them. Why would Aaron be interested in her during these years? It seems unlike Aaron to hide his feelings for any period of time. He expresses firm confidence in himself. He obviously has another side that has been hidden, private and deep feelings toward her which are fully unexpected. No one can fully know or predict another human, certainly not what another person thinks. Samantha knows one thing for sure in this situation. She cannot respond back to him favorably, even if this is her last chance to respond before she dies. Aaron must have thought that this might be the end of his life.

Her mind effortlessly recalls the day before Dr. David Falkner died, when he also told Samantha how much he cared for her and his regrets of his short lifetime, the things he couldn't do, should have done, then too late to do. She thinks about what her last thing to say would be, who to speak with if the last minute of her life had truly arrived.

Samantha texts her mom. "I love you Mom!" with no context of why she sends the message. She gladly holds no regrets in life, fully content, and happily knows that she would have done exactly the way she had lived, even if she were offered a chance to relive her life.

Chapter 29

What are you really thinking?

March 8, 2021

Two hours have passed, and Samantha is still at the same place, in the infant position under Aaron's arm, spooned by him. There are multiple emails from Dr. Levin, CEO of the hospital bringing his blow-by-blow news of what he knows, but still directing everyone on campus not to leave their location and not enter any hallway and remain in place. The location of the gunman is unknown. Samantha and the residents rarely speak. Crying has stopped. No longer do they ask each other what is happening. Occasional whispers between Carlos and Pihu are heard, but no one can hear exactly what they are saying. Amir and Aaron exchange occasional thoughts on techniques and strategies of how to tackle the gunman if he walks into the room.

Perhaps another hour passes with no activity or sound from the hallway until suddenly Samantha hears a distant soft padding from the hallway. Someone seems to be moving toward their door, footsteps more distinct. Aaron and Samantha bend their heads in unison, looking at the sliver of light under the door as it becomes obstructed. She sees white tennis shoes. A key struggles to find its way into the doorknob lock. The frustrated key is quickly pulled out, another key apparently chosen and forced into the lock. Aaron tenses his legs, slowly releasing his arm. *Is this my last breath?* Samantha wonders, pausing to exhale. As the key fully engages, the knob turns, and the door is shoved open by the intruder's foot as a blinding blast of hallway light swarms their darkness.

"Where is everybody? Why is it so dark?" Troy puts his keys in his right pocket, walks in and turns on the lights next to the door. Looking down at his colleagues tucked under the desks he asks, "What are you guys doing in the dark?"

"Close the door and turn off the light!" Aaron whispers.

"Why?" Troy asks, with little concern.

"Haven't you heard?" Aaron whispers. "A gunman is in our

hospital, and how did you enter the building?"

"I slept in last night. You know, in one of the beds saved for residents like us. I was on call overnight and some lunatic surgeon was doing brain surgery at 2:00 am and I got called in. So, I didn't go home. I slept in the hospital." Troy turns on his computer, looks for a pen, opens a desk drawer searching for paper and stops. He sees Carlos and Pihu hiding, looking up at him. Troy looks at them both, smiles and says, "What's going on?"

"Lock the door! Turn off the light!" Aaron commands again.

Troy shrugs and does what he is asked to do. "I don't know why you guys are all hiding down there but I need to get my work done. Dr. Huang is going to yell at me again if I don't show up by 9:30 at his office to sign out. I only have 10 or 15 minutes to organize."

"Forget about Dr. Huang," Aaron again commands. "Besides, he won't even gain access to the hospital this morning. It's all locked up. No one can get in or out right now. SWAT, FBI and police have surrounded our campus. Get down into one of the cubicles, Troy."

"I'm not doing that. The gunman dude can kill me if he wants, but I need to get some work done." Troy sits in his cubicle, leaving room for Pihu and Carlos to crawl out while he turns on his computer, bringing back light into the room. He shuffles his loosely arranged paperwork into the corner of his desk, then sorts through his pathology case slides by the light of his computer monitor. "It's so dark in here," he complains. "Can I turn on some lights?"

Everyone in unison says, "NO!" and someone else adds, "You idiot, we're gonna get killed!"

"Oh no, I'm gonna get killed," Troy mimics in a high voice. While looking at his monitor, he then speaks with a serious tone. "Nonsense, no gunman will walk into the pathology resident room. Nobody knows we are here in the basement unless the gunman is lost. I'm not scared of a gunman. I'm scared of getting another unsatisfactory evaluation from Dr. Huang." He speaks loud enough to be heard while everyone else is whispering.

"You don't understand, Troy, take a look online right now," Carlos responds in frustration.

"All right!" Troy opens up a video on his computer featuring his own campus hospital overrun with hundreds of law enforcement and military people in various uniforms wearing bulletproof vests, carrying heavy automatic weapons and running in a few directions. Countless are swarming toward the entrance of the hospital's ER area.

"Far out! No kidding! It's a war zone here."

"Yeah, we told you so. Look at Dr. Levin's emails," pleads Carlos.

"Oh no kidding, he sent us emails? He says dodge the bullets? Wow!" Troy laughs. "He must be peeing his pants! Ha!"

"Shut up, turn off your computer and get down!" Aaron again pleads, but this time with a firm low voice.

"Don't worry, chief, I will protect all of you. I will grab the guy, knock him down, throw formalin in his eyes and confiscate his weapon. If I fail, then, I will shield you guys and get shot. By that time, one of you should be able to get him from behind. Okay? You guys can thank me later after I'm shot from saving you."

Troy's confidence on display, as usual. He rises to retrieve a one-liter formalin bottle from the cutting room, opens the cap, and promptly returns to his seat. As a third-year resident, Troy is supremely laid-back, never stresses out about anything, White, tall, a little older than other residents and fairly good looking. He is criticized year after year by their attending pathologists for his tardiness. He self-proclaims that he is not a morning person, yet he works late and is usually the last person in the department to leave at night. He bewilders Samantha by his calmness in this type of circumstance. He intends to save his colleagues and is devising methods for attacking the gunman to save lives. She silently admires Troy's unexpected courage and self-confidence.

"I thought it was eerie in the hallway," Troy says. "Nobody was walking around. I saw no one from the third floor and all the way down to here. I even peeked into the stairwells, but no one was there either. I thought maybe I woke up in the middle of the night—like 4:00 am—but now it's obvious I simply overslept for a few minutes and didn't hear my alarm."

Troy places his formalin bottle-weapon next to his feet and proceeds with organizing several cases to begin diagnosing to sign out each case.

"Oh yeah, where are the biopsy slides? I only got the first ten or so. The histotechs usually come here at 2:00 am to cut the biopsy tissues. They must have delivered only the first cuts and then stayed in the lab. I guess they also hid under their desks and stopped working. They should stop hiding and come out. It's going to be a long day. I'll probably have to cancel my wife's birthday dinner for a second night in a row. Last night was her birthday dinner but I got called in at 8:00 pm to help a neurosurgeon—rush. He needed me to make sure he got clear margins. The entire surgery team waited 20 minutes, stopping mid-surgery for me to evaluate the margins and provide my diagnosis. I'm hot and stressed out thinking about it. Then I got called in again by the same surgeon."

Samantha knows they all empathize with Troy; any of them would have switched their call schedules if they had known.

Roxanne's voice interrupts their silence. "Oh, a SWAT team is entering the hospital! Now I see people leaving the hospital. There's nurse Ramos, my nurse friend from ER. She's walking out of the ER with her hands up. I don't understand why everyone has their hands up like captured criminals."

They all look at their phones, but Aaron responds to Roxanne. "Probably because police have not identified the perpetrator. They must keep their hands up to show they are not armed."

"Thanks Aaron," Carlos says. "So does this mean we are free to walk out too?"

"Oh, here is the email again from Dr. Levin," Troy answers. "He says the gunman is now captured. It appears he acted alone. There is no other gunman. We are now free to move about. He says anyone who feels shocked and unable to work is encouraged to visit the psychiatric clinic or go home. All right, let's just go home. I am traumatized!"

Troy is the least likely to be traumatized. He woke up in a bed at the hospital, insulated from any outside news.

Samantha's phone displays 9:50 am. They have been in terror, isolated for more than two and a half hours. Pihu scampers out from her cubicle and scrambles toward the bathroom.

Carlos pinches his nose tight and mumbles, "Man, I thought I would die with the stench."

"Why? Has she not showered lately?" Troy asks.

"No man, she lost her bladder control and peed here on my

leg. Look, I am wet. The whole carpet is wet," Carlos complains. Troy looks down at the scrub pants Carlos wears and sees urine stains near the ankles. "Oh wow, Carlos! She was terrified, wasn't she? Actually lost bladder control," Troy concludes in disbelief.

"Well, for your information, Troy, we were all scared to death. I'm glad someone did not lose their bowel control," Roxanne says irritably.

"Yeah, did you poop, Roxanne? I hope not," says Troy. "You know you can take showers and get fresh scrubs in the OR nurse bathroom and lockers. All of you should go and take a shower," he says laughing.

Roxanne yells back, "You know Troy, I appreciate the fact that you are willing to take the bullets for all of us, but I just hate your guts. You are such an insensitive jerk!"

"Wow, stop right there. Roxanne. You hardly know me to judge me like that." Troy then crosses his arms, as a referee calling time-out.

Quietness follows. Residents come out from underneath cubicles, and each takes a seat at their own desk, attempting to feel normal again until Amir murmurs, "It's probably a crazy homeless Black guy who had a gun."

"What? How do you know it's a Black guy? Maybe it's your country, man, violent Muslim Arabs!" Roxanne knows she went too far with that second phrase, but her shock from hearing another verbal blow to her race cannot be withheld.

"I am just saying it's all that Black Lives Matter business with demonstrations and looting that's happening and it creates angry people who lash out with violence," Amir retorts. "And those protesters were not even wearing masks and caused our hospital to accommodate countless more COVID cases. I am sick of handling more COVID cases in our hospital. What's that got to do with Muslims? We haven't done anything in this country, and we get all the blame for violence. We merely live according to our Islamic laws, and pray. You Americans are frightened only because of what we look like. We get that same racial treatment as the Blacks. Maybe even worse treatment, and we just bear it. You guys claim Black this and Black that, bringing up slavery history as if only you are victims." Catching his breath, Amir quickly adds, "and why don't you all just work hard and get an education, some degrees and try to live respectively without getting welfare and free money from the government?"

Roxanne is flabbergasted, unknowing how to respond. Her eyes enlarge, her mouth unable to make additional noise when Carlos interjects.

"The original cause is not the Blacks or Muslims, but the Chinese. It's the China virus that caused COVID. Those dirty Chinese brought the SARS-1 over in 2003, and now again this virus. They are the culprits of all our miseries now!"

"We are not all dirty! You Puerto Ricans are dirty!" Wang Li shouts back at Carlos.

Samantha stands up and raises her voice. "It's Trump's fault that COVID became this bad. He downplayed the consequences of the virus, presenting it as a minor nuisance. He dismissed the threat of the coronavirus because he was desperate. He was afraid the bad news might affect the economy and jeopardize his chances of reelection. He called the virus 'the foreign virus,' and then called it 'the Chinese virus' more than 20 times in March last year. His deliberate choice of wording was clear. He may or may not have racist intentions, but the words matter. And the intent matters less than the effect. Racist acts and harassment against Asians were already surging. We persistently hear words of hate. These words shape our world view. The adjective 'Chinese' is particularly problematic as it associates the infection with an ethnicity. Words like 'foreign' and 'Chinese' stoke anxiety, resentment, fear, and disgust toward anyone associated with that group. Ignorant Americans think all Asians are 'Chinese,' and we collectively are targets for xenophobia."

Samantha pauses, continues. "My mother was pushed, shoved and beaten in San Francisco for this. She almost died, and was hospitalized for three weeks in October. And just two days ago, on March 6th, a 21-year-old White male in Atlanta killed eight people at a spa, six were Asian females, and he told police 'that he was sexually frustrated,' which led him to commit the killings.

Really? A captain in the county sheriff's office said in an interview that sexual addiction was the motive, and the shooter had 'a bad day' and carried out the shooting to eliminate his temptation at the massage parlor—since when are we more interested in the perpetrator's opinion of why they killed people? Why is this even broadcast as if Asian American women working in a spa are all prostitutes? Those six women were Americans, of Korean descent. Isn't *that* anti-Asian hate crime? Do we need to hear excuses from a gunman?"

Samantha pushes on. "Action speaks louder than any words. An employee at the Atlanta spa who escaped during the shooting testified that the shooter proclaimed, 'I'm going to kill all Asians,' and 'I'm going down to Florida to kill more Asians working in spas and massage parlors.' Why do we even care to know the criminal's side of the story? We don't see the victim's faces, their losses, or their side of the story. Why do we hear this lunatic's sexual frustration story, repeated and recited by law enforcement officers while they talk about the shooting? Why does the media *not* focus their coverage on the people who are killed? Instead, they direct a spotlight on the shooters, like the crazy guy in Atlanta. Are media outlets ignorant? Do they not understand their sympathy is projected upon us by their stories that focus on the shooter's feelings, instead of what the victims feel? Anti-Asian violence is partly a product of Trump. He is careless, intentionally speaking disparaging, anti-Asian semantics."

"It's not entirely Trump's fault," Aaron swiftly replies. "Any president would have done similar things. Our president should not frighten Americans at the beginning of an epidemic. No one took the virus seriously. Look at President Bolsonaro of Brazil. He is macho like Trump, calling it the 'little flu' and accusing the media of hysteria. Bolsonaro said, 'stop whining about the dead and open up for business,' just like Trump."

Carlos promptly interjects. "That explains why Americans account for around half of the global number of cases and death rates, followed by Brazil and Latin America. How can a leader tell us not to whine about the deaths? If he lost his life or his child from COVID, he would not say that. Trump got COVID, but he got immediate treatment, the top doctors, top hospital, and top-of-the-line drugs, even the experimental drug. He got better quickly, but what about the poor people? Then Trump boasted it was no big deal to get COVID and we shouldn't be scared and not paralyzed by fear. But most Puerto Ricans who become infected with COVID are dying. We don't have money, secure jobs, or any status. We can't even come to a hospital to get treatment." Carlos then adds softly, "We just die quietly and no one even cares."

"But it's the Chinese. It's their fault!" Amir declares. "China had the level 4 laboratory in Wuhan, and they were studying the coronavirus. The American government even gave them funding. They obviously had spilled the virus, and it spread all over the world. The fact that they cannot find the zoonotic source, and the fact that the Chinese government continues to protect and insulate that laboratory says it all. They are hiding something from us. Their whistleblowers are threatened or even killed, meanwhile that government hides facts like they did with SARS 1 in 2003. Chinese scientists said that the new virus transmission was through the intermediary of Asian palm civets to cave-dwelling horseshoe bats, not too dissimilar to SARS 1. I guarantee you that Chinese scientists had their homegrown coronavirus and made it more potent by changing the genetic codes, genetically modifying it to adopt and attack human ACE receptors. Some idiot and untrained lab worker must have accidently spilled the virus and got infected, went to the seafood market and transmitted it there to several other people. Chinese people are blaming a seafood market because it's dirty just like our Chinatown in New York. Who wouldn't blame a dirty Chinese market for being the source of the virus? Even the Chinese people blame their own dirty seafood market. You can bet there will be another pandemic in our lifetime, and once again it will come from China." Amir's rage leaves him breathless.

"And how do you know so much about China?" Wang Li says, standing up and walking toward Amir as if to punch him. Aaron darts toward Wang Li and grabs his arm and waist, but a push-and-pull commotion escalates. Wang Li is the quietest of all residents, never losing his temper like this. Apparently he was not happy with Amir's idea about protecting everyone from the gunman, and was easily triggered to rise up and defend his own mother country.

"Stop that you guys, knock it off!" Troy says disgustedly. "The fact is, COVID is here whether it came from the lab or the seafood market or wherever. We have to deal with the consequences of this whether we like it or not. Blaming someone like Trump or someplace like China is not going to ease the pain or solve the pandemic problem. At this point, what good will it be if we know the exact source of where it came from, or whether the president should have done more to protect us? It's water under the bridge. Blaming Chinese or all Asians is not going to heal the pain." Everyone seems to agree with Troy, heads nodding.

Perhaps emboldened with support, Troy unexpectedly proclaims, "I am tired of Black Lives Matter and Stop Anti-Asian hate, all of it. How about White Lives matter! Our country is overrun with principles about protecting the interests and issues of minorities. How about the majority focus? Even entrance to medical school favors every minority applicant. I couldn't get into medical school for years because of stupid affirmative action programs. I don't fit into the quota—Latinos, Blacks, Pacific Islanders, American Indians, Brown people. What's all that for? This affirmative action program preferentially increases the chance to get accepted just because of colors of skin, not based on competence levels or scholastic achievements. Aren't they ashamed the action itself is discriminatory, based on race? Once in medical school, these people who got in under their affirmative action program do poorly. They make excuses like, 'I'm dyslexic, I lacked good exposure in my public school,' et cetera, et cetera. Meanwhile, I earned a 4.0 GPA, was an excellent student, competent, competitive, and cream of the crop. But I was rejected year after year, and they accepted dozens of non-Whites into medical school using lower standards. Why is rejecting White people acceptable, while favoritism is also acceptable? The Biden administration—no, the Democrats—welcome all colored people into this country, opening the door at the Mexican border for millions of people from El Salvador, Honduras, Guatemala, even all Central Americans and Mexicans. Kids are separated from their parents. It's a mess down there and we are keeping them alive, paying for the facilities, providing food and even kids' playgrounds."

Troy catches his breath before continuing. "What are we? We give and give until there is no money left to take care of our own people. Social Security is running out of money to provide for Americans who paid faithfully, and our own elderly are being shunned and turned away because the money is drying out. This country is facing trillions of dollars in debt. And yet, instead of thinking about young people like us who are trying to fund all of the programs to sustain our own elderly, we pay money to these immigrants, focus on equality of all humanity and the notion of racial balance. Rubbish to all of them. Who is paying for all of that? We treat all of these people, illegal aliens, with free medical care when they walk into our hospital. Immigration, especially illegal immigration is burdening our society and threatening our values. People wait years to arrive legally, while illegals arrive daily and our arms open wide. This country has gone far enough when it comes to giving minorities equal rights. As Democrats continue their rapid pace to accept more Latinos into this country, we will soon face minorities becoming the majority in America, pushing Americans out who were born here or anyone who is White. We will lose our identity as a nation. Blacks, Browns, or a person of any race for that matter is not the main reason why they can't get ahead. They are responsible for their own condition."

No one present seems to appreciate Troy's rambling.

"That's enough, Troy. I'm one of those Latinos," Carlos replies. "I am proud of my country and where I came from. America is not what you think. Your White people eradicated American Indians who were here first. America belongs to them, indigenous people, not the Whites. You guys are all immigrants from Europe who swarmed into this country by opening up Ellis Island less than two centuries ago. If America shut their door to European immigrants, you would not be here, not claiming American values, cultures and traditions. America is a melting pot just like here in New York City. In fact, right here, we have actual Americans. Whites, of course; Roxanne who is Black; me, Latino; Amir from Pakistan, Pihu from India, Samantha is Korean American, and Wang Li from China. I don't know where you and Aaron came from, but I will assure you, your ancestors came from somewhere in Europe and began humble lives in America. If we infiltrate our roots and tentacles long enough in this country as the Europeans have, we should have an opportunity to become politicians, rich enough to send our kids to college and live comfortably — if Whites are willing to share. We are, after all, immigrants. Every person here brings strength to this country. Diversity is a good thing." Nobody comments, and Carlos continues.

"You oppress us because you fear. You are afraid that we, the foreigners, will take away your privileged life because you are unwilling to share. We do not want to take your things. We merely want to live better lives here, and to eat in peace. My mother was an illegal immigrant when she came here and worked as a dishwasher in a restaurant. There was no law to protect her from being exploited and raped in her own country. Me and my brother work at McDonald's to fund our tuition, even during medical school. My father was an alcoholic. He lost hopes to survive in this country because of his heavy accent. He dug ditches, replaced roofs, did cement work, but people often withheld his pay, treating him as a second-class citizen. But we are not criminals, drug dealers, gangsters or troublemakers like the president claims. We the people of colors, recent immigrants, face more difficult paths toward acceptance and never achieve the sense of belonging in this nation." Carlos stops, tears in eyes from responding to Troy's remarks.

Samantha understands Carlos and eagerly explains to Troy, "You don't even know and appreciate how legally privileged you are, nor the economic status provided to you. Look around you. Who are the politicians? Overwhelmingly White, male, old dudes, naturally protecting their own interests. 'Law and order' is recited to oppress immigrants and to prevent their White supremacist origins being shaken. They must protect their status, enjoy their country club retirements and golf amongst themselves. They want a person who is a minority to carry their heavy golf bags, work in the kitchen, and serve them nice sandwiches. They can't have it the other way. They will not imagine Puerto Ricans or Latinos playing golf alongside them and beating them after a round of 18 holes. The last president uttered disparaging remarks recently against immigrants, arguing in favor of a Muslim ban even though he claims that he is a Christian. He definitely is not practicing the faith that teaches the 'love your neighbor' concept," Samantha explains. "He is an embarrassment to Christians."

Pihu walks in, her wet long black hair still dripping, wetting the shoulder areas of her new scrubs. She says somewhat shyly, "What are you guys doing? Aren't you going back to work? The gunman killed himself, I heard it from the OR nurses. They are starting to come back in and perform their routine work. They said he was a Latino who recently lost his pregnant wife and fetus to COVID while hospitalized here. She was admitted a few days ago and was refused to be given a single 8-gram dose of Regeneron's monoclonal antibody treatment like President Trump received. Our hospital administration decided not to treat patients with this experimental drug, but the patient's husband demanded it. He didn't have health insurance either. They are recent immigrants from Honduras. They have small children in their apartment in the Bronx. The husband, the gunman, thought that the hospital doctors and nurses were discriminating against them and not giving his wife the same drugs as the president received to recover from COVID. I think he got crazy with rage and got a gun and began shooting at ER doctors and ICU doctors. He rampaged through the ER and ICU killing 2 nurses and injuring several doctors. By the time police captured him, he shot himself near the ICU area. Can you believe this? Our own hospital?"

"Why does it have to be Latino again?" Carlos says despondently. Quickly Troy responds, "I told you; Latino immigrants are nothing but trouble for our country. Our president should shut the Mexico border like Trump did. He is encouraging people to come to the US." Without hesitation Carlos rushes to tackle Troy.

"You guys, behave!" Pihu shouts.

"Enough! That's enough!" Aaron yells, forcing the two apart.

Amir now chimes in. "It all started from this COVID. If it wasn't for this stupid China virus, we wouldn't face all of these tragedies." At once Wang Li interjects.

"I am sick and tired of hearing Chinese are this and that! We are Chinese, and we are clean. We immigrated from mainland China because we hate communism principles. We want to enjoy life, to eat, to buy the goods just like Americans. My parents worked 12-hour days and spent their entire savings to give up everything they knew in China and immigrate to New York City. Their sole purpose was to create better lives for their children. They sacrificed everything. We condemn the dirtiness of the Wuhan Seafood Market just like you do. That's why we left China. Now in America, no one likes us Chinese, and this virus has enhanced the hate toward people who look like me.

Where do I belong, then? I am hated by my home country and by America. Folks back home do not like us either, every time we visit China. Where do I call home? I want America to be my home. I am a citizen of America. This is my home, but you all hate me!" Wang Li exclaims.

Suddenly they all stop, and feel the sadness through Wang Li's voice. A majority of the medical residents are facing similar circumstances, leaving their own countries to live better lives in America but ending up facing bias, racism, not belonging anywhere and judged by the color of their skin.

Amir begins speaking softly. "My family came to the United States from Pakistan just a year after the Pakistani government passed a law in 2010 essentially permitting death to members of my community, the Ahmadiyya Muslim Community, sending us to death only for our faith. My uncle was killed. My parents gave up everything to come here. After the 9/11 attack, we saw hate groups grow exponentially in America against all Muslims. But Muslim people are not a monolith, we are persons of diverse and various cultures, traditions and practices. Even you guys make fun of me when I pray in my cubicle facing East, the direction of Mecca, kneeling on my small prayer carpet. I also do this while fasting during Ramadan. I ask only for a little respect as I practice and obey my religion, a comforting déjà vu of my birth country. I am hated in America; I can feel and hear murderous intentions against me and other Muslims. But I am a good Brown person."

Silence follows Amir. His colleagues return to their cubicles, sort out their thoughts, intending to focus on their day's work. Pihu quietly says "thanks" to Carlos as she avoids stepping on the wet carpet with urine stench. Carlos winks back at her with a smile.

Chapter 30

Containment

March 8, 2021

Pihu dwells on her plans to clean the carpet. First, she must wait until all of the other residents leave to sign out cases with their attendings. She will soak the carpet with water and a bit of soap, and repeatedly vacuum out the residual urine and eliminate the smell. Her colleagues and probably other people are aware that her scrubs and the carpet are wet because of her urination, released during the uncontrollable fear of losing her life. The situation is horribly embarrassing. She recently lost her mother, something she has not shared with others. Her mother was living in India, a tiny village called Mewla Gopalgarh in the northern part of the country and about a 90-minute drive from Delhi, the national capital. Her mother had recently traveled to visit her family back home to care for Pihu's grandmother, who was dying. Pihu assumed her grandmother was dying due to her old age of 90, but it turns out she had the Delta variant of COVID-19 that was later known to have originated in India. Her mother discovered the cause of Grandmother's illness only after arriving in India. She then determined to transport her mother to the government hospital but there was no available bed. An overwhelming number of villagers were becoming infected with COVID-19, so the village's practitioners of alternative medicine had set up an open-air clinic where the sick could lie on cots under a neem tree, alongside cows grazing around them. The reason for lying under the neem tree is that some believed it would raise their oxygen levels. Pihu's mother was one of them, lying under the tree, no one attending to her sickness, near Pihu's grandmother, who died a short time later. Her mother was then alone, and died just three weeks later. Pihu's mother could not get vaccinated before she went to take care of her mother in India. Nor could she get access to a vaccine in India, where vaccination was seldom available.

Pihu is unable to comprehend her reasoning for not sharing

about her loss. She feels ashamed that India brought this deadly Delta variant. She would have no shame if her mother died of cancer. Therefore, she has chosen to suffer alone and remains in disbelief that she lost her mother. Today she faced her own demise from an armed intruder in the hospital and lost control of her own urination, convinced this was her last day of life. Countless images of memories flashed through her mind, a sweeping film documenting her painful life, quickly followed by an overflow of yearnings she has yet to experience in life. This morning, her mother's fatality solidified into her reality. Pihu grieved. In those dark two hours, she softly sobbed, mourning the loss of her mother and her own likely demise while holding onto her unspoken words for her father, unmet dreams to be a doctor in this country, unlived potential to be married to a man of her choice and to carry on living through her unborn children.

India is the origin of the highly contagious Delta variant that began in October 2020, leading to massive deaths. By the end of India's second wave, the country had the second-highest number of recorded COVID cases in the world, with more than 31.2 million cases and 419,000 dead.

Aaron breaks their silence. "Let's get back to work. We have patients' lives that still depend on us. Each patient is waiting for our diagnosis." The goal of his encouragement is to resume their normal duty, without considering their months of working together in the residency program, no one finding an opportunity to open up and share sincere thoughts or feelings with one another. As physicians, they appear composed, intelligent and rational, but each has carried their own misfortunes and troubles in life from their own perspective. They each live different realities, perspectives and beliefs. When sincere thoughts are expressed with no inhibition and no background of tolerance, without politically correct terms or a background of plea for tolerance, then civil war is a natural phenomenon. It can be divided by Republicans versus Democrats, immigrants versus non-immigrants, Whites versus non-Whites, or bad versus good with no clear definition of who is good or who is bad.

****

In March of 2020, Americans began 'containment areas,' later known as 'lockdowns' by limiting exposures to an unknown and deadly virus. Initial fear of the novel virus unified Americans and much of humanity into believing, 'We are in this pandemic together!' One year later, we learned much more about the novel coronavirus, and the experience of the pandemic led to an unrecognizable difference; the unified voice of 'We are all in this together' had dissipated. The rich had become richer, the poor poorer, with significantly more deaths in Black, Latino and Brown people. It is a disease that makes disparity more apparent and obvious than any other illness. However, one experience became shared among all humanity — our persistent catastrophe had given way to the monotony of lowered expectations. The pervasive sense is that we cannot wait for the pandemic to end, and we must begin activities as usual. Businesses began to open despite the ongoing high numbers of deaths caused by COVID-19. The living must live to work and eat.

A question arose: When exactly will there be a finish, a specific point considered to be the finish line? With no clear ending of the pandemic in sight, individuals grasp for a sense of continuing life, perhaps with new norms. Prolonged waiting while one confronts life and death situations leads to constant alterations of human emotions, and survival instincts quickly engage. When a person is pushed to the edge of their fear, a very primal human response kicks in, a human stampede ensues from the principle of every man for himself. No longer is there a consideration for others or a respect for differences. A prolonged sense of defeat, everyday risks of exposure, feelings of danger, fear of losing life, and a dissipation of hope will alter a person's priorities and create a loss of security, and a loss of trust.

As a doctor, Samantha knows that during a pandemic, the only hope is vaccination, always considered the obvious solution until the outbreak of a COVID-19 pandemic. This virus evoked a surprising abundance of unforeseen diversity in beliefs toward vaccination. A majority of people in the US received vaccinations to hasten an end to the pandemic, yet many others refused vaccine shots without realizing this would later prolong the pandemic and eventually facilitate continual mutations of the virus. As vaccinations commenced, widely available testing became accessible along with better treatments for the disease:

death rates began to quickly fall. Yet as many people began refusing vaccination with claims that it jeopardizes their freedom, more and more mutations of the coronavirus appeared in different regions and different countries, prolonging the duration of a terrible pandemic.

Gradually, people are numbed by the pandemic, tolerating their situation, sick and tired of the pandemic and losing more hope. The hidden fear, depression, anger, frustration, defiance, unbelief, resistance, and unpredictability are welling up to manifest every man for himself behavior—through violence. Law and order are questioned by large numbers of Americans, and health care injustice appears prevalent among the 'have-not people.'

Respect for medical professions as a whole began to decrease—including the CDC—following inconsistent and frequent changes in mask recommendations, particularly at the beginning of the pandemic. Political viewpoints reveal sharp divisions and differences in perceptions of reality. It is generally agreed these wide gaps exceed what we have observed at any other time in the history of humanity. Groups of people label each another as irrational, often as cults. Gun violence becomes startlingly prevalent and increases to arrive at a point considered to be an everyday occurrence. Shooting incidents occur all around us in schools, grocery stores, workplaces, restaurants and highways. The pandemic successfully exacerbates our inequalities in race, health care, social and economic status within all states, from large cities to rural areas. It is a conflux of storms arising from the mass influx of guns, a recession, lack of trust in law enforcement, and psychiatric stresses commencing and flourishing within the pandemic.

In Los Angeles, drivers regularly ignore double-solid yellow lines at speeds exceeding 110 mph in full view of police officers in patrol cars, defying authority to vividly portray 'catch me if you can.' Neither law and order, nor restraint and patience seem to matter. Unchecked mental health, prolonged fears of infection and death, and a lack of regular jobs forms a significant insecurity in our lives. Naturally, unpredictable behaviors and acts of violence now accompany us.

Chapter 31

Theories of origin

April 16, 2021

The vaccination programs are well underway, and production at Ed Liu's company is swift and efficient, with no delays in manufacturing or production, where recognition of staff and accolades abound, and a stock price that is endlessly rising. At last, there is hope, not only in America but on every continent. The initial nightmare of vaccine logistics and distribution seem less problematic than expected. Each state in the US does their best to prioritize who is first to get vaccine shots and how to quickly distribute vaccines to their citizens. Countless individuals and organizations are involved in activities to proceed with inoculation. Calculations are made in scheduling, determining distribution sites, shipping, logistics, hours of operation, hiring health care workers to give vaccines, storage and inventory controls for the required temperatures of vaccines until each dose is used to avoid vaccine expirations, how to properly manage any vaccines left over at the end of each day and avoid waste, how to properly check the ages of each person receiving a vaccine including their geographic region and community. An ultimate aim is to properly register and record each recipient. These monumental tasks occur somewhat smoothly across the nation, but in certain communities and geographic areas they are less successful. The registration and record keeping was to be well planned and thoughtfully achieved, while respecting constitutional rights and privacy laws. Ultimately, it was decided at a federal level there would be no records kept of vaccinations.

Travel and vacation privileges on cruise lines and airlines would use an honor system or require a proof of vaccination, depending on individual companies. Unvaccinated persons were made responsible for awareness of their own risks of getting infection, especially when the entire country began opening nearly all businesses and schools.

Naturally, a pandemic of this scale deepened across the globe. Meanwhile, the public and the scientific community ask, "Where did SARS-CoV-2 originate? This question has become a prominent topic across the country. Partly out of curiosity but largely out of responsibility, Ed schedules a meeting with Dr. Steven Allen and a few scientists to discuss possible origins of COVID-19, adding 45 minutes to already crammed schedules.

Dr. Allen stands next to the door and peers at Ed who enters the room. Ed pulls a chair from the table and attempts to sit when Steven asks, "Ed, you traveled to the WIV in Wuhan. Our government sent you along with a few other scientists and doctors. What did you really find? Is the lab leak theory really plausible?"

Without pause, another scientist interjects. "There is evidence that the initial sequences of the virus were submitted by a Beijing virologist and posted on a website run by the NIH in late December of 2019, but removed a couple of weeks later for unknown reasons. Curiously, this data along with the original sequences that were retrieved from the cloud revealed that 13 of the 45 sequences were different from the version later posted in January. A deeper analysis of the variances in the two versions confirmed that sequences taken from people infected at the Wuhan seafood market could not have been the earliest cases of COVID-19. The missing sequences may be local or regional, or the national Chinese government's intent to hide something. So we may never find the underlying cause of this. If the virus did transfer directly from bats or another animal to humans, the Chinese government should provide us with genetic sequences from the earliest people infected, but they are not transparent. Therefore, the original hypothesis of a lab leak from the WIV will never settle." The scientist now looks at Ed.

"Yes, there are three hypotheses," Ed confirms. "One, the virus came from bats as a zoonotic vector, or from an unknown animal that infected a human. Two, the virus evolved naturally. For instance, an employee from the WIV became infected from a sample and accidentally leaked it into the community. And third, WIV scientists intentionally manipulated a virus sample, and accidentally or intentionally released the pathogen."

Ed leans forward and continues. "Let's look at the facts. The WIV is located in Wuhan, where the earliest COVID patients appear to be seen. The WIV is BSL-4, a level 4 lab which happened to be studying the coronavirus from a bat cave located about 100 miles away. Dr. Shei, who I met, is known as 'the bat woman.' She is a Director at the WIV. Dr. Shei had viral samples in her possession. And Sinovac, the first vaccine created by China, started distribution in China, June of 2020, which probably means they had been working on it for a while. As you know, their vaccines are produced from inactivated viruses which takes more time and effort than mRNA technology. We know quite well that production with inactivated viruses requires growing it in living cells in large bioreactors. This takes months. I hate to admit it, but here in the US, for instance, our company took almost 11 months to mass-produce a vaccine. Even if China had better technology (which I highly doubt) and superior manpower, they must have started their vaccine work in summer or fall of 2019. We can assume China was aware of patients with SARS-like pneumonia symptoms by late summer or early fall, and this is entirely possible. They have a known record of hiding SARS-1 beginning in 2013. Having said all that, it still does not prove that COVID's origin is from the WIV by accidental or intentional spillage. The very first data from Dr. Shei published in February 2020 detailing the virus known as RaTG13 showed the coronavirus found from bats were 96.2% same sequences as the samples from patients who died from COVID-19. As virologists, we all know it's not that simple to tweak genetic samples to create and convert the virus to SARS-CoV-2 that would then kill people with COVID. In natural environments, this kind of evolution takes 3-4 decades. As humans, we are not as intelligent as nature to make it in one decade, even though Dr. Shei is a superwoman. Also, if you look at RaTG13 and SARS-CoV-2, the differences are scattered throughout the gene and not in one single cluster. It is highly unlikely that scientists could snip and slice bits of a virus or tweak a pathogen's genome in such a way that would create SARS-CoV-2."

Dr. Allen and scientists at the table remain fixated on what Ed is revealing, so Ed continues.

"If we investigate the historical events surrounding how we usually experienced an epidemic or pandemic, the virus will gain zoonotic routes to infect humans. It's a more natural process. We still do not know the origin of the Ebola virus which first appeared in 1976. It is thought to have spread to humans from bats or nonhuman primates, but scientists have not identified the origin from a specific animal host. My logic and best educational guess about the origin of SARS-CoV-2 is that it arose in nature from an unknown host, like Ebola. But the Chinese government is not cooperating with any full investigation. The initial WHO report had numerous shortcomings which made us more suspicious of China. Their government has become susceptible to criticism from scientific communities across the world. A common claim in the US is that there were three research workers from the WIV who had SARS-like symptoms in November 2019. But the WIV is denying that. At this point, who to believe or trust is in the eyes of the beholder. Personally, I don't think Dr. Shei would lie to the world and to me. I met her personally. During my visit with her in early 2020, She was trying to help me and the US. I think that China should cooperate and collaborate with the WHO in their efforts to find the origin purely for scientific knowledge and to fulfill all curiosity of how the coronavirus evolved. Their opacity and uncooperative behavior brings unnecessary speculation and suspicion upon them."

As Ed concludes speaking, Steve asks, "But don't you think China is intentionally opaque because they have something to hide? And isn't it strange that China was first to invent a vaccine, before the US? It's as if they worked on this for a long time knowing there would at least be an epidemic, if not a pandemic that would arise. Don't you agree, Ed?"

"Not necessarily. Once there is a doubt, everything appears skeptical. The important fact at this point is that there have been three mutations from the people infected by COVID from the Wuhan seafood market that are unique from the original viral sequences. As we can predict, these three mutations require roughly 4-6 weeks of evolution, therefore the origin is likely not the Wuhan market. We can safely conclude that COVID occurred 4-6 weeks prior to clusters seen at the Wuhan market. The question is, where does the original COVID-19 come from? The WIV is located only 3 miles away from the Wuhan market, and WIV happened to be studying the coronavirus naturally leads us to suspect that their lab is the original source. We know that WIV received NIH funding from the US, and it is likely WIV is also connected to WHO. This could lead to unintentional but obvious political ties between American scientists and WHO employees. In turn, these scientists and employees may be trying to remove themselves as targets by diverting the suspicion of origin away from the WIV."

Ed stops speaking but no one moves, apparently waiting for him to continue so he says, "Adding to all of this, the Chinese government intentionally is not transparent. They have police who protect the perimeter around the WIV at all times. No one can access the facility without permission. All these factors favor the lab spillage leak theory. But let's look at other facts, like the 1918 pandemic. We possess a documented history of that pandemic, and it is consistent with how a virus naturally arises from bats—or an avian virus—these viruses usually go through an intermediary host and then to a human, so discovering the precise intermediary host requires several years or decades. It took 87 years to determine the origin of the 1918 pandemic. Therefore we can deduce the coronavirus most likely was not of man-made origin within a lab. I think it's entirely possible the intermediary zoonotic source is directly in front of us under a lamp; it could be our domestic cats or dogs. Pigeons, chickens and pigs are possibilities as well, even perhaps insects or rodents. Human knowledge and ability to alter the potency and virulence to infect human cells is not as good nor predictably reliable as nature's ability. For now, all the hypotheses are on the table and as scientists we need to look into every possible scenario. With our advanced technology, current understanding of science, and a vast number of scientists in the world, we should be able to expedite and understand the origin of this pandemic more quickly than before, after the 1918 influenza pandemic." Ed rests his shoulders, and looks for any response.

***

The 1918 influenza pandemic was caused by an H1N2 virus with genes of avian origin, and was the most severe pandemic until the arrival of COVID-19. The 1918 influenza pandemic resulted in about 500 million people (over one fourth of the world's population) to become infected with the virus, and at least 50 million died worldwide. This 1918 pandemic killed more people than World War I, in which 15-22 million died, including 675,000 in the US, much more than the 400,000 US soldiers in World War II who were killed. The time it took to pinpoint the origin of the influenza pandemic spanned several decades. The question of, 'Where did it originate from?' is a time-consuming question to answer. It is easier to know the results of the epidemiological evidence of lethality and the deleterious impact on global populations caused by a virus. Just like Hart Island in New York, the first devastating pandemic in 1918 had a mass burial site in the small ocean-side village of Brevig Mission, in Alaska, where 72 of 80 Intuit Natives lost their lives. This mass grave site marked only by small white crosses became seminal to the discovery of the origin of the 1918 virus by the 25-year-old Swedish microbiologist Johan Hultin, in 1951.

The entire burial site was frozen in permafrost and left untouched. Hultin obtained permission from village elders to excavate the site, believing that within the preserved burial ground he might still find traces of the 1918 virus itself. He successfully retrieved lung tissue from the bodies of four Intuit Natives, frozen in time. But he was unable to make the virus grow, and then 46 years passed. In 1997, Hultin read a scientific paper by Dr. Taubenberger, a young molecular pathologist working for the Armed Forces Institute of Pathology (AFIP) in Washington, DC. Their research was published in the journal *Science,* and it described his team's initial work to sequence part of the genome of the 1918 virus, and their discovery that the genome of an influenza virus consists of single-stranded RNA that belonged to a subgroup of viruses that came to humans through pigs, as opposed to birds. Hultin, now 72-years-old, contacted Dr. Taubenberger before going back to Alaska's Brevig Mission to obtain tissue from another body. After five days, Hultin uncovered an intuit woman that he named 'Lucy.' Her lungs were perfectly frozen and preserved, so he sent lung tissue to the AFIP's Dr. Ann Reid, who worked with Dr. Taubenberger. The team published a February 1999 paper in the *Proceedings of the National Academy of Science* (PNAS) journal entitled, *Origin and evolution of the 1918 'Spanish' influenza virus hemagglutinin gene,* having successfully sequenced the full length of the 1918 virus. They concluded that the virus most likely originated from avian, and had been adapting in a mammalian host such as human or swine before emerging in pandemic form.

In 2005, a CDC scientist took the virus's eight gene segments and inserted them into human kidney cells to successfully reconstruct the RNA of the complete 1918 virus, ultimately bringing back a historic virus from extinction. This finding was published in the October 7, 2005, issue of *Science*. All in all, it took 87 years to find the mechanisms of how the 1918 virus originated, causing a global pandemic.

***

In 1918, the world population was estimated to be 1.8 billion people. About a hundred years later, the world population had grown to more than 7.6 billion people based on 2018 census data. As human populations have risen, so have swine and poultry populations. This expanded number of hosts provides increased opportunities for novel influenza and other viruses from birds and pigs to spread, or from bats and other ill-known animals to spread, evolve, and infect people, respectively. To find the origin of the coronavirus that caused the pandemic in 2019 will likely require several years to understand, even with collaboration among numerous research scientists. It is too soon to determine with assurance whether or not the WIV, or other intermediary zoonotic, is the origin and source of the initial infection.

Chapter 32

Grabbing fog

May 30, 2021

Following a recent press conference, Dr. Steven Allen speaks to Ed, while pounding with his left hand on Ed's shoulder. "You should be the president of the US. You are a gifted speaker, not just a brilliant scientist. I am proud of you!"

Ed is never comfortable with men pounding on his shoulder causing undesirable energy his small body must absorb. While his boss delights in what Ed just said, others express comprehensive criticism.

Ed remains a foreigner, criticized as 'someone who does not understand American values and freedom of individualism,' and even as 'a guy who is ignorant about the possible dangers of unforeseen and long-term side effects from mRNA surrounded by fatty envelope vaccines,' while others discreetly comment that 'Dr. Liu is ignorant about the interests of ultra rich pharma executives pushing the vaccines globally to rake in the money. He is a little pompous Chinese man trying to make a name for himself.'

The criticisms are endless, ridiculous, and becoming personal attacks. Ed understands that his title and being a leader comes with a price of criticisms, and he attempts to brush these off. At other times, he is exhausted by the attacks, and his heart can no longer bear the weight of more burdens. He aches for a friend, someone like Samantha to share his burdened heart, but she is gone. He has no one to trust.

His parents are abundantly proud of him. "Ed," his father said on a recent call, "I am so proud of you. I saw the videos of you speaking in public. I can't believe you are my son. You are becoming the most significant person in the history of our time, discovering the new vaccine. You saved not just your mother and I, but much of the world. Your brothers—the medical doctors—could not have done what you have done and have accomplished." His mother interjects and says, "Ed, your brothers can comfort the sick and give treatment one by one to patients, but you have truly saved millions of people at once. We can't believe that our son is a true hero!"

Ed made them proud, the utmost compliment Ed could possibly hear from his parents. But strangely, these statements do not quench his soul to be completely satisfied. All he wanted to ever hear throughout his life was this one and only compliment from his parents, but once it is said, it happens to be no big deal. It is now done and past and he is lost for what he should accomplish or achieve. He found emptiness in seeking to fill his heart by performance and achievement and receiving compliments. He recognizes that he is a mere cog in the wheel of a performance treadmill made of his own ego-driven plans and hopes. When whatever plans and hopes are reached, there is nothing there to fill his emptiness. One more accomplishment or achievement or title or degree after his name will not quench his soul and no one is there to listen to his heart's cry. He can now lay down his lack of sense of self and his tireless performance to be accepted and approved by his parents' expectations. He finds freedom from this unconscious burden he has carried until now. But aside from this, he is truly lost in finding who he really is and what to strive for. And yet, whatever he strived for in the past was all illusion. Ultimately, there is nothing significant he can grasp or declare of what he has accomplished or finished. He now recognizes his lifelong disillusion of what success looked like. He has it all now, but he does not feel it. It was merely grabbing fog. There is nothing there in the end.

Ed had also failed to retain Samantha, the one thing in his life he had not successfully achieved. But now he can finally grasp an understanding of why Samantha had to leave him. She knew Ed; a man tangled up in his illusions that everything can be obtained, possessed, or to have. Samantha knew she would never allow herself to be an object to be possessed. The flowery times he and Samantha experienced together are assigned to 'normal couples,' and now Ed understands she must have comprehended that she was living an illusion with Ed. She had her God, who seemingly taught her what is real and what is illusion. Most likely, she was lonely with a man who did not share her reality. It is now the first time for Ed to recognize just a glimpse in understanding Samantha. He had always felt that Samantha did not accept him because he was not a medical doctor—but this had nothing to do with her rejection. Ed was caught in his disillusion of what a successful man looks like, and Samantha must have seen him in truth. She couldn't have continued her relationship with Ed. He had not listened to her nor understood her. Samantha surely knew her own identity; confidently knowing she lacks nothing in God.

Ed wonders, *Who is this God that Samantha trusted and believed? Would this God also accept me, or anyone without any title or degree behind their name?*

Through this painful loneliness, Ed starts to have curiosity about Samantha's God and attends a local church on Sunday in DC. He does not expect this God to say anything drastic or send thunder and lightning and he merely wants to know if there is such a being as God who can fill the huge hole of loneliness and emptiness in his heart.

Chapter 33

Push for vaccination

July 6, 2021

In early May of 2021, the goal of President Biden was to have 70% of adult Americans having received at least one shot by July 4, 2021, and 160 million Americans fully vaccinated. The expected outcome was to achieve safer family gatherings and small groups celebrating the US holiday of Independence Day, moving the country closer to herd immunity. The initial rush to receive vaccination continued from late December 2020 to mid-April of 2021, but the vaccination rush began declining, especially in the South and the middle of the country, mostly the 'red' states. The lowest rates of vaccination were in Wyoming, Idaho, Louisiana, Mississippi and Arkansas. In those states, it is estimated that only 40% of the hospital employees and 60% of the people in surrounding communities were still unvaccinated. More than 600,000 deaths due to COVID-19 appears to alarm many people to get vaccinated, but the state-to-state variations are stark.

The federal mass vaccination sites began shutting down in late May, and large supplies of vaccine doses with clear expiration dates were discarded, particularly J&J vaccines, even though creative methods were being introduced for alluring citizens to get vaccinated. These include free lottery tickets with a million dollar payout, tickets to sporting events, full-ride college scholarships for young adults, and other marketing enticements. Some communities introduced public warnings to adults. These warnings included facts that many who died from COVID-19 may well have avoided death, especially since the vaccines are safe, effective and readily available. Some call it a scare tactic. The federal government also began offering incentives to get shots by providing paid time off.

Nevertheless, as of July 4, only 45% of Americans have completed their vaccination; and only 65% of adults have received one shot; which leaves the US short by about 17 million adults that were expected to receive at least one vaccination shot by July 4. It appears about 160,000 million people (48%) are fully vaccinated by July 4.

***

A vaccination scare to the population arrived with news about the J&J vaccine. This arose following reports of strokes in certain people after their vaccination, particularly women of ages 18 to 49 who had thrombosis with thrombocytopenia syndrome (a condition involving blood clot with low levels of platelet counts) 3–15 days following vaccination. In sum, there are a total of 28 reports of women who developed blood clots among more than 8.7 million people who received the J&J vaccine. Although these were extremely rare cases, the news media exhaustively covered deaths that were likely caused by vaccination, inflaming fears among the population who were already skeptical of vaccines. The mRNA vaccines caused even rarer cases of anaphylactic shock, which is a severe allergic reaction 15–30 minutes following a vaccination. These are in the context of over 317 million doses with efficacy rates of 95% and 94% from two major companies.

The original clinical trials for vaccination from all three companies only included ages 18 years or older, and these companies soon began working toward an immediate authorization from the FDA for younger ages eligible for vaccination of 12 and up. Simultaneously, all three companies eventually began testing the efficacy in younger children, with FDA approval for children as young as 5 years old expected by November, and data for children as young as 6 months old coming in by the end of the year. The reason for separation of testing multiple age groups among the young is due to children's immune systems being very different from adults. In rare cases among children, mRNA vaccination caused myocarditis (inflammation of the heart muscle) and pericarditis (inflammation of the outer lining of the heart) among hundreds of millions of adolescents receiving a vaccine, particularly males under age 16 after a second dose. Most of these patients received treatment with good response.

The overall risk of vaccines is low, and the benefits are overwhelming, but many people focus on these extremely rare side effects, primarily because our media features these rare cases with increasing intensity, instead of highlighting 99.9% of the population who have no serious adverse event (SAE).

***

Ed's company faces multiple lawsuits from former employees who refused to get vaccinated and were therefore suspended from employment. Ed has indeed shifted his work from being a virologist to being at the front lines of HR issues, clearly against his desire but it seems he must be stuck with this. Perhaps by natural selection and his tendency of leading others well, he has become Dr. Steven Allen's right-hand person and primary spokesperson for the company. With this power and privilege, he decides to push forward with a global vaccination proposal of additional investments to increase their production of vaccine doses to 3 billion in 2022. These are for delivery to other countries, approved by the US government. Moreover, in 2021 the company raised manufacturing output to between 800 million and 1 billion doses. They also began work on variant booster candidates that will continue into 2022 and 2023, and are already undergoing clinical studies. On top of this, the company has decided to work on additional projects such as Zika virus vaccine and cancer vaccines using similar mRNA technology. Also, the company has expanded output by adding a production line in South Korea to make additional coronavirus vaccines for global purposes.

Producing more vaccines will not impact how people think about vaccines. Ed assembles a team of industry leaders to make an appeal to the general public by hosting a televised press conference.

Ed's closing comments are brief, and personal. "I understand the American people who still say, 'We will wait and watch.' However, many other countries are not privileged to receive any vaccinations. We are truly living in a rich and oblivious country, not knowing the products we have. Other countries are saying, 'We just want a chance at vaccination,' while we give incentives enticing people to get vaccinated, such as money and free childcare for parents and caregivers. These are signs of extreme privilege and ignorance in America, hoarding our resources and expertise. In Africa, there are fewer than 1% vaccinated, and in

India, more than 400,000 people died. Among those are 500 doctors who lost their lives from the Delta variant of COVID-19. These people and those in many other countries are suffocating and losing hope, unable to get the vaccines. They are desperate. I am in the position of watching and witnessing both sides; friends and employees who refuse to receive vaccines, and the other side of less fortunate countries who are eager but unable to get vaccines. We know our vaccine works. It's superior to many other currently available vaccines, and yet all vaccine manufacturing capacity has been limited to only 1.73 billion doses until now. We have a Delta variant of COVID observed in more than 74 countries, and the Gamma variant in more than 29 countries, and still there is no consensus on how to vaccinate our global population. While we Americans are vacillating on the idea of getting vaccinated, the spread of the virus will increase, and this vacillation will certainly lead to more mutations of the virus. The cycle needs to break, and until our global population gets access to vaccines and we Americans get herd immunity, this pandemic will prolong. We must have learned by now that one person, one small community and one country can make a difference by spreading or halting the virus. This is a basic fact that is still not learned. I hope social media tells the true story; that the risks from vaccination are extremely rare, while the benefit to end this pandemic is overwhelmingly in our favor. The time of when the pandemic ends is in our hands, our responsibility, and our control. Rather than spending time to find the origin of the SARS-CoV-2, it is our time to do what we need to do and that is to help by all means — and end the pandemic."

Chapter 34

Cost of one mistake

July 10, 2021

The chief resident gasps for his last voluntary breaths of his own volition. Aaron calls for Samantha before he is placed on a ventilator. He was admitted to the COVID-19 ICU room, fighting this ordeal for his life. Of course, he blames himself for contracting the Delta variant of COVID because he declined the free vaccine shots his hospital began offering last December. He was an anti-vaxxer who rejected everyone's recommendations and placed trust in his own health to fight this little, microscopic virus of which he had obviously underestimated its power. After all, he regularly spent time at the gym three times per week for vigorous exercise, swam 30 minutes twice per week and ate a mostly vegan diet. He always evaded the hospital policy of receiving an annual flu shot—he simply did not want any foreign stuff infused into his body.

***

After the gun shooting incident at the hospital, in addition to the COVID-19 pandemic, he became disillusioned about the meaning of his own life. Aaron's only goal in life had been to work exceedingly hard and become an excellent pathologist and obtain a premier position as a physician, but he began re-evaluating the meaning of life. Week after week passed. He grew weary, lacking motivation to work the expected 60–80 hours a week. As a chief resident, he was to be a role model for the other pathology residents and yet he felt imbalanced.

In order to re-evaluate and re-motivate himself to work, Aaron flew to his parents' home in Florida for a two-week vacation. That first night home he went to a party with his college friend Eric, who still lived with his parents in a mansion two blocks from Aaron's home. Eric's parents had just left for a two-week Alaskan cruise after 18 months of COVID travel restrictions were lifted. In their 70s, Eric's parents had been very careful to avoid infection. They had avoided travel or mingling with friends and received full doses of vaccinations. Prior to the pandemic, their reasons to host parties seemed endless; birthdays for themselves, birthdays for their son Eric and his younger sister Jessica, celebrations with fellow yacht club members, parties for their dog Manna and mingling with neighborhood dog owners, and their usual monthly BBQ parties.

Jessica lived six blocks from her parents, in a home she bought with a rich husband after meeting him during one of the yacht club parties. Their marriage ended in divorce after two years and Jessica promptly moved back to her parents' house. Eric enjoyed his freedom and never married, seeing as many women as he could explore. Eric grew up with Aaron and they attended college together, but he didn't get a medical doctor degree as Aaron. Eric never had any desire to be a professional. He reasoned that he possessed everything he needed, and saw no need to work for a living. While his parents explored Alaska on their cruise, Eric covertly hosted a party for Aaron. Numerous neighborhood friends were invited, including Jessica and her friends. His intent was to connect Aaron with Jessica, Eric's recently divorced younger sister. Eric knew she had a crush on Aaron when they were young. The party started with 20 to 30 people but somehow ended up with about 100 people filling the house. By 1:00 am, Eric had no idea who was who. The house was vast enough for about 50 people to roam freely and their commotion could not be seen from the outside. Sometime later the party swelled with unknown people Eric had not invited, and the crowd spilled outdoors. An array of alcoholic brands, marijuana and illegal drugs became as prevalent as the people. The swimming pool became populated with naked people having 'fun,' Eric would later say. Around 2:00 am the music became louder, as did the people who were uncontrollable. Aaron had a couple of drinks and maybe a couple more while dancing with women. His and other voices rose to the level of shouting to be heard, even without masks. A girl who was drunk and high on free cocaine wrapped her arms around Aaron and kissed him while dancing. Aaron did not enjoy unruly environments, but he did not avoid her nor sought to escape. He relished this liberation after COVID-imposed social seclusions and restrictions. He missed casual social interactions and innocent parties with people he had never met. Aaron imagined kissing Samantha while kissing this unknown and unnamed woman. Around 3:00 am, neighbors must have called the police and people quickly dissociated, music stopped, naked people quickly dressed, illicit drugs hidden as people ran out of the house. The aftermath was chaos; beer bottles littered every room in the house; the lawn and furniture damaged from cigarettes and other paraphernalia; garbage and assorted food strewn throughout the home, random clothes on the floors and beds. Eric's parents were prominent people and friends with the mayor and the police chief; the officers issued a verbal warning to Eric and then left. Eric, Jessica and Aaron began cleaning up but quickly decided to do that the next day. Aaron found one couch suitable to sleep on and began regretting. He should have been more careful.

Aaron contracted a COVID infection after this incident. He knew better about COVID. He had seen his own hospital in a severe COVID crisis. It only takes one time to be careless, just like a sexually transmitted disease (STD). Once is all it takes to forever change the course of a life.

***

Symptoms started with loss of smell, low grade fever and aching body. *It's COVID for sure*, he thought. Aware of his infection, he needed to go back to New York, perhaps to see Samantha for one last time. He hopped on an airplane and flew first class back to New York City, deciding not to return to work. The airports and the airline staff did not check for proof of vaccine or offer COVID testing. He knew his infection would be transmittable to others, so he remained in his apartment until he became seriously ill and called his parents. They cried, begging that he get help, so when his dad began sobbing and unable to talk further, Aaron agreed to call an ambulance and be admitted to his own hospital. His parents made immediate plans to fly and be with their son.

After days of exhaustive attempts from his fellow physicians to fight Aaron's infection using any and all current medical methods, his oxygen levels dropped dangerously low, and the doctors decided it would be best if Aaron be ventilated. The doctors also put Aaron on the list for a donor for bilateral lung transplants. Aaron finally realized his own health was not a match for a coronavirus on steroids called the *Delta variant*.

Normally, nearly every hospital will enforce a policy of no visitation for COVID patients, but since Aaron is one of their own doctors, his hospital makes a special exception for Samantha to visit Aaron. She arrives at his bedside, wearing full COVID PPE, masked up with an N95, a head cover, and a space suit with a tube protruding from the back. Aaron barely recognizes her. He sees her familiar and comforting eyes behind the small transparent face-covering portion of her suit as she looks down at him and asks, "Why did you do this to yourself Aaron? I told you that you should get the vaccine." Aaron's appearance is terrible, he lost considerable weight, his skin wet with perspiration, and pale. He actually does not look at all like Aaron.

"I should have listened," Aaron gasps, straining. "I was thinking that obesity, diabetes were not my problems."

He pauses. "Or hypertension."

Samantha waits.

"Besides, I am in my 30s, healthy as a stallion." Aaron chuckles, breathless, intermittently coughing.

He adds, "I saw my parents a few minutes ago. I wanted to see you before they placed me on a ventilator. I want you to know that I have always loved you, since the day you came to our program. You do not have feelings toward me. I know this is just one-sided love—but still, I want you to know. If there is no donor for the lung transplants, I may not survive nor come off of this ventilator. Even so, I am in peace with that. I merely wanted to see you and tell you that I love you. I never had courage to say that until we were hiding during the mass shooting, but I must say it again before I die."

Samantha remains motionless. "Aaron, I am so sorry. I wish you would not say that you will die. I want you to think about living, even on a subconscious level while you are on a ventilator and never give up on your life. You are too young and talented to just die."

"Can you at least tell me a lie, that you love me?" Aaron smiles sadly, almost pleading.

"I am sorry, Aaron. I will not lie to you. What I want to say is this: If you are going to let go of your life, please call out to the name of Jesus. Even in your unconscious level, God will hear your voice and save your soul. I want to see you in heaven as a friend. Please do not harden your heart in pride," she pleads. "Aaron, it is a life and death situation here, and in eternity. Call out the name Jesus!" Samantha releases her own sincere tears.

"I will do that," he says. "I will see you in your paradise, and there, I will kiss you as a friend." He smiles.

The doctors and nurses quickly surround Aaron. Samantha steps aside, and Aaron is placed on a ventilator. She watches him become unconscious. Finally, he appears peacefully asleep. The labored sound of breathing dissipates, his insistent coughing subsides. The room is quiet, making room for the regular and rhythmic sound of Aaron's ventilator. Samantha holds his hand and prays for his soul to be resting in Jesus. Although Aaron has not yet died of his COVID, there is no guarantee that he will be able to come out alive while on the ventilator, and his name is on the bottom of a long waiting list for lung transplants. She says goodbye to her friend, her chief resident.

In recent weeks, Samantha noticed a subtle drop in sympathy and empathy toward unvaccinated COVID patients who are dying in the intensive care units, notably from doctors and nurses. She sees this toward Aaron, a fellow health care worker, a doctor. About 12 months ago, most health care workers were sympathetic toward COVID patients. Samantha's colleagues openly spoke of how unlucky the patients were, and they provided diligent and tender care amid sadness for all dying patients. But now, powerful varieties of vaccines are available for receiving a shot. Even drug stores provide free vaccine shots. Yet any person who is not vaccinated, for whatever the reason — and ends up slowly dying in a hospital COVID unit — will often not receive the same degree of sympathy as vaccinated patients. Certain hospital staff feel resentment and anger toward unvaccinated patients who endlessly occupy hospital beds.

One of the doctors walking out of Aaron's room mumbles, "It's his own fault. He could have survived if he had accepted vaccine shots, free from our hospital, but he didn't. He should have known that vaccines are safer than any other treatments for COVID, all of which are experimental. Why is he getting all of these experimental drugs pushed into his body, yet he refused to get vaccinated?"

Somehow, Samantha feels responsible for Aaron's condition. Her sorrow grows for health care workers who continue caring and supporting the COVID-unit patients who refused to get vaccinated for one reason or another. Aaron's stubbornness in refusing a vaccine fills her with sadness. She could not imagine a doctor and scientist like Aaron could ignore his knowledge in exchange for his political viewpoints. Finally, her feeling of guilt arises from lacking a reciprocal emotional response of love toward Aaron, as he had shown toward her. Above all, she lost three men from her life; her father, Dr. Falkner, and now Aaron, all three doctors taken by COVID-19, although Aaron is technically still alive by machine. And Giti, her co-resident, also died from COVID-19.

Chapter 35

Americans ready to die for their freedom

August 5, 2021

Samantha learns Aaron died last night, four weeks after his ventilation. His parents are leaving immediately to take his body back to Florida for burial in their family's gravesite. Aaron was not fortunate in the search to find a lung transplant donor in time. No amount of money, wealth and power could buy functional lungs for him. His parents promised to donate a multimillion-dollar gift to the Bronx hospital if their health center could find a bilateral lung transplant for Aaron. His lungs were deteriorated and infested so badly with the coronavirus, that pushing the oxygen through the ventilator did not help in the end. The only advice the hospital administrators gave to Aaron's parents was to get vaccinated, but they quickly refused, fully aware that COVID-19 killed their son, and their home state of Florida had no more hospital beds to accommodate new COVID patients.

***

Death and illness are inevitable. This pandemic at our forefront reminds us of this more than ever before. We take living for granted each day and lose sight of this truth as we assume death and illness affects others, but not us. Time is the most precious gift we will ever have, and yet, we are lost in our delusions that life is permanent and that we can spend time doing menial things, instead of taking time to love and attend to the people who we love and cherish. Misfortunes of life happen to everyone. In essence, the only control we have is the attitude of gratefulness, appreciating what we have and striving not to focus on what we do not have. Once we count what we don't have, our life becomes more miserable, exhausted, and grumpy. No money, power, wealth, perfectionism, beauty, political gains, impressive titles and powerful positions, cognitive illusion of security or anything in this world we value and cherish can buy a single minute in a human life. The illusions we possess is a dysfunctional belief that we have control over our lives, cognitive distortions that if we are more perfect, the life will be better, an irresponsible allowance of letting destructive thoughts erode our minds to belittle our significance in life. Only God is in control. He knows our paths and the only thing we can do is to trust Him and know that God has a plan for each life. To understand one's purpose in life through God then becomes the primary thing which makes sense to pursue, since life itself is made by God. In life, it is truly sad to not know the Creator of this life, wasting breaths while thinking life is created by an accident.

***

Samantha wonders if Aaron relied on Jesus at the end of his life and called to Him, or if he relied on his own pride by rejecting God as he also rejected vaccine shots. Aaron inadvertently developed a sense of invincibility through his confidence; but he was not invincible. Her sorrow remains for Aaron, a man living life not knowing his Creator God while his mind and body were viable. How do people live without God? How lonely they must be.

Samantha remembers her conversation with Aaron after the shooting incident and his reasoning for refusing vaccine shots. A majority of health care workers have received the vaccines, yet approximately 20-25% of health care workers and hospital staff still refused to get the shots, just like Aaron. Their rationale remains puzzling for Samantha, especially as their refusal of vaccination continues to prolong the COVID-19 pandemic for everyone. Some days after she last spoke with Aaron, Samantha realized that America is fighting two different pandemics; a COVID-19 pandemic and a misinformation pandemic; an 'infodemic.' Unfortunately, falsehoods, just like gossip, tend to spread faster, further, and more easily than the truth. Deceptions spread at the speed of an out-of-control virus. Conspiracy theories encourage suspicion of all media, especially traditional media, and in turn deceive us about what is really going on. Many believe that pharmaceutical companies and governments are 'out there to make money,' and using humans as guinea pigs in research experiments for vaccines. In reaction to this, trust and belief in traditional, formerly trusted media outlets quickly began to retrogress.

Another theory spreads that the virus is caused by 5G cellular technology, leading certain people in one European country to burn down 5G towers—and Bill Gates is 'using the virus to enslave humanity' by enforcing a global vaccination and surveillance program. Another false narrative states that COVID vaccines cause infertility and death. The news of this conspiracy is proclaimed without proof or research data that would normally build confidence in any such claim. Countless claims have no basis in verified findings of facts and are hearsay, and yet countless people trust such baseless claims enough to participate in street demonstrations that block traffic while they hold up anti-vaxxer signs. In truth, we know significantly more things about the coronavirus now than when it began in late December of 2019. We also lack certain knowledge about the virus and the vaccines; even the CDC withholds large portions of their data. Therefore their position on vaccines, masking, and other topics can be vexing. Randomly, people have strong opinions on the scientific and medical nature of the virus and vaccines as if they went to medical school and became doctors with an infectious disease specialty.

The president of the US encourages false narratives by frequently criticizing the media as 'fake news.' With the spread of infodemic news, a lack of trust in our government and our health care industry spreads at an equal pace, so we see a decrease in willingness to follow restrictive measures that are known to curtail propagation of the disease.

Within a year of the virus outbreak, the handful of primary media outlets in the US promote stories primarily dealing with controversies, especially when violence is involved. Depression, fear and anxiety may have been a root cause of a higher susceptibility to conspiracy beliefs during the pandemic. This type of news is actually showing us the symptoms of misinformation. Controversies over wearing masks draws more viewership when outlets replay videos of violence on airplanes, violence toward health care providers, and violence at public meetings. The damaging effects of misinformation and disinformation are far reaching.

Samantha is pleased to recall that Aaron at least laughed at the previous president who had boasted, "Maybe we should drink Clorox bleach because it will kill the coronavirus." Some people swallowed this false and dangerous message, resulting in the consumption of highly concentrated alcohol disinfectants and other toxic liquids that have resulted in approximately 800 deaths and 5,800 hospitalizations worldwide. Samantha wonders, *Who can make any sense out of people who believe in such things as consuming bleach?* Samantha now understands why some people who believe in Jesus Christ have difficulty explaining to a sceptic why they believe in God. Truth reveals in the end, but falsehood spreads quickly like the virus. People forget that God is with science, for He also created science.

Samantha lost Aaron because he believed in some of these conspiracy theories and justified himself for why he should not take vaccine shots. He emphasized his freedom to choose and in his rights to fight for freedom. Americans are ready to die for their freedom of choice. Freedom is in our constitution; right to speech, right to protect oneself and to protect others. Getting no vaccine may have been Aaron's personal right, but in this case, it certainly does not protect others while also protecting his own rights, and so, in a way, it is a selfish act and a selfish freedom. His freedom caused his own death and massive inconvenience to the exhausted hospital staff. On his deathbed, he seemed to realize that he should have received the free vaccines. It was too late for him and futile for him to regret his belief in misinformation. He could only faintly speak out the truth to an empty audience. So, he died in a vacuum. No one will notice or learn of his newly found discoveries of self-regret, knowing the truth, and his own experience after contracting the Delta variant of COVID and awakening from living a life that hosted conspiracy theories in opposition to the miracle of COVID vaccines discovered by doctors and scientists. Indeed, America is a great country with excellent scientists, technology and resources, but tragic deaths follow people who possess incredulous and suspicious minds, who spin every good intention with political and financial manipulation; personal interpretations causing tragic deaths.

Once suspicious, forever suspicious.

***

Hospitals are now seeing more and more pediatric cases with COVID-19 and an increase in admissions. Nationwide, nearly 4.8 million children tested positive for COVID-19 since the early onset of the pandemic. Since the time of back-to-school, there is over a five-fold increase in COVID positive rates, an increase in hospitalizations and increase in death rates among children. Samantha's co-resident has two kids, one in kindergarten and one in first grade; both are admitted to the hospital and are now fighting for their lives. In a short time the parents also tested positive to COVID, but are asymptomatic for now. Both parents received two shots of vaccines, but the kids are not old enough to get the shots.

The CDC and Dr. Fauci announced, "It is less likely for a child to get infected in the school setting than if they were just in the community." Most schools are encouraging social distancing and adhering to mask requirements, but many parents vacillate and even force their kids not to wear masks. Like others among the population, some teachers and parents are also anti-vaxxers and refuse to wear masks in the classrooms when they are teaching or coming to a school campus to pick up their children. Many schools reopen amid the highly contagious Delta variant of COVID, causing uncertainty and anxiety.

One scenario arose after well-meaning unvaccinated mothers who opposed vaccine shots for themselves likely began transmitting COVID-19 to children under 12 years old, including their own. Also, there is a lack of education on how to properly wear a mask. Most kids and even adults began wearing a mask below nose level, not tightly sealing nor covering their mouth *and* their nose.

It became a delicate balance of growing the psychological, social, and academic wellbeing in children during closures of schools, while also protecting the physical welfare and wellbeing of children when opening up the schools.

After reopening, schools faced tremendous challenges of teacher shortages, outspoken and sometimes unruly parents who dispute mask requirements and oppose having their children quarantined after positive COVID-19 tests. Ultimately, some schools began shutting down for a second time in several states. Many states require that all teachers must be vaccinated and even obtain booster shots when they become available.

Booster shots quickly occupy much of the public discourse after 'breakthrough cases' (vaccinated people who test positive for COVID-19) are reported due to a decrease in antibodies in the body following six to eight months after vaccination. The booster vaccination requirements are not only for teachers, but also health care workers, military personnel, and many government employees. Even certain private companies and private hospitals are looking into mandatory booster shots for their employees, beyond just the two shots of an mRNA vaccine or one shot of the J&J vaccine. This discussion of booster shots erupts more anger from anti-vaxxers, and some declare that if breakthrough cases exist, then a COVID vaccine is not a true vaccine because the true vaccine should completely deter COVID infection. Citizens soon forgot that the mRNA vaccines and traditional vaccines never claimed 100% coverage of eradicating COVID-19 (only 95% at best), and the COVID-19 virus had mutated to an almost different species. The mutant variants are much more potent and highly infectious than the original Alpha COVID-19. Many overlook or are unaware that following a flu shot every winter, some people still get the flu. There are numerous variants of the influenza virus. Likewise, we now observe coronavirus variants. Hence we get the annual flu vaccine every winter season.

***

The most meaningful vaccination plan was to achieve herd immunity in America and then globally, following the 2021 initial vaccine coverage. This opportunity quickly dissipated. Obstacles included logistics in producing enough vaccines, lack of access globally to vaccines, objections to vaccinations alongside conspiracy theories of vaccines and the virus. Not enough people received vaccinations, and we lost our only opportunity to eradicate most of COVID-19. Now, another race has begun. It is a race to develop other and newer mRNA sequences of vaccines to cover the dominant COVID-19 variants. These complications dim the hopes for a world absent of COVID. So, hospitalizations of patients with COVID-19 and deaths continue, more common in the states with low vaccination rates, and an epidemic in this country seems endless.

Chapter 36

Vanity, vanity, all are vanity

August 23, 2021

Florida experiences its worst surge of COVID-19 by the end of August, averaging 25,000 new cases every day with more than 17,000 people hospitalized and 230 people dying every day; a new epicenter of COVID-19 with the leading number of deaths per capita. About 52% of Florida residents are fully vaccinated at this time, not as bad as Mississippi and Alabama with less than 38%. While nine in ten Florida residents over the age of 65 are vaccinated, Aaron's parents chose to be anti-vaxxers and ended up in ICU beds, helping to fill the last of the remaining seven percent of the state's ICU beds that are mostly filled with people under 40. Under a governor who has a relaxed—and sometimes oppositional stance toward masks and social distancing, the people in Florida pretty much live their normal lives at this time, making it a pleasant location for the virus to spread.

In the earlier stages of the pandemic, Florida enjoyed structural advantages in slowing down the spread of COVID-19, including the state's less-densely populated single-family homes, and the warm climate allowing residents to spend much time outdoors. But 18 months after the virus outbreak, the state sees lagging vaccinations amid a continuing relaxed approach toward virus prevention, even as a more virulent variant of COVID-19 descends upon the state. Florida is paying a steep price with 43,000 deaths, and by September 16, the State of Florida will report over 51,000 people have died from COVID-19.

***

Aaron's father drove himself to the hospital. He left his car near the entrance and collapsed into an empty wheelchair outside the entrance. Not a single ICU bed is available. He has many pre-existing conditions including hypertension, diabetes, and moderate obesity. He asked to see the hospital's president, who knows him well. Within an hour a bed was found for him next to his wife while four million dollars from his bank was transferred to complete the hospital's new children's wing. His wife was admitted into the ER three days ago for COVID symptoms. She had waited 24 hours in the screening area located under a plastic tent in the hospital's parking lot. Then, she was sent back to her home — there were absolutely no beds available in the ER. Her symptoms at the time were not severe, but the next day she could hardly breathe, and she was rushed back to the screening tent where her oxygen level was 89%. Normal level of oxygen is 95% or higher. Oxygen levels between 80-85% will affect the brain with vision change. By this time, she deteriorated even further with lack of oxygenation and endured multiple organ failures. Her demise from the nasty virus only took four days. Aaron's father watched as his wife died next to him, regretting their arguments eight months ago after she made an appointment to get her first shot of the vaccine. He should have let her do that to save her life. Now, it's too late. He watched his son and his wife as they died with COVID.

***

These are all too familiar stages which thousands of COVID patients endure, particularly the unvaccinated ones. The day after his son was admitted to ER in early July, he and his wife watched as their son received a supplemental flow of oxygen to 4 liters per minute, antiviral therapy, steroids, and anticoagulants. Aaron even received monoclonal antibodies, the same experimental drug the previous president received and who then got better. Aaron did not wean off the oxygen. His breathing became harder as if he was drowning. The bronchodilator treatment gave him little relief. His oxygen was then pushed to 15 liters per minute. Aaron could not get up from his bed to relieve himself. At this point he was transferred to ICU and was put on noninvasive 'positive pressure' ventilation, a large and bulky tightly fitted face mask that pushed oxygen more efficiently to pop open his lungs. Still, his arterial blood draw confirmed that the oxygen content was critically low. At this point, it was determined he would be intubated, and he and his wife were asked to leave the room.

Aaron then asked that he first be allowed to see Dr. Samantha Parker, a lady doctor whom Aaron had never mentioned to anyone. His parents were visibly alarmed to see a mixed-race Asian woman enter the unit and approach Aaron. They never expected their son could be attracted to a non-White race. She must be why Aaron declined to meet anyone they recommended him to meet, including the daughter of their friends, the lady both couples hoped he would marry. This was the last time Samantha and Aaron's parents heard Aaron's voice.

After a few minutes, the Asian-looking doctor left the unit, and they were allowed back in to see their son Aaron, sedated and paralyzed, fed through a milky white feeding tube, connected to a Foley catheter, and a rectal tube. The nurse and doctor visits became more infrequent. They could only turn and move his body around to avoid development of pressure ulcers—bed sores. Another group of staff came once every three to four days to bathe him as they waited for news of any donor for lung transplants. Lung transplants were discussed only because of his young age, a viable and able doctor just days ago. Very few people are blessed enough to have this discussion. More days passed. No news.

Then the doctors tried experimental therapeutics, weird drugs his parents never heard of, trying anything that might help Aaron. The positive pressure required to push the air into his lungs became extremely high. His lungs caused air blebs, in turn causing pneumothorax, then tubes were required for insertion to relieve air that would then cause a part of his lungs to collapse and shift. Even the ventilator could not relieve his COVID-infested lungs, so they got an ECMO machine which bypasses the lungs and oxygenates blood. Then, Aaron's kidney failed to filter the byproducts from the drugs and even with diuretics; his body retained fluid, requiring dialysis. His body and face were soon swollen to a degree no one could recognize him. With a depressed immune system, he became susceptible to antibiotic resistant staphylococcus (bacteria) from injection sites, and invasive vascular Aspergillus (fungal) infections in the lungs and nasal cavity which invaded into the brain. Doctors pushed antifungal and antibacterial drugs through intravenously. A dozen tubes of 'foreign substances' were entering into his body—all of it so that he could avoid a 3 mL mRNA vaccine shot. He developed a blood clot in his deep veins in the leg which lodged into his lung leading to pulmonary embolism. His blood pressure dropped despite the vasopressors. His heart then stopped, a flat line on the monitor. Doctors gathered and performed several rounds of CPR, desperately trying to get Aaron's pulse and circulation back. This was a sight no parents wish to see their child endure, not even to their worst enemies. Aaron's parents considered the difficult decision of letting him go. The only other choice offered was to let him survive in a vegetated state, forever not knowing if or when he might be awakened. This withdrawing or turning off the breathing machinery is an even more difficult choice for the parents, so they opted not to go that route.

"Let him go!" Aaron's mother abruptly screamed.

That decision appeared more humane; they signed end-of-life consent forms. With a young person's death such as Aaron, an organ donation opportunity is always on the table but with COVID-19, no such opportunity is granted. No organ from him would be beneficial to anyone waiting desperately for an organ transplant.

***

Now, Aaron's father must go through the same route, miserable to even fathom, an unwelcome familiar fate. Dying with a heart attack would be a blessing at this point. He lies motionless but his thoughts continue. *Who is going to make a tough decision for me, after losing my wife and only son? I cannot live in a vegetated state forever. A sudden death will be a blessing to me. What is the meaning of my wealth?* He is consumed with regret by his decision not to get vaccinated, especially when he overhears a doctor openly speaking to a nearby colleague.

"A total of five billion people received at least some sort of vaccine, almost two billion people are fully vaccinated, and 172 million in the US are vaccinated. Only very rare side effects have been documented." As the doctor speaks more softly in a deeper tone, he goes on to say, "What's more frustrating, is 95% or more of our patients currently hospitalized and dying are people who were not vaccinated. Our vaccinated patients eventually go home, in most cases."

Moments later, Aaron's father hears another person speaking.

"I know, it's frustrating! Most of my patients who were vaccinated and later became ill with low oxygen levels are eventually released after recovering with the aid of mild oxygen push."

Aaron's father asks a nurse to take his phone and call his lawyer. He instructs his lawyers to update his finances, donations, and his will, with advance medical directives not to receive any further medical treatments and interventions. He also requests funeral arrangements for him and his wife, and for his properties to be sold at auction and donated to his church. He declines ventilation, any further treatment including oxygen delivery, and dies within two days. In the end, his money, wealth and power meant little to him.

Under the umbrella of death which no one can escape, every human must kneel down, stripped of pride, and humbly return to dust, naked, as we came into this earth. No quantity of regrets will extend or buy a minute of life. All will subside from their existence. Money once deemed precious — sometimes more precious than life — will end up in someone else's hands to enjoy. He should have been more generous to his friends while he was living. Who will take care of his body after his death? Who would feel obligated to pay respect to him and manage a funeral service? All persons who were obsequious to gain finances or power through him are gone. Only the lawyers are surrounding him, who most likely will act like vultures, picking at the plunder. Not even his political party will save his dignity, regardless of his prior vast donations. Vanity, vanity, all are vanity.

Chapter 37

The great resignation

October 4, 2021

New York's Department of Health issued an order in September requiring that all health care workers receive at least their first COVID-19 vaccine shot by September 27. The US government also announced that the 17 million health care workers at facilities that receive Medicare or Medicaid funding must be vaccinated or regularly tested. Approximately 92% of New York State's 650,000 hospital and nursing home workers were vaccinated, but others still refused to be vaccinated against COVID-19. Other states imposed similar requirements but offered their employees opt-out options such as weekly testing and religious exemptions. New York State proceeded to fire 1,400 employees despite at least eight lawsuits on First Amendment grounds, and the fired employees were left without any benefits, and ineligible for unemployment insurance. The state allowed no vaccination opt-outs.

Health care systems already were struggling with staff shortages, and many hospitals once again are rapidly limiting elective surgeries and are reducing inpatient capacity by 25%.

***

There is no organized religion that has come out in opposition to the COVID-19 vaccines, including Jehovah's Witnesses, Christian Scientists and the Catholic Church. The Pope has declared getting vaccinated 'an act of love.' Only one medical reason will always justify exemption from the COVID-19 vaccine: severe allergic reaction called anaphylaxis, most likely due to polyethylene glycol (PEG), an ingredient in an mRNA vaccine and polysorbate in the J&J vaccine.

Dr. Wells, the pathology residency director at the Bronx hospital is one of those who applied for a religious exemption. "Human life is sacred," Wells said. "The Bible clearly says that your body is a temple. The vaccine is made from aborted fetuses, and the mandate directly violates religious beliefs and hence violates the First Amendment."

In fact, actual vaccines do not contain any fetal cells. It is known that historical fetal cell lines were derived in the 1960s and 1970s from two elective abortions, and have been used to create other vaccines such as hepatitis A, rubella, and rabies. The fetal cell lines used to produce some of the potential COVID-19 vaccines are from two sources; HEK-293, a kidney cell line that was isolated from a fetus in 1973, and PER.C6, a retinal cell line that was isolated from an aborted fetus in 1985. While actual vaccines contain zero aborted fetal cells, pharmaceutical companies prefer human cell lines in their research phases, in particular fetal cells, since a virus needs cells to grow and tends to grow better in human cells. Fetal cells can be used longer than other cell types, and fetal cells can be maintained at low temperature, allowing scientists to continue using cell lines from decades ago. Use of fetal cell lines from aborted and viable fetuses appears to be the main argument in favor of religious exemption from vaccines, but as a class, mRNA vaccines are not designed, developed, or produced in fetal cell lines.

The entire department of pathology had received vaccine shots, except Dr. Wells. No one had known this fact until he submitted a resignation letter to the hospital and promptly walked out. He had joined a protest a week ago, holding a sign *My body, my choice!* as he and others walked around the hospital entrance. No one in the department had known of his vigorous stance opposing vaccinations. Dr. Wells regularly participated in prayers and proclamations that God would provide healing if he were to get COVID, and if he were to die from it, he believes that God has called him home. He also believes that God would punish nations for the sins of some of its citizens and that natural disasters including the pandemic are a sign from God. After his resignation, it became known that he believed people who have faith in God will be rewarded with good health and protected against COVID infection.

Many of his Christian friends and colleagues pleaded that he take the vaccine shot and avoid losing his job, arguing that even Jesus would have taken the vaccine. Thus far, over 77% of Christians have received a vaccine shot. Many had reminded Dr. Wells that President Trump gladly received two doses of vaccine, and committed $18 billion in government funds to Operation Warp Speed, a public-private partnership to develop COVID-19 vaccines at a breakneck speed. For some unknown reason, the COVID vaccine had become an exception for Dr. Wells. He willingly received other vaccines as conditions of employment at the hospital such as MMR, hepatitis B, poliovirus, annual flu shots, and other shots like tetanus every 10 years. Perhaps the dermatopathologist in Boise, Idaho had influenced Dr. Wells. The Idaho doctor infamously stated COVID vaccination is 'needle rape.' Dr. Wells argued further with colleagues by declaring the new vaccines are 'experimental' having not undergone extensive clinical trials — even though the Pfizer vaccine received full FDA approval.

***

Following the unexpected departure of Dr. Wells, urgent meetings within the department were held. The hospital educational committee met. It was essential for them to protect and continue a smooth residency program. After the death of chief resident Aaron, the chief residency position was given to Samantha, as selected by the pathology faculty. She was immediately overwhelmed by these additional responsibilities. Furthermore, Giti's recent death caused the department to backfill Giti's position by instituting double shifts in work rotations for all pathology residents. Dr. Wells' departure as director of the residency program had created a nightmare.

Samantha must now attend more meetings as the representative for all pathology residents. She works an additional 20–40 hours per week in order to provide just basic services. This is against the policies for residency training. But who could possibly follow ACGME rules and not work 80 hours per week during this pandemic?

Samantha is also emotionally challenged by her fellow residents; a few even hurl verbal attacks upon her for views held by Dr. Wells, since she too holds Christian beliefs. She responds to these attacks, explaining that she does not share his radical, political, White evangelical viewpoints — and yet their sarcastic and cynical comments toward her continue. Hateful comments about Christianity in general also continue to be unleashed against her. She is thankful to God that Roxanne, who is also a

Christian, consoles Samantha and helps her in many ways.

Once it became known Dr. Wells was forced to resign after refusing to be vaccinated, faculty members in the department of pathology became intensely competitive in their zeal to obtain the vacant leadership position. Bickering and backstabbing erupt, the atmosphere becomes more toxic. Samantha's new position affords her one vote for selecting Dr. Wells' replacement, and many of the attending physicians oddly offer bribes to Samantha. Some offer lunch, coffee drinks, an opportunity to house-sit at an expensive home, tickets to Yankees baseball games, New York Philharmonic tickets, and any number of random gifts she presumably might like. *How funny and odd people become when you have some power*, she thinks. Most of these bribes come from the assistant professors, who are typically younger and competing for any position offering more job security, status, and pay. The senior faculty who would normally deserve this position are calmer, quietly seeking and asking the proper questions to probe Samantha if they are being considered or may qualify for the position.

Dr. Stevens is one exception, a forensic pathologist and medical examiner who Samantha admires. Last year Dr. Stevens asked Samantha to accompany her to a crime scene and provided great instruction during the experience. Dr. Stevens was recently promoted to associate professor level. But since she does not hold the position of *director*, she is not visible in terms of getting such a title as residency director. Most of the directors are male. Female pathologists are not visible in any of the hospital leadership circles, although certain faculty are pushing that females should hold at least some of the leadership positions. Samantha hopes that Dr. Stevens will at least apply for the position, but she lacks courage to speak directly with Dr. Stevens, the committee, or the department chairman since Samantha is a voting member of the committee.

While Samantha quietly observes the behaviors among faculty, an email arrives from the chairman of the department that the interim pathology residency director will be Dr. Paul Weinberg, a surgical pathology director who is a full professor, perhaps an obvious choice to become the residency program director. The email also mentions a search committee will be created to proceed with a national search, and encouraging anyone in the department to apply for the position. Peace appears on the horizon, advancing ahead of the political and unruly tsunami of people competing for the position.

One morning, Dr. Wells had simply left without personally saying goodbye to any resident. Samantha was sad to see her leader leave while at the peak of his career. His sudden resignation and the hospital's COVID policy limiting gatherings to less than 10 people prevented the residents from hosting a farewell party. Some had assumed Dr. Wells would resign and practice pathology in the Midwest where many states are not imposing vaccine requirements for health care workers. If Dr. Wells had not resigned and was later fired, he risked suspension or revocation of his medical license from the state of New York, while others assumed Wells would struggle to get a new job after being fired.

One doctor even asked, "Who would hire a doctor who believes the coronavirus was intentionally created?" Another doctor said, "Dr. Wells ignorantly claimed that COVID risks are exaggerated. He had crazy conspiracy theories. He also concluded vaccines are often ineffective, because 4,000 fully vaccinated people were later killed by COVID-19," and then a hospital pulmonologist exclaimed, "How can Dr. Wells arrive at *that* conclusion? That guy has never personally seen *any* patient in ICU dying from COVID. He's a pathologist. He never sees patients. If he had seen dozens of people die, day after day due to COVID-19, he would be more reasonable and not so gullible."

Samantha learns that 59 other health care workers are forced to leave her hospital, either from resigning and/or firing. Security officers briskly enter offices and explain to each person they have 30 minutes to gather their belongings. Each person is then escorted out of the building holding a cardboard box.

Samantha's life and career are at the height of chaos. She lost Dr. Wells, who was a significant advocate for residents. For 12 years he was their director of residency, a consistent strong voice protecting the interest of residents. His vacancy triggered aggressive behavior, roaming Alpha wolves seeking a top position. Some play power games, others bribe residents, and several faculty members secretly slander and whisper insults toward Dr. Wells before his departure. This defamation is now directed toward Dr. Weinberg, their interim residency director.

Everyone has something secret, ugly when it is shaken to dust. For Dr. Wells, these were only petty things, and he did not hide his opinions. Samantha was fond of Dr. Wells, she respected him. Her opinion of him will not change. Her one unmet wish was not met, to be given the opportunity to thank him before he left the institution.

Chapter 38

Paranoia

October 10, 2021

Emily assumed that she was getting better, and slowly began trusting people in public places. She has fewer thoughts of someone hitting her or pushing her simply because she is an Asian American. Last year Emily had nightmares and post-traumatic stress disorder after experiencing her head injury from the hate crime incident. As days passed, she could not entirely brush off her horrible experience of someone beating and kicking her. At night, she dreams of someone chasing her and attempting to repeatedly beat her. Eventually she will awake, drenched with sweat, her heart palpitating, struggling to go back to sleep. She once again dreads leaving her home, shopping, or going anyplace alone. She always will ask Mrs. Kong to accompany her. Once outside, she is told by Mrs. Kong that she constantly looks back, checking to see if someone might be following her with a hammer or a gun. She screams uncontrollably when there is an unexpected loud noise. Nagging doubts cling to her, fearing for her safety expecting someone will hate her because she is an Asian American. She is exhausted. She trusts no one, as if everyone is out to get her either by physical violence or somehow taking financial advantage of her. She recently began mistrusting people who she formerly trusted. Her husband Robert is no longer there to help ease her paranoia. She hesitates to call on the handyman to come into her house to fix even minor things; her list of things to fix, her honey-do list formerly tossed to her husband Robert. This list now awaits Samantha who will soon visit her. So many inconveniences continue being added to her single life with no husband. Emily does not trust people coming into her home and becomes practically paralyzed to remain at home. Images of her handyman invade her sleep, dreams of him breaking into the home to take advantage of her and to rob her. The large house became her nightmare, overwhelming her with responsibilities.

She sleeps with every light in the house turned on. Her electric bills are immense. She does not care; she needs her sense of security. Sometimes she wonders, *How does Mrs. Kong handle her nighttime fears?* Her friend Mrs. Kong lost her husband two decades ago. She concludes Mrs. Kong must be a strong woman. Emily also concludes that she cannot wait an entire year for Samantha to move in with her. She is tormented from constant memories of being beaten. She is alone and terrified. *I do not like being in America,* she decides. *I am no longer safe anywhere in America.* The pandemic is resilient, so she stops attending church services and seeing her friends. Her social life pretty much stopped, and Emily is aware that she has become more of a reclusive homebody. She only sees Mrs. Kong, once a week mainly for grocery shopping. She is not much of a phone person, and Zoom meetings with her friends from church are awkward and not rewarding. She cleans the house, cooks occasionally for herself and watches Korean dramas. She discontinues the weekly house cleaning services of a lady, for she has no need of such service.

Samantha and Mrs. Kong encourage Emily to see a psychiatrist about her PTSD, but she doesn't trust psychiatric help, which she needs. Emily believes only a few trusted friends are needed to share her deepest emotional feelings. No need to spend money for unnecessary psychiatric help. She knows her thinking is old-fashioned and traditional, but her true reason is her disbelief that a psychiatric doctor will cure her problem. The last thing she wants is to revisit the incident and experience the horrible emotions. Her best thing to do will be moving to another country where she doesn't have to worry about hate crimes against Asians. She will forget and move forward.

One day, Emily impulsively picks up her phone and calls her sisters in Korea. She longs to see them. Without interruption she speaks quickly, "I am coming to Korea to see you. Then we need to visit Jeju Island. We'll stay there for about a month and look for a property where we might live together, taking care of each other as we grow old. I will pay for your trip. Think about it. Let's talk later." She hears no response. "OK. Goodbye, I love you."

This thought of living in Korea seems attractive and

comfortable to Emily, a place where there will be no discrimination among Koreans where they all look alike. Emily would fit in very well, at least in physical appearance. Now older in age, her affinity toward Korean food has increased. She becomes obvious of missing the food her mother cooked. Instead of 'getting used to' American food, she begins to buy more Korean food than ever. Three days after calling her sisters, Emily purchases a plane ticket to South Korea. Convincing her sisters to visit Jeju Island with her can be done after she arrives in Seoul. She has no idea how expensive homes are on Jeju Island, but nothing will be more expensive than her San Francisco home. Also, they don't need a huge house, just something big enough with rooms to accommodate each of them. Plus a kitchen and living room overlooking the ocean, certainly. Emily knows that her two older sisters will need her help, but she won't mind taking care of them. She wants to live with them so they can enjoy each other's company very soon, while Emily is still able. Her sisters are in their 70s, one is a retired teacher, and the other has never worked. Both are fairly wealthy, each well cared for by a son and daughter-in-law, but Emily is pretty sure they want to live with her and be fully independent. She is confident they will be intrigued by her idea. They'll at least be willing to look at some properties on Jeju Island. Emily is excited about this trip and her only hesitation is how to break this news to Mrs. Kong. Of course she will be disappointed with Emily's idea. For two years Mrs. Kong has been unable to visit her hometown of Wuhan. She dreaded the long days of quarantine the Chinese government required, and ultimately visas were provided only if there was a death in the family.

One day prior to her trip to Korea, Emily invites Mrs. Kong to her home for a simple Korean dinner and tea. Emily is surprised by her neighbor's response.

"I knew this day would come some time ago," replies Mrs. Kong. "I have been thinking about moving to my first son's house. I should sell my house when you are selling yours. My home is too big for me to take care of. My knees are no good. No one comes here anymore. COVID is bad. No grandchildren visiting and no family coming to see me. All I do is clean the big house. Dust everywhere. No matter how many times I clean the house, there is still dust everywhere. I am tired of this big house.

And Emily, you are paranoid about American people coming to kill you. I know because you constantly are looking behind us when we are out. Now I look behind me when I walk outside. Too sad to live like this here. Even in San Francisco with a Chinatown home to many Chinese people, we get beaten by Americans. If they do not come to beat our bodies, they still beat us mentally. We, Asians, are in constant defense mode, fighting with Americans, regardless of who is present among us. They are in our heads! The other day when I took out my garbage, I had no pepper spray in my bag, so I panicked and rushed back to get it and fell in my own backyard. My knees are no good for running anymore. After I fell, I was still looking back to see if anyone followed me. This is no good. Too scared to live in my own house. Nobody will defend this old woman here. I couldn't get up. I stay in my backyard for 30 minutes, no phone to call you, and my front gate wide open. I think anyone can come, walk into my backyard and finish the job of killing this old lady. Thank God I didn't break my bones. I laughed and cried. It's too sad. Nobody respects old life, not Asian life for sure anymore. They think Asians brought COVID that kills Americans. Emily, you go, and you visit and move to Korea. Live in peace. Don't need to look back to see if someone is following you to give you a beating. None of this nonsense. You are old enough to do whatever you want and need to do. No one is stopping you. You earned your right to do whatever you want. I am happy you told me first. I was going to tell you what I have been thinking but I didn't know how to tell you. We both old. We paid our duties long enough. It's our time to live however we want to live."

Honesty always pays well. Relief comes at once while the ladies listen to each other, recognizing their mutual toleration of the status quo. They hug tight, tears on their cheeks. This is their ripened moment in time to make a change and prepare for their last phases of life. Emily must move on for her own life, even if Samantha is inconvenienced by the absence of her mother when she moves back to San Francisco. Emily has done enough, sacrificed her life to be a good mother and a wife. This is a time to meet her needs and live her life as she pleases.

Chapter 39

Hating the heroes

October 25, 2021

COVID-19 deaths in the US are now at 736,000, with 45.4 million people who have become infected. COVID-19 infections globally are 243 million, with 4.94 million people dead. The United States still has the highest number of incidence and death rates, followed by India and Brazil. It is ironic that the US developed the most effective vaccines in the world, yet has the highest death and incidence rates. The price of freedom costs the lives of American people. The CDC released all data of incidents per 100,000 people spanning April until the end of August, before and after the Delta variant of COVID hit. For the unvaccinated, 736 infections per 100,000; J&J-vaccinated, 171 per 100,000; Pfizer-vaccinated, 135 per 100,000, and Ed's company-vaccinated, 86 per 100,000. So, the CDC data shows an unvaccinated person had at least 6.1 times greater likelihood of testing positive, and 11.3 times greater likelihood of dying from COVID-19 compared to a fully vaccinated person.

Breakthrough cases among the combined vaccinated people are 114 per 100,000. Among unvaccinated people, breakthrough cases number 666 per 100,000. The COVID-19 death rate for the breakthrough cases is 0.7 per 100,000, compared to 9.1 per 100,000 for unvaccinated people. Medical science shows that breakthrough cases which lead to death are normally seen in people who are over 80 years old, with underlying immune suppressed conditions such as patients with cancer, or those with cardiovascular disease, lung disease, diabetes, and those who are taking immunosuppressive drugs.

***

Ed's company celebrates another landmark. The FDA recently approved the combination approach of vaccination: people who initially received a J&J vaccine may now receive a vaccine from Pfizer—or from Ed's company, because their vaccines are rapidly delivered to drug stores and therefore his vaccines are in higher demand. Also, the CDC approved kids younger than 12 (ages 6 to 11) for a lower-dosed vaccination following a study that involved 4,753 children. Pfizer had tested their vaccine efficacy in children of ages 5-11, with 91% effectiveness. Oddly, Pfizer's vaccine has consistently been granted approvals prior to the vaccine from Ed's company. Therefore, initial bursts of public attention places a focus on Pfizer, even though the vaccine data from his company shows superior effectiveness. The inclusion of children and adolescents in vaccine programs is essential to end the pandemic because they can transmit the virus to their adult parents and others in their community.

Ed and his team continue to be jubilant by their ongoing success with vaccine discoveries. Meanwhile, Ed has private discussions with Dr. Steven Allen about the efficacy of their vaccine, and possible origins of COVID-19.

One morning Steven drops by Ed's office and asks if he can sit and discuss his recent thoughts. "You know Ed, I am a bit disappointed in the mRNA vaccine. It's not like the polio vaccine where you receive the vaccine, and you are forever immune to poliovirus. This mRNA targets the coronavirus spike protein and yet it seems the antibody levels diminish over time. You can still get COVID-19. What's with all these breakthrough cases? What happened to the T-cell functions, and memory B-cells? And booster shots; those were not required with the polio vaccine."

"Remember Steven, about the hepatitis B vaccine? Later, they realized the immunosuppressed people may need a booster shot for Hep B vaccine. There was a recent study for mRNA vaccines in regard to T-cells. The initial dose of vaccine elicited a rapid response from helper T-cells — the CD4, but the killer T-cells, the CD8, appear in large numbers only after the second vaccine dose. Some people challenge the idea that the mRNA vaccine works well. But we do know that the memory T-cells and memory B-cells persist for at least 6 to 8 months, and continue to evolve and mature, and none of that information is relayed by current antibody testing." Steven seems to understand what Ed is saying, so Ed continues.

"Our studies could determine the longevity of T-cell response to vaccination. The antigen specific memory B-cell also increased after the second vaccine dose although the memory B-cell response declined slightly with age in their small numbers. We really do not know much about the longevity of mRNA vaccines in regard to long-term efficacy of the memory B-cells, CD4, CD8 and killer T-cells. What's more complicated are the elderly — and immunosuppressed individuals — is this vaccine fully effective for them? Breakthrough cases are seen in these people, and in younger people who are immunocompetent. We have a puzzling question, Steven. Why do certain younger people get COVID-19, even after two shots of our vaccines? And we see other types of people infected by COVID-19 who never became sick from it. Why are these asymptomatic people not sick? It's another puzzling question. Since the mRNA vaccine is not functioning like the polio vaccine, maybe we shouldn't have called it a vaccine in the first place. And because the coronavirus is rapidly mutating, somewhat similar to influenza virus, the vaccine efficacy also may escape. So, we should get a COVID vaccine like a flu shot that you get every year. We continue to call the flu shot a vaccine, but it is not forever protective against influenza virus. Likewise, we should also get the coronavirus vaccine annually. That's why we are trying to combine flu and COVID vaccines together, for annual shots. Plus, we are recruiting cohorts of 300–500 participants from Southern California to test new mRNA vaccines against Beta, Delta, and a combination of Beta and the original strain. We are also planning to test a Beta–Delta multivalent vaccine. As you know, Beta variant carries mutations that make it more resistant than any other known variant for the current vaccines. Pfizer has already begun recruiting 28-month-old infants to age under 5 for their vaccine trial. We are a bit behind on this. There is a new strand called Delta plus, AY.4.2, a daughter of the Delta variant from the UK which already has reached California and New York."

Ed does his best to inform Steven about the current news since his CEO is often unaware of activities currently underway in the company.

"So, Ed, Mr. know-it-all. You've been to Dr. Shei's lab in Wuhan. What do you think about the lab leak theory?" Steven smiles deviously. "After all, four and a half million people have died globally."

Ed immediately reacts. "I didn't get to see much in her lab. She denied everything to the WHO."

"Well, do you believe her? Of course, she would deny the origin of COVID-19 and the patient zero coming from her lab. But how do you explain the potency of COVID-19 spreading to at least twenty-six countries in one month? Most viruses that need an animal host and are circulating in the wild are not very good at transmission. COVID-19 seems designed to be like a human virus. It must be the twelve nucleotides, a furin cleavage site in the spike area which has the unusual ability of binding to ACE2 receptors in human cells. This furin cleavage site is inconsistent with expectations from evolutionary theory and more consistent with an engineered product, don't you think?"

Ed looks directly at Steven, perplexed. "But the journal *Nature Medicine* in March 2021 published that SARS-CoV-2 had naturally spilled over from a bat, evolving into a pandemic virus either in an animal host, or, unnoticed in humans, and the authors concluded that the virus is not a laboratory construct, or a purposefully engineered. The virus most likely resulted from a natural zoonotic spillover. And you know that the presumed patient zero—actually three WIV researchers—had fallen ill with COVID-like symptoms in November 2019, much earlier than the December Hunan Seafood Market cluster cases. The market is more likely a victim, not the origin of the novel virus. Steven, don't you think that the location of the WIV is just a coincidence? They have the largest library of bat coronaviruses in the world; some nineteen thousand samples are stored in its labs. Not only that, but Dr. Shei had also published her work on chimeric viruses in 2016, rumored to have been done in a BSL-2 lab that would not require proper PPE and all other restrictions.

With barely a pause, Ed continues. "Here's another interesting thing. In 2002, the SARS-1 virus spilled over from bats to civets at an urban market. This was found within just four months of the outbreak. MERS emerged in Saudi Arabia in 2012, after the virus spilled from bats to camels to people, and this was found within just nine months. But why isn't the SARS-CoV-2 intermediate host yet to be found? It's been almost two years. Chinese officials told WHO that their scientists had tested more than 80,000 livestock, poultry, and wild-animal samples across thirty-one provinces, collected both before and after the outbreak, but found no evidence of virus. Can anyone trust or challenge the Chinese government? Another interesting thing is that Dr. Shei and two other scientists submitted a $14.2 million grant proposal to the US Defense Advanced Research Project Agency (DARPA) with a plan to identify, model, and test the spillover risk of novel SARS-related bat coronaviruses, and to develop a vaccine to preempt viruses from jumping into other animals or people. The plan specified they would insert "human-specific" furin cleavage sites into SARS-like bat coronaviruses. This proposal was submitted in 2018. As a scientist, we know they must have completed a somewhat successful pilot study before applying for this major grant. Now, isn't that anther crazy coincidence, Steven?"

Hesitantly, Steven asks Ed, "Did they receive the $14.2 million?"

Ed is shocked by the question. Apparently Steven was not even aware of Dr. Shei's grant application.

"No, it was rejected. But remember, the NIH had given her a grant at the beginning of her research. And don't you think it is odd that the Chinese had released the vaccine against COVID-19 remarkably fast, within six months? This means their work on a vaccine had likely begun *prior* to the COVID-19 outbreak. Other virology scientists think that if you look closely enough, you can see a tiny WIV signature on the SARS-CoV-2. And Steven, it's not that Dr. Shei wants to hide the science, but the Chinese government will not allow her to share her scientific genius work. If the WHO finds the details of a lab leak, the scientists are culpable of an accident. Even if it was from a wildlife farm of zoonotic origin, it would still implicate the policies of the Chinese government. That's why China prefers swirling the storms of other possible sources. They claim US soldiers brought the virus to Wuhan in October 2019 from Fort Detrick, Maryland. Another claim captured attention by blaming imported frozen food. China is still not cooperating to find the original source of this virus."

Ed pauses, and then adds his final conclusion. "In looking at all of the theories of origin, I still think that nature is the best bioterrorist. It's far more creative than any scientist."

Steven scoffs, and begins standing from his seat. "You are a Chinese descendant. Perhaps you don't like to be blamed for this pandemic that was caused by a virus which came from China, or from a Chinese scientist."

Ed pushes his own chair back and stands, pointing at Steven. "That's a racial remark, Steven. I am deeply disappointed and disgusted that you said that."

"But it's true," Steven says, shuffling his feet back. "I sent you to Wuhan to meet with Dr. Shei at the WIV. I made you famous, made you our company spokesperson, and you are protecting Dr. Shei and her work that may have contributed to this pandemic disaster. You told me almost nothing about her, or her work. How did you even manage to bring her virus to us? You must be involved or knew about this furin cleavage site insertion and never told us about it."

"That's enough! I work for this company, and I went to Wuhan for you because you didn't want to go there at the time, either because you feared catching COVID-19, or you didn't know much about virology. I went there and came back successfully, and even obtained the virus with specific genetic codes that caused the original COVID-19. I had successfully cloned the virus in a Petri dish. I successfully led and managed hundreds of scientists to develop our mRNA vaccine in a short time, and I made you a multibillionaire. And now, is this what I get from you, Steven? A racial slur?

Steven steps closer to Ed. "Those were not racial remarks. I am just saying that it is plausible to protect Chinese people if you are Chinese."

Ed shakes his head at the foolish man, turns his body to avoid something toxic, then walks around Steven as he leaves the office.

"Hey, Ed, I am joking! You know that!" Steven shouts out as Ed closes the door behind him and thinks, *Yeah, right. It's a joke. White people usually say it's a joke when it pertains to racial discrimination.*

Steven opens the door to release one final plea. "Ed, come back! You can't take it seriously, it's not personal! Hah! It's a joke!"

Such petty comments are familiar to Ed. *Of course it is personal. Why would I not take it seriously? You blatantly condemn my heritage. If I explain that you are a redneck country bumpkin, an*

It's a blatant racist remark and ignorant display of discrimination against all Chinese scientists like Ed. When does a scientist become ignorant about the color of a person's skin, or a person's heritage? Can a scientist simply receive respect for their accomplishments? Ed is an American-born scientist with no Chinese accent, educated in the states, an American citizen just like Steven, devoted to American values, loyalty and pride. His American loyalty is questioned only because he is descended from China. If he were not proficient in the English language or spoke with an accent, he cannot imagine the extent of racial discrimination remarks he would have received. This foreign treatment from his own country of America is not new to him, but he is heavily disheartened each time it confronts him. For that reason, Ed is pleased that a genius scientist like Dr. Shei exists in this world. Whether she is a culprit of the pandemic or not, no one can deny her powerful research and immense collection of coronaviruses. Ed is certain she confronts an equal dosage of criticisms, doubts, and hateful comments from all over the world. However, her success and mere presence encourages all Chinese scientists who live in America. Clearly, Americans are frustrated at the secretive and deceptive nature of the Chinese government, but are not necessarily frustrated at the individual people in China. What is not clear to Ed is to what extent the hatred and frustration is toward the Chinese government, or toward all people of Chinese descent. All of Steven's celebrations and praises for Ed ironically disintegrate into nothing at the moment Steven exposes his true self, through one racially motivated remark revealing the truth of a person. One negative experience can instantly destroy any relationship, regardless of the number of positive experiences that had built a false mutual trust in a human relationship.

Ed briefly considers joining the mass exodus of staff leaving the company, but recognizes his own anger is driving his thinking. He will appear to brush it aside. He will process it as a careless joke from Steven, as he has done a thousand other times in life, placing it among the dirty moments of his life, the 'Chinese' jokes accumulated throughout his life that dig down deep into the dirt for somewhere to hide, learning to laugh about it. With any amount of success he accumulates, he must bear these jokes. No money, power, effort, titles, education, or protective policies to discourage discrimination will stop the put-downs and unspoken bias for being a Chinese American. There will be someone else to spit out another joke and salt his wounds, and not in the distant future. He is certain of this. Likewise, his brothers who are doctors often face ignorant patients who refuse receive help from the 'chink doctors,' especially during this pandemic. Medical doctors who are non-White are confronting growing discrimination from fellow Americans who come into their medical offices, and doctors of all races are commonly berated by patients who demand treatment. Physicians in some hospitals consider themselves lucky if they are never shouted at, or beaten with blows to their heads, or other forms of physical violence some have witnessed.

Last year, before the release of the mRNA vaccine, Ed imagined a possible scenario of being seen as a hero by the American people, or globally recognized as a Nobel Prize winner, perhaps saving many in the world from the COVID-19 pandemic. Part of the dream has come true; he has developed an mRNA vaccine. Well, not by himself, but through collaboration with many scientists in his company. Sadly, he held an assumption that Chinese Americans would no longer face violence and outspoken discrimination. His assumption dissolved. It is here to stay. No matter how significant a scientific breakthrough may be, regardless of the science and the lives saved, such contributions from any Asian American in this country will be diminished, or perhaps even disregarded. The anti-Asian semantics will exist forever. His only choice is to live with it.

Chapter 40

Unintended accusation

November 23, 2021

Ed decides to meet up with Lifang Shei, the daughter of Dr. Shei. Ed and Lifang had first met in China back in late 2019. It was a blind date arranged by Dr. Shei, who had disapproved of Lifang's boyfriend, a dark-skinned, struggling jazz musician, and the date was a condition she imposed upon Ed before granting him a tour of her lab at the Wuhan Institute of Virology. His sole purpose of going to China that year was to learn how Dr. Shei had sequenced the coronavirus from bats. Of course he agreed to the date. Lifang lived in London where she worked in a vaccine manufacturing facility, and was visiting her mother in China at the time. Ed's blind date with Lifang was brief, although the two remained in contact over the past year and a half, brief business discussions about vaccine manufacturing and an occasional email.

In a recent call, Lifang informed Ed that she broke up with her boyfriend. Her father had unexpectedly visited her in London, and a stormy argument erupted with her father when he realized his daughter was living with a man. He demanded the relationship to end, and immediately rented Lifang a flat near her workplace. Lifang was already planning to end the relationship, so her father's unwanted reaction compounded her frustrations. Her boyfriend had grown more dependent on Lifang after losing his job in a jazz club as a saxophone player during the pandemic shutdown. He never tried to get any type of job after that and their apartment became more unkempt, so she was never sure exactly what he did during the day. She felt the abusive emotions and reactions they both emitted, and their relationship went from bad to bitter.

During her call to Ed, Lifang went silent, and then her voice quickly brightened while announcing her recent promotion to assistant director, in quality control. She enjoys her new position and adores her new flat full of newly found freedom and where tidiness abounds. Slowly, she casually invites Ed to visit her in London, promising him a tour of her factory. Ed hesitates. All of England and every European country is withstanding another wave of COVID-19, referred to by the media as a Delta 'plus' variant, and Omicron. Nevertheless, Ed is lonely. Spending another Thanksgiving holiday alone in New York will inevitably be boring.

That same day, he booked a first-class seat on a flight to Heathrow, with a plan to stay until Sunday morning, and no hotel reservation. Ed wants to venture out, maybe see other women besides Samantha. *Let's see what will happen,* Ed mumbles to himself.

Lifang arrives at the airport driving a small red MINI cooper, and Ed grins. Without hesitation she drives zipping around the streets of London, her excitement to see Ed carried by the energy of her car. As she opens the door to her flat, Ed is met by a wonderful aroma from her homemade American Thanksgiving dinner; golden brown hens in a slow-cooking oven, along with baked potatoes and green beans, and white chocolate chip cookies resting on a counter. Ed is astounded that Lifang could be such a good cook, just like her mother, Dr Shei. Ed has gone for months without any homemade Western-style cooking, so their meal together is a wonderful treat. After dinner, they work out a system to clean the dishes. Ed and Lifang stand next to each other, and Ed begins scrubbing the largest pan. He blurts out, "I did not reserve a hotel room."

"That's fine. You sleep on my couch. I didn't expect you to reserve a hotel."

Lifang gathers hot tea and cookies she had prepared, and they sit once again at the table.

"How is your mother, Dr. Shei doing these days?"

"Not so good. The government and international attention are focused on her. Nonstop. And pressure from the WIV; it's getting to her. She can't sleep well. I can't imagine what she's going through.

"Why is she bothered by the government?"

"The Chinese government? Ed, are you kidding? Day and night they are upon her. They want this data and that data, everything since October of 2019, even her personal information. She receives protection from the government in her home, at her worksite in her lab, 24/7. She can't talk to the media, the WHO, and definitely no international news outlets. She is restricted to only certain places, and government officials follow her everywhere. She is in prison in her own country."

"I'm sorry Lifang. I didn't realize that."

"You don't know China, Ed. You don't want to become famous in China. They have a lot to lose if the world learns the origin of the SARS-CoV-2, whether it originated from her lab, the Wuhan Seafood market, or maybe elsewhere. In any scenario, China will have problems answering questions about the origin. I think they are hiding something." She takes a bite from a crumbling white chocolate chip cookie and says, "They probably know much more than we think."

"Do you think your mother was partly involved? It does appear a little suspicious. What are the odds that the first case in humans—patient zero—is located in the vicinity of the WIV, the largest BSL-4 facility, and site of the largest collection of bat coronaviruses with researchers who work on sequencing the viruses? Wouldn't some people assume this outbreak may have come from your mother's lab? It may be a stretch, but maybe the most obvious site the WIV could blame was a dirty seafood market that sells live, caged animals. Why would the first case of COVID come from the urban city of Wuhan, while the bat SARS virus is found 1,000 miles away in the Yunnan cave?"

"What are you saying, Ed? Are you finger pointing to my mom as the origin for COVID?" Lifang's sarcastic tone reveals her anger.

"I am only pointing out a coincidence; that the sampled bat-coronavirus sequence has been offline since September 2019. If your mother had proposed a theory to carry out a study to tinker with the genomes, and tried inserting it into the virus to make it more susceptible to bind with human ACE receptors and make it more infectious, it may have worked. She would be a genius. Lifang, what do you think?"

"Ed, what I think is you flew across the ocean to accuse my mother of being the culprit for the pandemic. Are you sugar-coating an accusation with a compliment that she is a genius? I am done with this conversation. You are ignorant of the whole story. In China, obviously they are frantic and curious to determine the origin of COVID, and the government continues extensive analysis. Of course they would look at my mother. They concluded that it most likely came from raccoon dogs sold in the Huanan Market. As you may not know, Ed, analysis of spatial patterns seen in early cases indicated animal-to-human contact from live markets in China. When looking at the clustering of the early COVID-19 and observing the sequences from patients' samples, it was independently found that the most plausible origin was from the Huanan Market, starting early to mid-December."

Lifang pauses, glaring at Ed. "You guys—Americans, are unaware of the entirety of events and facts, and yet Americans spread more rumors than facts, torturing my mother, who has nothing to do with this. My mother received hundreds of threatening letters. She can no longer safely leave her house, and here in London I must hide the fact that I am her daughter, otherwise letters will arrive addressed to me with threats to kill me. I don't need you coming to my flat and telling me this nonsense. I am tired. I'm going to bed."

Lifang pushes her chair from the table and marches into her bedroom, leaving Ed with her cold tea and partially eaten cookies.

Ed had not expected that he would upset Lifang. He was merely curious and wrongly assumed Lifang would offer other ideas or share more information with him. He was utterly insensitive, not grasping that she is a daughter of Dr. Shei, an international target of blame and accusation for over a year. He gathers the few dishes used for their tea and cookies and places them in the sink, then quietly washes them. He dries his hands with a small towel from the counter, and sits on the edge of a lone couch in the corner. There is no pillow or blanket. Ed started this relationship poorly and it's going to be a cold night for sure. He regrets not reserving a hotel, but decides to stay. He gathers his thin down jacket and covers himself from the waist up. He's still cold. He should have been kinder and more sensitive to Lifang. After all, she is the daughter of world-renowned Dr. Shei. Lifang obviously would do everything possible to defend her mother's ethics and protect her from accusations of being the culprit of a pandemic killing millions of people.

Well, this is the punishment I get for using my tongue unwisely.
Ed braces for a cold night.

Chapter 41

Unforeseen excitement

November 24, 2021

Ed wakes up under a nice warm blanket covering his body. He has no memory of being cold last night. Lifang must have placed the blanket over him. An aroma of coffee fills the room, and he turns and sees Lifang making coffee. Warm morning sunshine touches her cheek and black hair.

"Good morning, Ed. Sorry I had to wake you up," she says with a jolly undertone. "It's already 10:00 am and I have a headache. I need caffeine. I hated to wake you up from a deep sleep." Ed wonders if she has a multiple personality disorder or early Alzheimer's.

"That's fine, Lifang. I flew here to see you, not that I must acclimate myself to the time change. I slept really well here. Thanks for the warm blanket."

"No problem. The sofa could extend out to become a bed, but I didn't want to wake you up. Are you okay? Any back pain?"

"No, fortunately I feel fine, maybe a little stiff." Ed smiles, and Lifang responds,

"I am sorry, I left rather abruptly last night. I have been fed up with the relentless criticisms about my mom. No one is harder working and dedicated to their work than my mom. I don't really like her myself, and yet if someone else criticizes her, I become really sensitive." Lifang lowers her eyes, and Ed says,

"I am sorry if I had a critical voice, Lifang. I didn't really mean it. It's just that my company required me to answer these exact questions after I saw your mother in China. People think that since I am Chinese, I know everything about the origin of the virus. I totally understand your position."

"No one in my company knows that Dr. Shei is my mother. I told no one. No one suspects that we are related."

"That's a good idea, Lifang."

"I took the rest of the week off for a vacation. But today or tomorrow I want you to come with me to work," she says excitedly.

"Isn't it closed for the Thanksgiving holiday tomorrow?"

"No, the British do not celebrate the US Thanksgiving holiday."

"Oh, yeah, I forgot. The UK is different."

"Yeah, I know. You Americans assume the whole world revolves around the US. We British celebrate our own holidays. Thanksgiving is not one of them."

"Sorry, I am so accustomed to the American way. Sorry for my ignorance."

"That's okay, we are used to Americans. Just remember that the UK is not an extension of America. We are a sovereign country."

Ed stirs the milk in his coffee and asks, "Has the UK also experienced anti-Asian violence during COVID?"

"Yeah, there are some reports which cite a rise of 300 percent in hate crimes towards Chinese people. But unlike the US where your president passed the COVID-19 Hate Crimes Act, the problem here is still widely ignored and anti-Asian sentiment will remain the norm for decades to come because the UK government will not take appropriate action to correct a century of state-sanctioned exclusion and exoticization."

"You'd be surprised that the COVID Hate Crimes Act does not hinder everyday anti-Asian sentiment in the US. I face some of it in my own company."

"I'm sorry to hear that. But let's not talk about it. It depresses me. Let's just enjoy each other's company for this short time you are here. I'd like to take you to many different places to eat and fully experience the UK." Lifang's tone turns serious when she adds, "And if we experience such sentiment or violence, we will fight back with my pepper spray and my umbrella that I carry in my bag. See? I have my gameplan." She smiles and proudly displays the contents of her bag to Ed. He sees a small tube of pepper spray. Or maybe it's lipstick. He smiles and asks,

"I heard the UK is seeing an increase in COVID numbers?"

"Yeah, we have been rather nonchalant about COVID for a while. We lifted almost all COVID restrictions in the UK on July 19th, following one of the world's fastest vaccine rollouts. I think two factors are contributing to our rise in recent infections. One, after a rapid and successful vaccine campaign, we didn't realize antibody levels in many people who tested positive for COVID plateaued in May, and then continually dropped, not realizing neutralizing antibodies are waning. We thought that the vaccine would be effective forever. Then came the Delta variant's mutations. Israel is seeing similar findings. Our company's Oxford-AstraZeneca vaccines are still 91% effective at preventing hospitalization and death. Relatively speaking, the UK has around three times as many infections as the US, but only two-thirds the daily deaths."

Ed nods and replies to Lifang. "The UK Merck had approval for Molnupiravir—the antiviral pill—in early November. I think that may be a game changer because they are not targeting the spike protein of the coronavirus, but inhibiting replication of the virus. Soon after, Pfizer came up with Paxlovid. More recently Sotrovimab from GlaxoSmithKline."

"Yeah, we are very excited about our UK product. What is currently in development at your company?"

"I can't tell you that," Ed replies, smiling. "You should know that."

"Okay, I thought I could gather some of your secrets. Well, let's see if you can keep them secret by the end of this weekend. Let's go out for brunch, and then I want you to meet my boss. Get dressed, but not too casual. Maybe my boss will try and fetch you to join our company."

Is Lifang joking? Ed is unsure. But looking at it objectively, it appears she is partially serious. So, he dresses accordingly in semi-casual business attire. Her boss might be awaiting Ed. He imagines living in London, Lifang at his side as a real girlfriend. An unforeseen excitement grows from this small possibility of a life with this sparkling and unpredictable lady. Perhaps a time to bury memories of himself and Samantha that are no longer useful, and to face new perspectives. This vacation is dramatically refreshing after two years of nonstop, fast-paced work. Being with Lifang is nice, an entirely different woman who is spunky and uninhibited. Ed wonders, *What would my parents and brothers say about Lifang?*

Chapter 42

Hot commodity

November 25, 2021

The day is fun with Lifang. They arrive at her company, not much different from his own in the US, but much larger in scale and manufacturing processes that are intriguing to Ed. Lifang happily introduces Ed to her boss, Ian Dorskin, the director of production. He is a tall, skinny man with a heavy East Sussex accent which Ed has trouble understanding, even though Ian speaks the English language.

Apparently, Ian and Lifang had a mutual understanding of recruiting Ed. Every senior leader at the company would have known Ed's name, the lead scientist at the US company who discovered the mRNA vaccine. Ed quickly perceives his visit to the plant was prearranged with a purpose to recruit. Ian is extremely friendly and obliged to show every aspect of the company to fulfill Ed's curiosity. The company CEO had even agreed to meet Ed at almost any time or any day during Ed's visit in London. Ian and Lifang escort Ed to dinner at a Michelin-starred restaurant. Ian orders exclusive wine selections and the finest, most expensive appetizers. Ed had not expected to be lured in by their charms, nor by the imagery they created for Ed to visualize a unique, enticing perspective of working in their London-based company. Ian explains that more than 8.5 billion doses of vaccines have been manufactured worldwide thus far in 2021. The highest number of manufactured vaccines have been from AstraZeneca, followed by CoronaVac and then Pfizer. Ed's company is fifth in the line. The world's most vaccinated nations are the United Arab Emirates, Chile, and Cuba, and the least vaccinated nations are Tanzania, Afghanistan and Papua New Guinea. Ed had no idea the AstraZeneca vaccine is currently at the top of the chart of doses distributed in the world. Their profit must have been exponentially high compared to Ed's company. He feels appreciated and welcomed, even though the UK may have similar problems with anti-Asian sentiments. At least for a brief time, his talents and skills are more important than his race. Especially meaningful for him was Lifang introducing Ed as her friend during dinner, then expanding that when she said, "maybe more than that in the future."

After the meal, Lifang tells Ian the story of how she and Ed met in Wuhan. "I had no desire to meet him. My mother thrust the date upon me. I was constantly pressured to meet someone of the same race and nationality. I was not happy with my life at that time, so I agreed to the blind date. Now, things have changed, and I admit that perhaps mothers know best."

Ed silently enjoys her passive, thoughtful efforts to grow their relationship since he arrived in London. As the conversation deepens and the effect of wine progresses, Ed welcomes the idea of meeting with their company's CEO. Ian promptly makes a call and schedules the meeting for the next day. It is that simple. A new job prospect is just a phone call away. For scientists, it's often about who you know, not what you know, to get a job. This would be a lateral move for Ed, maybe even one level below but it would be a different job in a different country. A person with proven scientific discoveries and experience in vaccine technology is a hot commodity in their world with a pandemic. He calculates the first thing to do is shop for clothes to make at least a decent first impression. Ed had packed only a small carry-on bag with casual clothes for the long weekend in London. His interview with the CEO of a large global company was never imagined. He begins to worry. If the situation in London becomes tempting and he accepts an offer, what would he say to his boss, Dr. Steven Allen?

Chapter 43

A London decision

November 27, 2021

Ed boards the airplane late at night and reflects upon the unexpected events. Lifang had tears in her eyes, hugging him at the airport. They bonded with each other after only three days. It was fast and unexpected. They were inseparable. He wanted to experience her favorite places, they had fish and chips and went to other remarkable, lesser-known eateries she knew of, visited museums, and finally, Ed would meet the CEO and other executives. A series of meetings went exceptionally well. Everyone he met during interviews seemed impressed and clearly expressed their eagerness for him to join their prestigious company.

He recalls his unusual conversation with the CEO. They were meeting one on one when the man began speaking with more exuberance while holding a white envelope in his right hand. He said, "Ed, you know we want to have you here." Ed looked at the moving envelope. "Our offer is a superior salary to what you must be earning now. We always pay our people highly competitive salaries. We have numerous stock options, bonuses twice a year." Ed tracks the envelope as the CEO pauses and presents the envelope to Ed. A single page; a title of Executive Vice President, Research and Development, a place to live in one of the most expensive neighborhoods in London and a dollar amount in British pounds sterling. Far too good to pass on, but Ed politely stated he would need time to carefully think about it, and would respond within a month.

While on the flight, Ed assesses that the job will not be a lateral move, and much better in many ways than he had expected. He is determined to return home and to his current work, sort things out, allowing him to seriously think about leaving the US and moving far from his family. Considering the compensation offered, he would fly first class several times a year to visit his family or friends. In addition, his new role will require frequent business trips to the US. Two things hinge upon his decision; one is to work fewer hours, and two is Lifang. How does he feel about her? Can he have a serious relationship with her? Can they get married? Is she the person he can commit a married life with? Can he truly forget Samantha? Ed wishes that he had more time with Lifang to figure out all of these questions and answers. The long distance, different countries, their age gap, and even different cultures — even though they are both Chinese — all these facts are hindering him to find the underlying cause of his questions about Lifang. Dr. Shei would be happy if he and Lifang were to marry, and perhaps his parents as well. Ed has no interest in the idea of dating and playing games with his heart. He is ready to get married and settle into a steady life. He wants to have a few kids and be with a loving and supporting wife, regardless of whether she also pursues a professional career. Sometimes he has thoughts of comparing Lifang with Samantha and finds himself asking, *What would Samantha do? What would she say?* He spent more than a decade with Samantha as a woman he loved. But recently, his mind holds fewer thoughts about Samantha. The time away from his office gradually allowed Ed to understand why his dilemma should not puzzle him. They practically grew up together throughout college, and beyond. He had no other girlfriend during his life. Even though he and Samantha had broken up, he felt as if he was cheating on Samantha when he was with Lifang, especially when he would kiss Lifang. He and Lifang had not slept together, and one thing that bothers him is the fact Lifang was recently with someone else before seeing Ed. With Samantha, he never questioned her, so when they were kissing, the irritable thoughts and questions about, "what was it like with the other guy?" never came up. When he had no personal relationship or feelings for Lifang, none of that bothered him, but now as he experiences a closer relationship with Lifang, irritating thoughts and images of Lifang possibly having sex with her recent boyfriend really bothers him. Love is truly possessive and unforgiving. Can he let it go and be with Lifang? But then, who at his or her age has not had another serious relationship?

What about his current job in the US? He likes the job and has liked working with his boss, except his last conversation with Steven full of insensitive and ignorant remarks. As with any job, it comes with problems. His job started in a company that was a start-up, basically a nonexistent company which quickly became a multibillion-dollar entity. His bonus this year will sufficiently equal the salary promised by the London company. And that is just the beginning. His current company will grow exponentially, and so will the stock options, potential bonuses, and even his salary. All of these sources of compensation will likely increase and surpass what the London company is offering. Ed's current position and title as Scientific Director is sufficient enough. Ambition or ego to achieve a better title is not something he ever sought, really. Instead, he poured his life, efforts, and all concerns into the company from the ground up. He hates the idea of giving up his collective efforts, his life at the company and his career with Steven.

Still, his company is younger and smaller than the one in London, and his current company will inevitably experience growing pains and restructuring in coming months. Sadly, Ed is not convinced Steven is prepared or has the courage to advance him above his current level, nor is Ed assured if better prospects will be available in the future. Somehow, over time, Steven had become comfortable using Ed as his personal assistant. He might be unfamiliar or uncomfortable with seeing Ed as Vice CEO, President, or even a Senior VP. Ed might always be seen by Steven as nothing more than his right-hand assistant. Ed wonders how long he can maintain workdays of 12–16 hours, no work-life balance. Ed practically lives in an office. Because his company and their collective work are not as established as AstraZeneca, Ed has been pulled into everything from HR, quality control, public relations, and strategy for recruitment of human subjects for the phase studies, among other roles. He is not doing what he was trained to do, the scientific work. Engaging in scientific work, leading research and development is solely what he wants to do. The new job will provide exactly that.

As his plane begins its descent, he concludes he must think about this further. He needs more time. He will return to his current job for a while and then decide whether to accept the new position in London. One fact he is most pleased with: people are enthusiastic to hire him and recognize his contributions, regardless of his race. Most surprising is knowing

that he is valuable to a wonderful, spunky woman awaiting him
in London.

Chapter 44

Omicron

December 2, 2021

Following his England trip, Ed became sick with flu symptoms, loss of smell, back and joint aches, sniffing, sneezing, coughing, nausea and general malaise. He immediately assumes it is COVID-19, most likely from the Omicron variant in London that had been spreading like a wildfire. *Thank God I received two vaccine shots,* Ed thinks. *And a booster two weeks before I traveled to London. Otherwise this might get really bad.*

***

Omicron has spread across the world faster than any previous variants such as Alpha and Delta. The Omicron variant is remarkable, its genome possesses more than 50 mutations when compared to the original coronavirus seen in Wuhan, China, with about 30 of these mutations contributing to changes in amino acids in the spike protein. These untamed crazy mutations have two benefits from the standpoint of the virus: one is an increased ability to bond with a twenty-times stronger grip to the ACE2 receptor protein, and the other is its ability to gain entrance to the host cell after being engulfed in an endosome, and not adept at fusing directly with the cell's membrane. And hence, the Omicron variant is superior at evading the virus-blocking neutralizing antibodies produced by vaccinated people, or people infected with earlier variants. It also consists of three distinct sub-lineages, named BA.1, BA.2, and BA.3. The BA.1 and BA.2 have taken off globally, first detected in South Africa and Botswana in early November 2021. But retrospective testing has found earlier samples from individuals in England on November 1st and 3rd. Omicron variants are multiplying 70 times faster than the Delta variant, but the evidence suggests it is less severe than the Delta variant because it has less ability to penetrate deep lung tissue, and hence, Omicron infections are 91% less fatal, with 51% less risk of hospitalization. While the Omicron variant is less fatal due to its increased transmittable infection, the total number of patients requiring hospital care—and associated death rates—are expected to be higher than Delta's peak.

The US government asks people to get booster shots for better protection after evidence showed a third vaccine shot boosted effectiveness against infection to around 75%, and 88% against severe disease. However, breakthrough infections in people who are vaccinated are likely to continue, especially when cold weather arrives. People will spend more time indoors, travel during the holidays, and grow fatigued with the CDC guidelines and warnings. This will be a perfect storm for the arrival of Omicron, the highly infectious variant that will prolong the pandemic phase instead of moving us toward an endemic phase.

The UK infection rate increases during late November and on into December, and is tentatively expected to decline in mid-January of 2022. The Omicron variant arrived in the UK just as mask requirements were lifted, even as people started to enjoy their normalcy of going back into work, restaurants and bars. The UK and South Africa sternly warn the world that the Omicron variant is not to be ignored. This is mostly dismissed in the US where citizens are enjoying their decrease in the Delta variant. Eager to see family and friends during the Thanksgiving holiday, millions embark on travelling in the US for the first time in almost two years. Even higher travel rates are expected to swell the airports during the Christmas and New Year holidays. Fatigue from the COVID-19 pandemic weighs upon people, so imagining that another variant is just around the corner is too heavy to consider. Many are resigned to the fact that Omicron has already entered the US where it is rampant in San Francisco, New York City, Washington DC, and other large cities. Early data comes out from Africa and the UK showing the Omicron variant is expected to be less severe, primarily causing flu symptoms. This encouraging news is quickly embraced.

***

Ed walks into his company's employment office for a COVID test using PCR, a company benefit he helped introduce in early 2020. Within two hours, as he expected, his test came back positive, with instructions to go home immediately. He is expected to work from home for at least ten days, even though the CDC guidelines had changed to five days if an employee retests before returning to work. Ed calls Steven to inform him of the situation, but withholds information that his Omicron infection was likely a result from a trip to London. Fortunately, his illness feels mild, so he expects to accomplish many things from home by using his laptop computer. A dry and irritating cough nags at Ed, along with a moderate but persistent headache. He sleeps more than seven hours each night and can work more than eight hours per day. Ed considers his good fortune of living during this time in history, a recipient of the mRNA vaccine and thus avoiding hospitalization or death from COVID. Meanwhile, one of his work colleagues had chosen not to be vaccinated. They often had lunch together. One day after Ed tested positive, his colleague was fired and left with no health insurance. Ed learned of the situation upon returning to work and walking down the hall and seeing his colleague's empty office. A nearby assistant gave Ed a note with a phone number of the hospital room. Ed promptly called.

"I was admitted two hours ago, Ed. I've gotten really sick from the Omicron variant. My oxygen saturation rate is 85%, they say my breathing problem is severe. They're rushing to transfer me to the ICU for immediate ventilation." Ed strains to hear the weak voice. "I made a bad decision. We all worked hard to make our vaccine. One simple shot. That's all I had to do." He sobs, gasping to speak. "My stupidity to believe in my own healthy body to fight the virus. I grossly underestimated the little virus's power to knock me down. I'm a healthy, muscular 210-pound man. I'm only 34."

Ed detects only the beeping sounds from a monitor, then hears his friend gasping for air and finally saying to Ed, "I may lose my life, but medical bills for my family to pay is my biggest regret. I leave them a heavy burden." Ed hears other voices and additional commotion in the background, sounds that fade. He imagines a good friend and colleague being rushed toward the ICU, and wonders if he will ever again hear his voice. Ed empathizes with the doctors and nurses who continue treating the stubborn people who choose not to get vaccinations, fueling a prolonged COVID-19 pandemic. He had closely observed his brothers and Samantha carrying immense burdens to care for their patients. Persons throughout the health care system often endure sleep deprivation, lack of proper self-care in nutrition, rest, and valuable personal time. When anti-vaxxers get COVID, they often become critically ill and come to the hospitals to lay their bodies upon other people who must risk their lives to care for them. These are often neighbors, people they may know who have children and relatives of their own. Patients who shun vaccines are often more demanding of treatment, sometimes pushing and shoving the very workers who are assigned to treat them. These patients often require immediate hospitalization, leading to contamination and infection of workers who are exhausted or at their breaking point, even while shortages of health care workers are rapidly increasing. In turn, patients with cancer, cardiovascular problems, diabetes complications, orthopedic concerns, and myriads of other illnesses requiring health care are pushed aside or delayed in treatment. It is now commonly understood by medical staff that anti-vaxxers have contributed to widespread delays in treatment, have pushed their agenda under the protection of their own individual freedom, have ignored or became ignorant of how their own behavior affects other people and our entire society, effectively minimizing and shunning mRNA vaccine technology and the scientific breakthroughs by American scientists who deserve recognition and celebration.

The mRNA vaccine is truly a scientific miracle, not only in the discovery but the time of delivery. Especially during the spread of Omicron, millions of people ignorantly state that it doesn't matter whether one is fully vaccinated or not because everyone will get it anyway, downplaying and denying the significance of vaccines. It is true, mRNA vaccines have not entirely lived up to initial expectations when it is shown they block 95% of all infections, but then over time, that level of protection against infection declines. Even booster shots are shown to wane in their effect after 4-6 months. Still, the mRNA vaccines clearly altered hospitalization rates and reduced death rates from COVID-19. Modeling is conducted by numerous scientific organizations to display what it would be like without the vaccines. One model completed by the Commonwealth Fund reveals that an additional 1.1 million Americans would have died from COVID-19—and this data modeling is prior to the massive

Omicron wave. Further, the 1.1 million deaths did not factor in the impact of substantial shortages of hospital beds and a significant reduction in hospital services and capacities the additional deaths would have created.

These were the fastest vaccines ever developed, less than one year after Chinese scientists shared the genetic sequences of the SARS-CoV-2 virus, an exceptional human achievement in the history of vaccines. In comparison, the Mumps vaccine took four years, and faster than any scenario that was predicted by Dr. Fauci. He had predicted one to one and a half years, at best.

***

Ed had begun to experience short memory loss following his COVID-19 infection. He was aware that brain fog can also be one of the long-haul symptoms which thousands of COVID patients were currently experiencing. These patients often express a loss of focus in addition to memory loss.

Ed first recognized that his own short-term memory was a problem after forgetting one of his daily routines. Entering his apartment on a recent evening, he could not recall where he had placed the keys to his apartment and car. About 30 minutes later, his heart began palpitating rapidly while searching for his keys. He called to mind reading about people who had recovered from COVID-19 were often showing stark increases in cardiovascular problems during the course of a year following their infection. About 20 such cardiovascular problems have been reported. Other studies are showing that people who recovered from even minor symptoms of COVID had a 52% more likelihood of having a stroke than the contemporary control group, meaning that, out of every 1,000 people studied, there were around 4 more people in the COVID-19 group than in the control group who experienced a stroke. Also, the risk of heart failure increased by 72%, or around 12 more people in the COVID-19 group per 1,000 studied. The long-haul sequelae of COVID-19 are beginning to unveil, and at a minimum, hospitalization increases the likelihood of future cardiovascular complications.

Ed locates his keys and determines to rest more. Falling asleep helps him to release the worries and paranoia arising from his COVID symptoms. The absolute last thing he wants to experience is the loss of brain capacity. He would cease working as a well-functioning scientist. He depends on his quick thinking, a coveted brightness and creativity in thinking. Chinese herbal tea becomes a priority. He steeps a small pot then settles down to binge-watch a Netflix Chinese historical drama of eight episodes featuring a heroic Kung Fu Master. When was the last time he ever had this kind of time to relax and savor time alone, with no internal or external pressure to be productive?

Chapter 45

Power of a woman

December 16, 2021

Ed's memories of his experience in London begin to wane during a time of guiltless relaxation at home. He completes the required ten days of quarantine at home, returns to his office and tests negative for the virus. He comfortably embeds himself into the routine work schedule. His company is now a global company by any definition, and Ed soon begins working 12 hours per day, sometimes 16 hours with no end in sight. On a typical night he will wake up at 1:00 am to lead a Zoom meeting with a South Korean manufacturer, or meet with a South African company to answer genetic sequence questions in the race to target the Omicron variant of coronavirus. He makes himself available for working nights, days or weekends. There is no balance in his mentally exhausted life. He accepts his inability to perform the job. He's had enough, and heads to Steven's office for permission to delegate some of his responsibilities, especially the HR component.

Steven looks up from his computer, nods for Ed to sit, and listens to Ed's situation. Without a pause, Steven replies.

"Ed, you're right. We need to increase headcount; it's long overdue on my end. We also need to restructure the company, and look at what role you'd like to fill."

Ed takes advantage of this opportunity to shift the conversation.

"Steven, I also came to tell you about a job offer I received in London, an offer I am seriously considering for two main reasons. First, a work-life balance. It is not a gradual change; it would occur on day one. Secondly, there is a woman in London that I have reconnected with."

"Well, okay Ed. I can't match the woman part, but I can match the salary, and I can match whatever title they're offering. I also agree to limit your responsibilities as you discussed." Lifang immediately enters Ed's thoughts. He painfully misses her, and his decision immediately becomes clear.

"Steven, I appreciate your offer and immediate response. I miss Lifang, the woman. I need to take the London offer."

Looking downcast, Steven looks up after some time and says, "OK."

The very next evening after Steven failed to retain Ed, Steven placed additional duties upon his valuable young scientist. Ed must oversee the hiring of his own replacement, interview each candidate, attend the hiring committee meetings, and ultimately extend an offer to the candidate Ed selects. Then, Ed must train his replacement. He must also complete his current workload, and find additional time to transition portions of his current duties to four other people, each with their own individual titles. These additional duties had arrived via an email from Steven a few minutes before midnight. Ed scanned the email and went back to sleep.

As a last resort, Steven backpedals in the afternoon and nervously appears in Ed's office, pleading that whatever position Ed would like to have, he will honor that. He'll make the change effective immediately. He can give up the duties of company spokesperson, HR responsibilities, quality control—whatever he'd like to give up so that Ed can focus on research and development, and he would give Ed the title of Senior Vice President. Ed does not reply.

"Ed, I know I can't compete with your female companion, but I know a few Chinese ladies, wonderful scientists! I can set up a few blind dates. There is one lady I did research with; she has long, shiny black hair, beautiful eyes. Another is tall—great smile. Funny, too!" Still smiling, Steven blurts out, "Come on, Ed. I'm sure one of them has a British accent."

Ed just laughs and politely passes on the opportunity.

The company keeps Ed busy as they concoct a new vaccine formula for the Omicron variant of coronavirus which broke out in Africa. This variant might evade the original vaccine, having some 32 mutations in the spike protein. Ed is needed constantly. He does his best to fulfill his duties, but his heart and mind had already begun separating from his work. There is no passion in his work, and his colleagues appear to know of Ed's situation. His colleagues become cautious to discuss any potential proprietary vaccine formulas or components with Ed. Likely, their change in behavior is from fear: Ed may unknowingly reveal components of their work to his new company in London. Feelings of resentment and excitement become mixed within Ed's heart. Resentment when forced to train his own replacement, arriving at work each day while his ethics are in question, and yet his excitement expands while contemplating a new life in London.

In the meantime, Ed and Lifang have daily video calls that last for hours, depriving Ed of sleep as he awakes groggy and tired each morning. Their conversations fascinate Ed, his longing to be with Lifang heightens. She calls Ed late one night and promptly exclaims, "Ed! I want to see you. Can I visit you in the US during the Christmas holidays? British people celebrate Christmas big time! Can I?"

"Well, I guess so. Sure. Okay." Ed loves the image of spending more time with Lifang and suddenly she exclaims, "OK, terrific! Goodnight! Talk to you tomorrow, Ed."

Startled but now awake, Ed decides to extend his decision whether to accept the London offer until the ultimate deadline of January 1. Even though Ed has already decided to quit his job in the US, he will await Lifang's visit and spend more time with her to better understand himself before accepting the offer. So, it will entirely be his relationship with Lifang that will determine his future job. Love is unpredictable. She may even want to get a job in Ed's company and move to the US. If that happens, he will humbly crawl back to Steven and ask to resume his position.

Chapter 46

Another immigration

December 24, 2021

Ed decides to pack up and leave for London instead of waiting for Lifang's visit to the US. He calls the London company and verbally accepts their offer. Surprisingly, he is told a deposit was made on a premier London apartment as part of their recruitment package for Ed, so they're thrilled with his decision and Ed is relieved not to hunt for apartments. He has no home in the US to sell and only a few things to pack, mostly books and clothes. A coworker who Ed had recently hired has just relocated and is thrilled to accept Ed's rarely used furniture. Perfect timing for them both. Dr. Steven Allen is not thrilled. Still sad and disappointed by Ed's decision to leave for a woman, Steven says, "There are so many women in America, why do you need to have a girl in London?" He jokingly provides Ed a summary, "Women often have strange power over men. That's okay. I promise to hold your position open if things do not work out in London. I'm also giving you the end-of-year bonus, even though it's not required by company policy. And I'm adding a little extra."

Ultimately, Steven displays decency and respect for what Ed has done for the company. He also arranges a congratulations party by Zoom, with Ed's colleagues joining from their office workspaces and many others join from their homes. Their congratulations and laughter erupts unhindered, their celebration runs free. Steven offers the final comment by promising Ed that he will keep a position open, and reserve Ed's office in case he returns from London next year after recognizing his mistake in leaving the company.

It is strange for Ed as he prepares to leave the country from where he was born and grew up. First, he visits his parent's house in Ohio to say goodbye, promising to return for a visit at least once or twice per year. Finally, he pulls out his phone and opens up some recent photos that bring him joy. An image of

Lifang appears, and the stoic faces of his parents. He smiles from deep within.

The excitement and joy from his parents is overflowing as they closely inspect his photos of a Chinese woman who can also speak Chinese. This is a different degree of acceptance than when he introduced Samantha to them a number of years ago. Ed's two brothers are also visiting his parents during the holiday. They quickly grab his phone, raise their voices and shout their congratulations. They are not yet married and have been waiting for Ed as the oldest brother to make a move. This pressure is something Ed persistently felt as they waited in line behind Ed before they would marry. He now explains to them that he has wanted to change his job and live elsewhere for only a short time; to try out different things for a while, especially because of Lifang. This is a huge commitment for Ed, a decision to try out a new job and deepen a new relationship with Lifang in London, a foreign country where there are no familiar faces, no friends waiting for him. This is also an important step he will take in order to let go of Samantha from within his memory. It is a big step he must take to forget his first love who lingers in his heart. It is strange to Ed that a woman has such an important and crucial influence on his decision. He hates to admit this, but it is a reality he cannot escape.

***

As the Omicron infection rate doubles over the course of the holidays, many airlines cancel their domestic and international flights due to fewer and fewer availability of crew members who are calling in sick with positive COVID-19 tests. Airports are saturated with travelers during the holidays and passengers scramble to book flights that are mostly sold out, packed like sardines as the airline industry faces the most highly transmissible Omicron variant in densely populated airports and flights. Tensions rise, leading to a prevalence of violent behavior from travelers who gather courage often induced by alcohol. Verbal and physical confrontations are occurring in the air and captured on streaming videos. Certain passengers defy airlines' mask requirements. After boarding of flights and just prior to take-offs, flight attendants announce the federal laws and masking instructions, with actions that might be taken if passengers refuse to wear masks. The irony is laughable as the flight attendants announce the *'punishable by law'* commands, which are quickly followed by, *"We're so happy that you chose to fly with us!"*

Ed eventually boards his plane headed to London. As he closes a tiny window shield and settles into his first class seat, he silently says goodbye to the American sky. His parents had immigrated to this great country to have better lives. It is peculiar that he grew up in this dream country, made a successful life, and yet now he is immigrating to another country to have a better life. Where is a better place than America? Yet, his heart is set on a woman who lives elsewhere and that is the better place, wherever that is under the sky.

He thanks God that he did not work for the J&J company. A panel of experts from the Centers for Disease Control and Prevention recently made a unanimous decision recommending people not to get the J&J vaccine if those developed by Pfizer and Ed's company are available. While it won't matter much to J&J as a business—in the third quarter their vaccine generated only $500 million of the company's $23 billion in revenue—it is unfortunate the company receives a direct 'push to the back' from the CDC due to rare but undesirable side effects, such as blood clots and thrombotic thrombocytopenia syndrome. J&J is under the weight of a mountain of bad PR, unbeatable bad luck with a tragic ending. If he had worked with J&J, he most likely would not have been offered a job in London.

A thought of Samantha briefly comes to mind, but Ed decides against sending her a text that he's leaving the US and moving to London. He sets his phone to airplane mode.

Chapter 47

Garbage pileup

December 27, 2021

It has been two years since the world woke up to meet COVID-19 which originated in Wuhan, China, and the world has never been the same. Two Christmas holidays have passed and COVID-19 is still not over, remaining resilient to infect people even though remedies exist to fight it. This variant thrives in the upper airways and becomes contagious fast, dodging many of the antibodies in vaccinated people and among some previously infected with COVID. Omicron had arrived at a perfectly opportune time, in terms of the virus. The cold, winter holiday season in the US offers the virus a larger pool of hosts, allowing its infection rates to skyrocket at a time when many people became weary and indifferent to wearing a mask. Although the Omicron variant purportedly brings milder symptoms, the sheer number of infections causes hospitalizations to increase — including children. Millions of people line up for booster shots and thousands of testing sites are quickly booked for COVID testing. These are sought-after precautions against Omicron before employees return to workplaces and children return to schools. CDC has shortened the quarantine time to five days after a person tests positive for COVID. However, the person must be asymptomatic, in part because of the shortage of workers in aviation, hospitals, and schools. This new 5-day requirement surprises and confuses citizens who were recently told quarantines should be 10 days, which followed the initial 14-day quarantine requirement near the start of the pandemic. Numerous experts believe the new CDC declaration is non-scientific. The incubation time for Omicron is widely known to commence 2–3 days before symptoms begin, and continues for at least 5 days after the symptoms. The CDC and other health organizations are apparently rationing in favor of businesses rather than acknowledging the actual scientific data of infections.

Common themes are now appearing. The Omicron variant is much like a common cold; infections are considered as ordinary upper respiratory infections; recovery times are short, within one to two weeks. But the long-term effects are still unknown.

Meanwhile, the word *'mandate'* became problematic, wrapped up in semantics and scorned within discussions, often separated by red and blue concepts rather than looking into the main point of interest to protect people's lives, particularly in a freedom-seeking country such as America. Wearing a mask became a requirement in New York State in July of 2021, when Governor Cuomo mandated that all state employees must receive vaccinations by Labor Day, or undergo weekly testing for COVID. These included workers in education, hospitals, health care, police and fire departments, correctional facilities, transportation, and sanitation; essentially within all governmental and civil service departments. Going further, vaccines would be mandatory for all 'front-line' workers at state-owned hospitals. No allowance would be offered to avoid the vaccine requirement by undergoing frequent testing.

By late October, an estimated 9,000 unvaccinated New York City municipal workers had left their jobs, unpaid, after the mayor required City employees to be vaccinated by November 1. This led to immense garbage pile ups in many areas of New York City as roughly 17% of the City's sanitation workers refused to get the vaccines, in turn causing an alarming increase in rats, many which carry diseases including hantavirus and leptospirosis. This situation threatened another epidemic, if not a pandemic crisis.

Chapter 48

Over my dead body!

December 29, 2021

False accusations against the government are spreading. The number of COVID-19 deaths are presumed to be exaggerated; the government is covering up deaths tied to vaccines; ivermectin is claimed as a better treatment for COVID-19 in face of the fact that ivermectin is a broad spectrum antiparasitic agent used mostly for the treatment of onchocerciasis—also known as river-blindness—for strongyloidiasis, for soil-transmitted helminthiasis, and even for scabies. Skepticism and anger increases. Baseless notions arise that the vaccines cause infertility, or cause COVID infections. Void of any proof, claims are made that the vaccines contain a microchip; the vaccines can alter human DNA and may eventually screw up our bodies; the vaccine liquid contains harmful and impure substances; the vaccines use or contain aborted fetal cells; and pregnant women should not receive a COVID vaccine. Claims based on fear abound by comparing vaccine mandates to medical experiments conducted by Nazi Germany and Imperial Japan. These beliefs are not the source of truth, but tyranny will continue. One bright spot is that one particular false narrative that was rampant in 2020 has finally died down; hydroxychloroquine is now widely understood to have no evidence for treating COVID-19, and it can cause serious side effects. Surely, there will be more skepticisms and even more creative ways to attack the integrity of science and the government. Gossip and false information is viral, spreading like wildfires. Ash dust travels in all four wind directions until settling. In time, the truth will be seen and be known.

***

Samantha reads in her hospital's email newsletter that ER has reported one of their patients came with COVID-19 symptoms and demanded that the ER doctors treat him only with ivermectin. His 'ferociously loud tone and demeanor' exploded while he refused all other treatments including oxygen, antiviral injection, and ventilation. He absolutely refused to get a vaccine jab. The patient stated, "Over my dead body will I get a vaccine shot!"

Immediately one of the ER doctors replied, "You can get the ivermectin drug from the drug store, and we do not provide ivermectin from this hospital."

The doctor then refused hospital admission to the patient. Immediately, the patient and his family shouted countless profanities never before heard in hospital corridors, ensuring everyone in the ER would hear their cries. He also threatened to sue the doctors and the hospital, including malpractice upon COVID patients. Even while dying in bed, countless patients like this man have pronounced that 'they will never get the jabs.' The trust, respect, and reliance toward medical doctors has visibly declined during the pandemic. The basic etiquette of respect is eroding before our eyes, and expectations of basic politeness and appropriate behaviors is futile in preserving human dignity. It is difficult and often impossible to accept or treat such patients, humans who are ignorant of the medical truths about the virus, who think they know better than doctors and demand certain treatments they believe in, embracing misinformation and outrageous lies as truths that are pouring out like waste from social media.

Scientific studies, however, show that without a vaccination program, there would have been approximately 1.1 million additional COVID-19 deaths (3.2 times higher) and more than 10.3 million additional COVID-19 hospitalizations (4.9 times higher) in the US at this point in time. Since one in five eligible people have not received vaccinations, 551,126 unnecessary additional COVID deaths in the US have occurred. Sadly, the rapid development of a successful vaccine program had no chance of being celebrated, a program that had advanced our boundaries of scientific discoveries, a truly breakthrough technology program. Instead, it became a program heavily politicized, impossible to celebrate due to polarized opinions.

Considerable numbers of people have been questioning, "Why vaccinate?" This thinking seems based upon assumptions; that breakthrough cases are common with Omicron, that

Omicron is a less severe form of COVID and therefore beneficial because it can infect more people and then we can finally achieve herd immunity. It is true that Omicron is seen to be associated with a 53% reduction in the risk of symptomatic hospitalization, and a 74% reduction in the risk of intensive-care admission, and a 91% reduction in the risk of dying. However, a staggering number of people are seeking emergency care and hospital admissions as infections soar, particularly in California with an astonishing average of 101,000 cases a day that is far above last winter's record of 46,000 cases a day.

Chapter 49

Who is left to help the sick and dying?

December 30, 2021

Nearly one out of five health care workers in the US are estimated to have opted to retire early, quit their jobs, or walked out on their jobs. This is even prior to the large-scale walkouts of municipal workers seen in New York City during October. Many nurses in Samantha's hospital quit their jobs and became on-call or 'floating' nurses. Other employees, particularly those who were flexible to move or without family ties, moved to whatever states or positions that were in need. These jobs frequently offer higher pay within better organized systems. Very often they would also receive more respect. While certain nurses might make more money than physicians, they would lose many employment benefits. Respiratory technologists also became high in demand, and like nurses, their positions were hard to fill in most states even prior to the pandemic.

More importantly, the remaining health care workers are increasingly becoming infected and draining our hospitals that are desperately short on staff. Who will attend to the sick and dying?

Samantha commonly sees close colleagues who suddenly become infected with COVID and cannot show up to work. This occurs nearly every morning. The entire team of pathology physician assistants (PAs) in her department have called in sick or tested positive following COVID rapid tests. Most are now unable to work. Many residents across all specialties also began calling in sick due to positive COVID rapid tests. Chaos at work swells amid an urgency of retaining the bare number of qualified people who can perform critical work for patients. The healthy people must pick up additional and unexpected duties in addition to their already heavy workloads. Sickness never staggers conveniently to prepare appropriately.

Every morning someone must assess who is actually showing

up at work and divide the duties among those who show up at work; fluid models need to be adopted. As an example, at the end of December, more than a dozen histotechnicians at Samantha's hospital who make the pathology slides are sick with COVID-19. Hence, physicians cannot do their work even if they come to work. Heavy loads of work depends on a few histotechnicians; those who make the slides have become the most important people in the department since they are positioned most upstream in the department. All those who are downstream must wait, including the pathology attending physicians and the pathology residents. This topsy-turvy and chaotic work is not unique to the pathology department. Samantha sees it in all departments of the hospital. The most visibly vulnerable areas in hospitals are the COVID units and the ICU, due to a lack of nurses, a news story repeated nearly evening across the country.

Samantha still serves as the interim chief resident, and it looks like the demands and challenges of her job are here to stay until June of next year when she moves to San Francisco for her fellowship. Her department is shattered by this pandemic. Employees also need long-term mental care to recover, exacerbated by Dr. Wells' departure. Samantha currently covers more service levels than her job requires, or her time allows. She must now perform the role of a pathology PA: The person who cuts the gross specimens.

Samantha assumes the national board exam scores for residents will be lower for all those who endure the COVID-19 pandemic during their years of residency training. Paradoxically, medical school applications have increased significantly, up nearly 20%. The admissions department attributes this to the 'Fauci effect.' In essence, Dr. Anthony Fauci became the most famous and visible physician who inspires a new generation, while angering others.

Increasing demands at workplaces inevitably leads to internal fighting, further inflamed amid growing strains from politics, in parallel with rampant disbelief in the government. The mental health of citizens continues to roam unchecked during the COVID-19 pandemic, and large numbers of health care workers are suffering for nearly two exhausting years.

Good morale is absent among the attending physicians and residents in many hospitals. In Samantha's hospital, many who have *not* tested positive are not even showing up at work unless specifically required, citing emotional or physical exhaustion, lack of sleep, work-related dread, compassion fatigue, and burnout. Unspoken symptoms abound; low self-esteem, relentless anxiety of COVID exposure, and suicidal thoughts. Even her department chair does not come into work, and people will generally follow their leader.

As the end of another year approaches, hospitals also see an influx in non-elective cancer surgeries, elective procedures, and elective surgeries. Hospital beds swell above maximum capacity with COVID and non-COVID patients. Surgeons schedule operations on weekends and at nights, and these require pathologists like Samantha to stay late into the night with surgeons. Hope dissolves as patchy increases in workloads climb higher. Communication from leadership is absent or vague, and frustration leads to anger by a persistently insufficient allotment of PPE—even when performing autopsies where COVID-19 is shown to be the underlying cause of death.

Among Samantha and her fellow residents, anxiety sets in as they acknowledge their insufficient training. Concerns and anxiety had surged after their colleague Giti died from COVID-19, and surged again during their harrowing gun incident, and again as their chief resident Aaron died from COVID-19. Their remaining stability was lost when Dr. Wells, their residency director, walked out of the hospital. This fostered more insecurity and fragility to their wellbeing. They lost trust in their leaders to represent their voice of residency issues, and their entire residency program has no structural protections that remain. Medical training has become a remote priority for the hospital leaders, blatantly apparent as very few attending physicians show up at the hospital to train residents. Those who do show up will fervently maintain their distance from residents, even while wearing a face mask. They speak at a low volume, some with heavy accents, all of which creates a hit-or-miss form of teaching. After 20 or 30 minutes of training with residents, the attendings often leave for home. Samantha confirms with her former med school classmates that this same situation is occurring in residency training programs across the country.

Every man for himself has become the norm.

Chapter 50

Jeju Island

December 31, 2021

While Samantha manages unforeseen difficulties as interim chief resident, her mother calls from Korea. Emily cautiously explains that in late November she had an overwhelming desire to visit her sisters for a month or two, and describes to Samantha how they eventually bought a home together.

Shortly after her arrival, she and her sisters took the short flight from Seoul down to Jeju Island for a vacation. Emily is the last child of five kids, with two brothers and two sisters: one sister three years older than Emily, the other five years older. They all have families of their own and live comfortably in Korea. It is Emily who suggested the idea of living together and day by day the sisters discussed what that would look like. The idea of three elderly women living together is precarious according to traditional Korean thinking. The connotation and judgment that will follow is that the children of these women are not filial enough to take care of their own mothers. Emily was vaguely aware of this traditional Korean thinking, but not willing to close the chapter on exploring new ways of living. After all, she had grown tired of living in America and experienced an anti-Asian attack — even in San Francisco. Her large house is too big and burdensome. She is saddened by only one thing — missing Samantha.

One evening while the sisters were watching the ocean on the patio of a coffee shop, the waves soothing. She calmly speaks.

"My daughter was recently accepted to a famous school, the University of California in San Francisco, for a year-long fellowship training to be near me. I never wanted to burden Samantha. I will not prohibit her from getting the best education and the best opportunity for marriage. I cannot allow my daughter to carry the baggage of taking care of her own mother. This is how I feel. I will tell Samantha."

The next day the sisters began looking at homes while they

discussed and considered the option of living together. Two weeks on the island passed and their search for an appropriate house became nonstop. So, Emily convinced her sisters to move into a home on Jeju Island. The three sisters selected a house which she would then buy, for them to live together. Their new house overlooks the ocean with four bedrooms and four bathrooms; one for each sister and one guest room for family visits. She plans to hire workers with helpful hands to help them cook and clean daily. Her sisters had eventually agreed to live their elderly lives in this unconventional way, joyful being together and catching up after years of separation following childhood. They entered the home to pick up the keys, and began crying and hugging.

Samantha is startled, and thrilled her mother is happy returning to her birth country and living on Jeju Island. She also feels a deep loss, even a bit of betrayal because she had signed a contract with UCSF for a year of fellowship training located near her mother's home. Her cross-country move from New York to San Francisco is 3,000 miles, and now she must also help her mom by moving her to a different continent that is 5,600 miles away, and also help manage the sale of her mother's home. When Samantha lost her father, she considered a new way of life to live near her mom and develop a more intimate relationship with her. But now, her mother is defending the decision to move further away, claiming this will give Samantha more freedom and allow her to be married without the 'parent baggage.' Samantha has never felt burdened by her mother nor considered her as 'baggage.' She had carefully pondered her options and had concluded to live with her mother and take care of her. Samantha also wonders about Mrs. Kong, her mother's friend and neighbor. *What happens to her?* Samantha asks herself. Perhaps reading her mind, Emily explains that once Mrs. Kong learned of her move to Korea, she also decided to sell her enormous house next year and move into her first son's home in Texas. Her mobility difficulties have increased and even going to the grocery store is a painful experience. Emily had been Mrs. Kong's companion and even her designated driver as her vision grew dim and forced her to stop driving. Aging is no joke. Every day has brought them both new challenges. Things in the past seem a distant memory for the once vibrant ladies.

The elderly find themselves their own places to rest and die. It is up to the younger generation of people to either follow the elderly and risk losing their own identities, or live without them and gain self-identity. It seems ideal if the elderly are able to sacrifice and follow the younger people, but often that is not the case. Emily does not budge in her decision no matter how convincing Samantha becomes. Stubbornness is a lasting character trait that will increase with age. Samantha can live near her mother, but only if she follows her and moves to Jeju Island. To Samantha, Korea is a foreign country. Although she can relate to them on some levels, even in her DNA, she is unfamiliar with anything Korean: the language, culture, upbringing, education, and to some degree, even food. Samantha will be a non-functional person in Korea, unable to speak their language to start with. She cannot practice medicine in Korea, at least for a while. Her own identity and the work for which she aspires would be lost.

Samantha makes her decision. Early next year she will help her mother sell the San Francisco house, the very house she grew up in. She will honor her contract and search for a small campus apartment when she moves to UCSF to complete her fellowship. After her fellowship, she can pretty much go anywhere to get a job. Most likely, New York or California. Samantha had envisioned herself providing care for her elderly mother, even holding her tight in her arms in the last minutes of life—this dream is shattered. Some people tell Samantha that she can finally enjoy complete freedom. What is the price of complete freedom when one loses the person one cares about the most? It is in the bonding and social interaction where one truly finds complete joy and freedom.

This pandemic changed everything for Samantha. Her mother's decision to move was rooted from the Anti-Asian attack upon her, preceded by the demise of her husband. Samantha lost her father at the beginning of the pandemic, then her encounter with Dr. Falkner and his rapid death from COVID-19 after performing autopsies, followed by her friend Giti's death, her roommate and colleague. Less than a year later came the tragic loss of Aaron, her chief resident, countless changes in her residency program and the departure of Dr. Wells. Everyone either separated or scattered. Nothing seems the same, but this life goes on for her. Every new day brings challenges, seemingly insignificant and menial things to fulfill like eating, working, waking up and getting up, cleaning, but each activity is a blessing in life. She witnessed hundreds of COVID-infected patients lying sick in bed, some dying in a comatose state, unable to undertake any single mundane activity. The seemingly boring and mundane things in life are the true blessing. Life is taken for granted without understanding the significance and blessings when we have life. Time is the most important gift in life. Samantha must cherish every day as a new day, worshiping God, counting her blessings in wonder, embracing what the next day will bring as long as she has the breath. We are born alone and die alone. But when we are alone, in solitude, God speaks and draws us near to Him.

Chapter 51

Wedding Invitation

February 22, 2022

Samantha receives a London wedding invitation from Ed and Lifang, with an explanation of why they chose a marriage date of 2/22/22:

Twosday is a once-in-a lifetime palindrome date that reads the same forward or backward. In the Chinese language, 'two' and 'love' are similar concepts in a love relationship, and the words are phonetically similar. Hence, 2/22/2022 is to be an auspicious day for love. The date is also the 22nd day of the first month of the Lunar calendar and falls on a Tuesday, the second day of the week — making it a day full of twos that won't occur again for another 200 years.

The wedding invitation includes their photograph. Ed appears happy, his cheek touching Lifang's cheek, and both have big smiles. Their wedding is to occur on a patio at his company's headquarters in London, a rather small wedding with a minister, parents from both sides, a few friends, so Samantha assumes perhaps less than 50 people are planned for the gathering.

No way, of course I won't attend, Samantha concludes. It would be awkward.

Samantha is happy that Ed found his love, but surprised how fast his wedding came to fruition. She possesses a mix of feelings, without knowing her exact emotions. She has known Ed for more than a decade and never reached a point of marrying him.

She wonders, *How long has Ed known Lifang in order for him to arrive at a point of marriage? Did he know Lifang while he was still dating me? This is a man commonly perceived as a serious type of person who would not rush a loving relationship toward marriage without weighing things out carefully; pros and cons decided by logic. Lifang, by her appearance in the photo, seems at least ten years younger than Ed. When did they meet? Did Ed rush into marriage to not prolong his pain of separation with me?*

STOP!

She dislikes her own thoughts. *Just be happy for them, Samantha. I have nothing to do with Ed anymore! I am the one who terminated the relationship.*

Then she hears her mom's voice. *You are not getting younger. Your biological time is ticking. You should think about having a baby before your ovaries get dried up. Ed is a good man who loves you very much.*

Samantha knows all of this. She had chosen never to sacrifice her own life for the sake of her reproduction time bomb. She created extensive changes to herself only through significant effort from within, and ultimately she matured into understanding and accepting that she cannot live to fulfill other people's expectations. Any man who she might love would be required to accept and love her the way she is, even if she may not fully know or understand herself. This was shown to her from Dr. Faulkner, holding her while letting her be, with complete freedom and without any of his expectations or judgments. There was room to breathe, freedom to find herself within the relationship, without suffocation from mutual families. Most of all, Samantha felt religious freedom with Dr. Faulkner. She did not have to attend and respect the religion of Ed's parents, of Buddhism and their ancestral Buddhist temple ceremonies. She could not picture herself bowing down to an image of Ed's great grandfather and grandmother in the annual ancestral rites and celebrations, accompanied with clusters—small mounds—of carefully selected food items. She would not bow down to any gods or dead persons. Being a woman in that Asian culture, she would be required to fulfill all of the family requirements and be submissive to the authority of numerous and unknown family members. Her whole relationship with Ed slowly suffocated her, seeing herself in torment with her own identity. She would not step into a relationship of marriage knowing that it would kill her over time. The expectations of being an Asian woman in Asian culture would be to lose her identity as an individual while gaining an illusion of power through a long endurance of self-disintegration for the sake of family in the end, aged and old. She observed this in her own mother as well, even though she married an American man.

Something about that is beautiful, as well as sad. While Samantha is still figuring out who she is and is to come, she cannot bear to live in such a stifling and restricting environment where other people will define for you who you are, and who you should be. For this, she was very proud of her strength to fight back and terminate her relationship with Ed.

***

Death seemed more imminent when the Omicron wave arrived, killing more than 2,000 people a day as it reminds Samantha how precious life is, to not waste any single day in a bondage of other people's expectations of who she should be. The Omicron wave has been deadlier than the Delta surge. More than 120,000 people in the US have died since Omicron became the dominant variant in December, with death rates 14 times higher for unvaccinated adults. Millions of people died with COVID-19. Remembrance of the dead will fade quickly, and living will pursue next menial things to do.

Life will go on. COVID-19 will go on. The pandemic will exit from people's minds regardless of longevity or viability of the virus. Samantha moves on to prepare for her fellowship. Ed goes on to his blissful marriage in London. Emily will finally sleep with ease among her sisters on Jeju Island, able to speak freely in her own language without correcting her grammar. One thing is for sure; everyone will go on living. No one is guaranteed to have another day of life on this earth, and Bible scripture gives us a promise that says, "The Lord himself goes before you and will be with you; he will never leave you nor forsake you. Do not be afraid; do not be discouraged" (Deuteronomy 31:8).

Later, David also wrote in Psalm 37:3–4, "Trust in the Lord and do good; dwell in the land and enjoy safe pasture. Take delight in the Lord, and he will give you the desires of your heart."

Writer's point of view

The Black and Purple Deaths

In human history, the bubonic plague was the most fatal, initially called the *Black Death.* About 50 million people died, mostly in the European and Mediterranean regions, from 1346–1353. It wiped out 60% of Europe's entire population.

The second deadliest? The influenza virus, also known as the Spanish flu of 1918, and initially termed the *Purple Death,* claimed more than 21 million lives. During that 1918 influenza pandemic, an estimated 103 million people lived in the US and the virus killed 1 in every 150 Americans, compared to 1 in 500 who have died from COVID-19 among 331.4 million Americans. The 1918 pandemic did not have a vaccine.

The recent pandemic of COVID-19 had claimed over 7 million deaths from around the world from 2020–2024. In the US, there were 1,199,333 deaths and over 6 million hospitalizations due to COVID-19, primarily during four distinctive waves: Alpha, Beta, Delta, and Omicron. The spread of the virus is much more rampant due to global traveling and its accessibility of transmission to every part of the world in a modern society. Through the rapid discovery and use of vaccines, we were able to claim far fewer global deaths when compared to the bubonic plague and influenza pandemics. As of this date, it is estimated that at least 3 out of 4 people in the US experienced a COVID-19 infection at least once. This includes those with or without vaccinations.

Long COVID

Of those people with a COVID positive infection, data has shown 17.6% experience what is known as *Long COVID* (45.4 million adults), which is a condition that occurs when patients still have symptoms at least four weeks after they have cleared the infection. It was first detected during an autopsy study among those who died with COVID-19. The patients with Long COVID had detectable viral RNA in the stool, urine and blood plasma. The culprit is likely due to lingering virus, harboring and replicating viral RNA found in the brain, muscle, gut, and lungs. Symptoms include prolonged respiratory problems, dysautonomia, and brain fog with cognitive deficits, most likely caused by microclots. Dysautonomia is an umbrella term for abnormalities in the autonomic nervous system which cause disruption of heart rate, breathing and digestive function. Long COVID is also generally defined as having fatigue or other characteristic symptoms at least three months after infection.

The race of vaccines and mutations

New vaccines always lag the speed of virus mutations. Certain coronavirus mutations that gain hyper-contagious status, and more potent variants, can almost be guaranteed. Unless the coronavirus mutates to a non-virulent level by accident, or people collectively accept the level of impact the virus inflicts endemically, its rampant infection will continue. For example, the CDC estimates that between 2010 and 2023, the influenza virus known as the flu resulted in 4,900–51,000 deaths annually, 110,000–710,000 hospitalizations, and 9.3–41 million illnesses. By default, these rates are considered acceptable by health experts, governmental bodies, and the general public. In comparison, the CDC tabulates that a little over 47,000 deaths in 2024 were attributed to COVID-19, as listed on death certificates. People will have differing opinions as to what constitutes an acceptable level, and the debate will continue where the benchmarks should be. One thing almost for certain: There will not be a complete end of COVID-19, no on-off switch; perhaps a dimmer switch at best.

Who made mistakes?

Looking back upon the evolution of COVID-19, there are many complexities and mistakes in handling the pandemic crisis. This includes WHO, lack of sharing information internationally, US political parties, scientific and health care communities, communication to the US public—or lack thereof—and media coverage. Non-health experts and self-proclaimed experts spoke too much regardless of their expertise, while the scientific and health experts spoke too little and too late. Conjectures about science and politically based conjecture should be clearly delineated by medical experts, our leaders, and the media, especially when public health is acutely in the balance as seen during this global pandemic. The pandemonic activity caused by COVID-19 within the US government, the CDC, and the NIH arrived amid an overall lack of preparation, with no strategic goals and a delay in communications. COVID-19 policies were left to each state, county, university, workplace, and school district, leaving an uncontrolled experiment with every strategy and often no strategy, all at once.

There were many unintentional mistakes and certain misinformation that was provided by scientists, including infectious disease specialists, epidemiologists, virologists, and public health experts, and these mistakes often undermined virus potency, including comments like 'it is just like a bad flu,' and 'this only affects the elderly,' and even 'you don't need to wear masks.' During the initial stage of a pandemic, people need to know what it is, how it could be transmitted, risks involved, how to prevent becoming infected, and what to do and what not to do. But scientists were not delivering this information with speed nor with clarity. Virologists and medical doctors were not in sync with their messages. Conspiracy theories quickly evolved, making confusion of who might be telling the truth. As scientists interpreted rapidly evolving data to deliver unbiased viewpoints, competing information became distributed by non-scientific, non-expert faceless figures who generated personal income by higher numbers of people who viewed their claims. These people quickly disseminated unsubstantiated claims mingled with political agendas, facts versus opinions, and effectively degraded the quality of scientific findings. Suddenly, everyone became a physician without an appropriate license.

Herd immunity

At one point, we thought herd immunity by vaccination would end the COVID-19 pandemic. But we did not factor into the equation roughly 30% of our US population: Anti-vaxxers. This factor meant herd immunity could not be achieved. Unwillingness to vaccinate infants and toddlers of vaccinated parents would bring the total to more than 50%, making herd immunity even more unlikely.

Waning immunity

Another component of the equation would be the waning immunity gained by vaccination, and unequal potency of vaccinations caused by the variety of vaccine choices. All of these variables created a haven for researchers to collect myriads of data for their publications. An overly optimistic herd immunity became a distant hope by a virus constantly mutating into more transmissible forms. Vaccine works best if the virus is stable, not airborne transmissible, and newer variants that are few in number. SARS-CoV-2 and influenza viruses are not stable, mutation occurs frequently, and hence the goal cannot be complete eradication.

A better goal

An effective goal is to manage outbreaks and reduce the rates of moderate-to-severe illness and death. Booster shots and annual updated shots is a hopeful scenario as we observe a waning of antibody titers, new variants, and antigenic drift. Wearing masks may be here to stay with the added benefit of preventing flu as well as the coronavirus, even as a barrier to certain air pollution and allergies. But this too has become a political statement rather than a personal intelligent choice under the umbrella of freedom. Many states began lifting mask requirements even before the Omicron variant began to subside, and even as the BA.2 variant of Omicron began emerging.

What else stays with us forever?

One, political opinion differences and beliefs. On September 18, 2022, President Biden stated that the pandemic stage of the virus was over in the US, but in August of 2024 California experienced their highest spike of cases since the summer of 2022.

Two, disproportionate numbers of sick people are in poverty and at higher risk of infection. Additionally, one study has shown that for each 100,000 Americans (of their respective group), the highest actual mortality rate from COVID-19 showed 256 for Indigenous people, followed by 180 for Black people and 147 for Latinos. White and Asian people were shown to have the lowest death rates.

At the start of the pandemic it was common to say that we are all in this together, but in the end, more poor people are seen dying with the virus than from any other disease.

Third, we may never know the origin of COVID-19, unlike most other pandemic viruses.

Fourth, there will be another pandemic. It is a matter of when, not if. The next one could certainly be deadlier than COVID-19.

Fifth, skepticism.

The March of Dimes

In 1955, millions of mass inoculations of children in the US against poliovirus was tumultuous, not dissimilar to the COVID-19 vaccination program. One of our highest points of respect for scientific discovery was the introduction of a Polio vaccine. Infantile paralysis affected mostly children in the US and peaked in 1952, with nearly 60,000 children affected by poliovirus—21,000 cases resulting in paralysis, and killing 3,000 children. Scientists had no idea how the virus was transmitted, causing people to shut down pools and keeping children inside their homes. When the polio vaccine was approved for use in 1955, church bells rang in jubilation, people were thrilled, and parents eagerly waited in lines to sign up their kids for a shot. Physicians and scientists were overwhelmingly trusted, and citizens commonly contributed to research funds. Armies of mothers went door to door asking only for a dime. Hence the name, 'March of Dimes' following its initial name as the National Foundation of Infantile Paralysis. The foundation was established in 1938 by President Franklin D. Roosevelt, who personally became infected with the virus in 1921 at age 39.

One of the six labs that first manufactured the polio vaccine was Cutter Laboratories in Berkeley, CA. Cutter made a terrible mistake and manufactured a defective Salk vaccine composed of the live virus instead of the killed, or 'inactivated' poliovirus. As a result, batches of the vaccine went out containing the active poliovirus. Ultimately, at least 40,000 children were infected with the poliovirus, 164 were severely paralyzed, and 10 died. This led to temporarily halting the vaccination process. After pinpointing the problem, the vaccinations restarted within weeks. People generally understood and accepted that the risk of contracting poliovirus was a much greater threat than the risk posed by a vaccine. The country continued to trust in science. Because of that trust, the poliovirus was essentially eradicated in the US. The poliovirus continues to infect hundreds of people each year where vaccinations are not given, according to some estimates. The Gates Foundation notes that polio could make a resurgence to 200,000 per year, and yet polio could be eliminated from the planet if all populations accepted vaccinations.

Murky origins of SARS-CoV-2

Facts about the genetic sequence of SARS-CoV-2, which in turn led to COVID-19 vaccine development, remains a bit murky. In February 2020, WHO predicted a vaccine against SARS-CoV-2 would not be available for at least 18 months. However, the very first vaccine originated from China on June 24, 2020, merely seven months after the virus itself was identified. It is not surprising that China was the first country to manufacture the first vaccine, because Chinese researchers mapped out the virus and quietly uploaded a nearly complete sequence of the virus to a genetic database on December 28, 2019. This was at least two weeks before Beijing even revealed details of the deadly virus to WHO, described below. The genetic database was GenBank, run by researchers at the US National Institutes of Health. Dr. Lili Ren at the Beijing-based Institute of Pathogen Biology, as part of the state-affiliated Chinese Academy of Medical Science, was one of the researchers who isolated and mapped out the virus's sequence. The US Centers for Disease Control and Prevention in Atlanta stated that the SARS-Cov-2 sequences were shared within China, specifically with China's equivalent of the CDC, on January 5, 2020. On January 12, 2020, China shared the virus's sequence with the WHO. However, the viral sequence that Dr. Ren provided on December 28, 2019, was never published — and was quickly deleted from the database on January 16, 2020.

China's CanSino was the first vaccine introduced for limited use in the military, and their two inactivated virus vaccines were introduced for emergency use in high-risk occupations. On August 11, 2020, Russia announced their approval of its Sputnik V vaccine for emergency use. Both of these vaccines were not used nor available in the US, where a record number of fast-track vaccines were being developed. The two primary vaccines from

Pfizer and Moderna both use mRNA technology. On November 20, 2020, Pfizer released the mRNA vaccine BNT162b2, and the United Kingdom was the first country to approve this vaccine and the first country in the 'Western' world to approve its use. On December 11, 2020, the United States Food and Drug Administration (FDA) granted an Emergency Use Authorization for the Pfizer COVID-19 vaccine. A week later, the FDA granted an Emergency Use Authorization for the Moderna mRNA-1273 vaccine. As mentioned in my book, AstraZeneca and Johnson & Johnson vaccines are not mRNA technology, but were important in the early months of slowing the pandemic. Although developed and used later in the US, both vaccines faced very few but undesirable complications causing blood clot and deaths on rare occasions.

Devastation by lies

Scientists have found that mRNA technology used for COVID-19 vaccination results in very rare cases of myocarditis in certain people, but the benefit of controlling infectiousness of this virus and dampening the death rates is well worth such risks that are extremely rare. Even more striking, COVID-19 vaccines mutated into a fight for freedom, first amendment demands, and the rights of individual choice in a battle against vaccines. Just like Salk in 1955, American scientists discovered amazing technologies to fight a virus. Today, discovery that mRNA can be used against COVID-19 has led to the most effective vaccines ever seen in the world. Losing millions of lives is devastating, but most of us who practice medicine have sorrow amid a frustration from misinformation, false rumors, and conspiracy theories with intention to confuse others while pushing deeper political purposes, often for personal and financial gain. The waves of misinformation have spread and mutated beyond the scope of scientific studies or proven facts, ignoring any review of fact-based literature which in turn fosters the viral spread of fear and lies. This lowers the level of trust in our government, health care institutions, and efforts toward public health and safety. The rights and beliefs of an individual person easily overrides our American mentality during chaotic times of uncertainty. While the world is fighting a pandemic, it is also fighting an 'infodemic' in which falseness spreads quicker, further, and easier than truths. Meanwhile, our scientists are unseen or silent, or far too late in debunking misinformation. Misery seems to compound all at once and ugliness comes out in chaotic times. Time will tell what is true.

Perfectly designed

COVID-19 did exactly what was expected from it; to become more infectious with increasing potency. Looking at historical facts of pandemics, only with quick and effective vaccinations were we able to survive without experiencing 50 million or even 21 million deaths described above.

Many who oppose COVID-19 vaccination are ignorant of one important fact: mRNA technology is not new; what is new is COVID-19. Scientists have been working on mRNA for many decades, and its use in vaccines could have been a cause for another jubilation; church bells should have once again rung in celebration.

Doubts, faith, and facts

Doubts about the vaccine? Look at the data. Look around us. Look at the patterns. Jesus in the New Testament performed at least 37 documented miracles. One of them is the story of Lazarus, a man who died and four days later was raised back to life by Jesus, who said at the time as recorded by John, "I am the resurrection and the life. The one who believes in me will live, even though they die; and whoever lives by believing in me will never die" (John 11:25–26). He then asked, "Do you believe this?"

How many people at the scene actually doubted, even after seeing Lazarus walk out of the tomb, and alive? Many likely assumed Lazarus had never really died, even though it is recorded that he had a stench. Skeptics who witnessed the scene came up with different scenarios and conclusions. Conversely, how many people in the vicinity—but did not witness the miracle—believed that Jesus did indeed raise Lazarus from death? How many of us today have some doubt that the Lazarus story is true? There can be numerous, different twists to this story that our minds can create. Perhaps Lazarus had undergone deep sleep by a barbiturate substance and appeared dead.

Perhaps Lazarus and his sisters Martha and Mary plotted and made up a story that he was dead, so that it would appear Jesus possessed infinite powers of resurrecting the dead. Perhaps the people who saw Lazarus walking out of the tomb were all delusional. Perhaps some people acknowledged this miracle, but still would not believe it. Perhaps Jesus never even existed. Perhaps there is no God. Perhaps there will be no hell or heaven.

Where is the limit for the doubt? When does trust begin? Where is our faith? What is the truth and what is the fact? Did false prophets exist even in the Bible era? What did they look like? Were they distinguishable from common people? Why is God silent? Why is God quiet about the vaccine? Why did God allow this pandemic to occur in 2019? Did George Washington, our first president, really exist? In the year 2021, did anyone see George Washington? How do we know he even existed? It takes faith to know George Washington existed since no one from this era saw him. Why do we believe in history textbooks? No one currently has seen George Washington as a living human being, but nearly all of us have no doubt that he actually existed, led an army to victory at Yorktown and was the first president of the US. Why do people believe these events today even without meeting Mr. Washington, and yet not believe in a vaccine that exists today where one can actually see the benefits of significantly fewer hospitalizations and lower infection rates than unvaccinated people?

Some Christians carry microphones along a street to deliver their message about the hell that exists even in their own loving hearts and pour out the message of a salvation that is available to all. Some watch, others step aside, some listen with interest while others are irritated, some ignore, some are oblivious and some intentionally reject the message of salvation. No matter how a scientist, doctor, friend, loved one, politician or celebrity sends a message about vaccination, the message is ignored by some, while others become irritated, and some will comment 'of course I was vaccinated,' while others may proclaim 'you will not violate my rights and freedom!' Some will deny even while becoming cyanotic, their faces bluish in color as they lay dying and unvaccinated. People want to believe what they want to believe. Ultimately, the consequences to others or themselves are their own choice. Free will is the most powerful weapon we have, but it comes with a hefty price of consequences. The only sure things in life are death, paying taxes, and perpetual mutation in viruses.

A parade of variants

We continue to experience variants with varying degrees of transmissibility with SARS-CoV-2. Such a virus is always a few steps ahead of our capacity to catch up to the antigenic changes affecting vaccine protection. By April 2021, there were at least five major variants depending on the regions they were found, labeled by the CDC as *Variants of Concern*, or VOC. Other variants will likely be added to the list.

B.1.1.7 (Alpha), first detected in the UK and known to be 50% more transmissible, and found in Florida, Michigan and Colorado.

P.1 (Gamma), first detected in Brazil and Japan, and the US had reported 323 cases of this variant.

B.1.351 (Beta), first detected in South Africa, again 50% more transmissible and the US had reported 224 cases of this variant.

B.1.427, first detected in California, 20% more transmissible.

B.1.429, another variant first detected in California, 20% more transmissible.

All these variants have not provided clear information on whether the vaccines can protect from infection or have significant effects on neutralization by antibodies. *However, the trends reflect that states in the US with successful vaccine deliveries also have a decrease in death rates from COVID-19.*

Other important variants include:
B.1.617 (Delta), originated from India.

C.37 (Lambda), originated from South America, particularly Peru.

B.1.621 (Mu), identified in Colombia in January 2021. It had been detected in 43 countries and was added to WHO's *Variant of Interest,* or VOI. Mu looks potentially clever at immune evasion from vaccines.

AY.4.2 (Delta plus), a daughter of Delta, originated from the UK.

B.1.1.529 (Omicron), a South Africa variant. The BA.2 subvariant is known to be more infectious.

JN.1 (Variant from Omicron), the US in 2023-24.

There are many thousands of variants of SARS-CoV-2. The naming of these variants is done by the WHO, in collaboration with partners, expert networks, national authorities, various institutions, and researchers who established the nomenclature systems for naming and tracking SARS-CoV-2 genetic lineages. For example, the Global Initiative on Sharing All Influenza Data (GISAID) was established in 2008. *Nexstrain* was established in 2017 and provides an open-source toolkit to track SARS-CoV-2, and *PANGO* (short for Phylogenetic Assignment of Named Global Outbreak lineages) is a dynamic nomenclature system for classification and naming of genetic lineages of the virus.

The letters of the Greek alphabet, i.e., Alpha, Beta, Gamma, Delta and Omicron were chosen to be more practical for discussion among non-scientific audiences. The working definition of Variant of Concern (VOC) of SARS-CoV-2 are Alpha, Beta, Gamma, Delta, and Omicron variants. All meet the definition of a Variant of Interest (VOI) plus one or more of the following changes:

Increase in transmissibility or detrimental change in COVID-19 epidemiology, an increase in virulence or change in clinical disease presentation, or a decrease in effectiveness of public health and social measures or available diagnostics, vaccines, therapeutics.

The *Variants of Interest* (VOI) definition of SARS-CoV-2 are variants with genetic changes that are predicted or known to affect virus characteristics such as transmissibility, disease severity, immune escape, diagnostic or therapeutic escape and to cause significant community transmission or multiple COVID-19 clusters to suggest emerging risk to global public health. VOI includes Eta (B1.525), Iota (B1.526), Kappa (B.617.1), and Lambda (C37) from various countries. The Lambda variant met the definition of VOC, and the Mu variant has met the definition of VOI.

Coronavirus continues to mutate. Variants of Omicron include XBB.1.5, XBB.1.6, EG.5, BA.2.86. The most common variant in winter of 2023 was JN1.

Vaccination goals achieved during COVID-19 were not seen

during the influenza outbreak in 1918, and our current vaccinations are reducing the outbreaks and are preventing severe complications. Although current death rates have continued, these began to diminish significantly after January 2022. Similar to the history of deaths related to flu, COVID-19 related deaths will likely continue, and unlike influenza, reinfection rates after COVID-19 are higher, (5% reinfection rate in a January 2023 paper published in *Nature*) and therefore waning vaccine immunity is expected over time, needing booster shots.

When exactly is the end of COVID-19?

COVID-19 is not going away, ending at a discrete time. No specific date or magical metric in the near future can be identified when COVID-19 is objectively and undeniably over, and we can expect only a gradual dissipation by wearing of masks and acute awareness among people. Similar to the 1918 influenza pandemic, the world continues to live indefinitely with both viruses as endemic. Most likely there will be two 'flu' shots or a combination; one for influenza and one for coronavirus. This means the coronavirus will keep circulating in many areas of the global population — and in America — for years to come, but its prevalence and impact will likely come down to relatively manageable levels. But what are the acceptable and manageable levels? How many deaths and infection rates are allowed or tolerable? COVID is here to stay with us from the pandemic phase into the endemic phase, just like the flu.

The aftermath

Among students, the damage of this pandemic included the loss of academic learning, emotional and social strains that may lead to anxiety or depression. Students experience shortages of schoolteachers and staff, and our society and economy has faced the great exodus of employees from workplaces, permanent closures of businesses including restaurants, hotels, and others in the tourism industry. We see a profound disruption of our lives requiring extensive time to create stability. Many of our routines may not recover, pushing us toward creating new routines.

What can we learn?

How can we move forward, what did we do right and what did we do wrong? Looking back with 20/20 retrospective vision, we can thank each health care provider who went forward as a first responder in the pandemic while given no proper PPE, sacrificing their personal and family lives to care for those who were dying with COVID-19. We do the same for those who served in our military. We can be grateful for scientists and researchers for a job done well with the discovery of mRNA technology used to create vaccinations at lightning speed, and thankful toward medical experts who volunteered time to speak in public, offered interviews on public radio and attended town hall meetings in front of angry audiences.

The next pandemic

Communication, communication, and communications. We need to do better in executing communication strategies in future public health crises to deliver accurate, credible, and impactful communications authored by scientific influencers (both community physicians, and public health leaders) in order to ensure citizens are hearing above the cacophony of misinformation.

Faulty theories around experimental uses of hydroxychloroquine and ivermectin as COVID cures are still perpetuating in social media. This kind of misinformation needs to be corrected with necessary resources and agility from the scientific community, business leaders, teachers, and politicians. True leaders dispel false information immediately during a pandemic with a united front. Americans need to understand the differences between public health issues and individual rights. There should be no fighting in the public about a mask wearing policy; *wearing a mask reduced new infections by 53%* according to worldwide studies that are compiled. *Handwashing was found to have a substantial reduction of COVID-19 cases by 53%.*

Irreversible reality

I witnessed dead bodies piling up in the morgue, bodies lined up in the hallway of my hospital and then piled one on top of one another into an already overloaded morgue that began running out of body bags. I witnessed a mass exodus of ICU nurses and certain ER doctors who carried an enormous sense of defeat. Therefore, my reality of COVID-19 may be drastically different from the rest of our population who are not health care workers. All hospitals began overflowing with COVID-19 patients, delaying much needed cancer surgeries or oncologic treatments, and causing triaging even of trauma cases. Goodbye to preventive care.

The reality in hospitals and among patients became irreversibly terrible conditions; patients with liver failure, renal failure, and heart attacks in which hospitals had to delay treating, and sit on for weeks. Most health care workers became overwhelmed with burnout and to top it off, the requirement of risking their own lives.

The sordid irony of their danger became strikingly visible while treating COVID-19 patients who refused vaccination, often belligerent and vocal about the traditional hospital care, but still yelling for hydroxychloroquine or ivermectin from their dying beds. I saw the hospital lacking PPE, rationing one thin mask per person per day, and asking us to recycle N95 masks for all health care workers by autoclaving them with proper name tags and then reusing them. Health care workers dedicated their lives to save humanity in the darkest time in modern history.

My last breath

As a medical doctor during the dark hours of the pandemic, I awoke each morning and traveled to a hospital fully occupied and spilling over with patients in outdoor tents who were dying from SARS-CoV-2, risking my own life. I sang while driving on a ghostly vacant 12-lane Los Angeles highway knowing these could be my final hymns to Jesus, thanking Him for the opportunity to serve my fellow citizens in America until I took my last breath, hoping and praying to not infect my beloved husband if I arrived home.

About the author

Sophia Kim Apple, MD is a breast cancer expert and professor emerita at UCLA. Dr. Apple contracted the polio virus as an infant in South Korea. Her family moved to Japan after her fourth grade, where she lived for almost four years but was unable to attend school because of the stigma from her disability. She came to America with no knowledge of English, and later graduated from NYU with a BS and MS in Biochemistry. She completed medical school in Ohio followed by six years of residency and fellowship training at UCLA.

Dr. Apple is the author of over 70 original medical research papers, and editor of *Breast Imaging: Expert Radiology Series*, and has taught hundreds of medical students and physicians-in-training in Pathology, Radiology, Surgery, and other disciplines.

At the age of 17 she was hit by a car while crossing a street in New York City, and God changed her life perspective of who she was and the purpose of her life ever since. Her perspective of life and as an author is unique, as an Asian American immigrant, a female physician, and a person with a physical disability.

She practices medicine as a pathology physician in Southern California, and lives with her husband of 38 years. She blogs at unseendoctor.com.

For inquiries contact unseendoctor@gmail.com, or www.unseendoctor.com